The Urbana Free Library

TROUBLE IN
ROOSTER
PARADISE

TROUBLE IN ROOSTER PARADISE

—

A Gunnar Nilson Mystery

T.W. Emory

coffeetownpress

Seattle, WA

coffeetownpress

Coffeetown Press
PO Box 70515
Seattle, WA 98127

For more information go to: www.coffeetownpress.com
www.twemoryauthor.com

Cover Illustrations by T.W. Emory
Cover design by Sabrina Sun

Trouble in Rooster Paradise
Copyright © 2015 by T.W. Emory

ISBN: 978-1-60381-996-1 (Trade Paper)
ISBN: 978-1-60381-997-8 (eBook)

Library of Congress Control Number: 2015932881

Printed in the United States of America

To My Folks

—

I'd like to thank my publishers, Catherine and Jennifer, for their input and support.

Chapter 1

—

An assisted living home in Everett, Washington
Monday, June 2, 2003

"WELL, YOU'RE A WELCOME improvement," I told the pretty young woman standing at the threshold of my open door.

"*Excuse me?*" she asked.

"You're not wearing scrubs yet, but you're looking in on *me*, and you've got that concerned caregiver face worn by all the staff. So, I gather it's *you* who's replacing Amazon Sally."

"*Amazon Sally?* Oh, you mean Sally Jennings."

"Uh-huh. A big Amazon of a girl. Her height reminded me of a tall waitress I knew back when telephones were black and a call cost a nickel." I turned my wheelchair to face my visitor.

"I didn't get a chance to meet Sally, but yes, I'll be taking over for her, starting tomorrow." My cheery caregiver entered the room and came over on a sleek pair of legs with cute dimpled knees that brought back memories of a girl I once knew—one who liked to dance to music with a heartbeat.

The new girl was standing in front of my wheelchair now,

so I had to glance up to see her shrewd eyes and moving lips.

"I'll be working here for the summer. I'm not on duty yet, but I wanted to pop by and meet everyone." I detected a hint of community college in her voice. "My name is Kirsti Liddell, Mr. Nilson."

"Nice to meet you, Kirsti. And please, call me Gunnar." We shook hands.

Kirsti Liddell wore a light blue blouse, red twill shorts, and tennis shoes. She was on the tall side of short, had big blue eyes, blonde hair cut in a pageboy, and a pert little bust that didn't jounce as she moved about. I placed her age at about twenty.

"I understand you'll be with us until your broken leg mends," she said in a dulcet tone.

"Right," I muttered. "You might say I found out the hard way that it's high time to pay someone else to clean my gutters."

Kirsti gave me a broad smile. Her airy, nimble movements provided a stark contrast to the sumo wrestler clunkiness of her predecessor. And whereas Amazon Sally had reeked of salve and her breath of far too many cigarettes, Kirsti's scent was vanilla and jasmine. In my day, Big Sal was what we called a B-girl. Kirsti would have rated a hubba-hubba.

Kirsti and I got better acquainted in the next couple of days. She was a nail-biter who favored multicolored ankle socks. By the third day I'd sized her up as one of those terminal romantics, the type who have more than five senses, hear tunes we don't, and view ordinary events as headline news. By the close of her first week, she was remembering to call me Gunnar and I was calling her Blue Eyes. By the second week of June, she was electrified to find out what I used to do for a living.

"Why you've been holding out on me! Mrs. Johnson says that years ago you were a private investigator in Seattle."

"That biddy's the one who's the snoop."

"It must have been exciting."

"That was donkey's years back."

"What?"

"A long time ago. Long before Seattle became the current land of Oz."

"You mean the Emerald City?"

"Yeah, whatever."

"I'll bet you've faced danger."

It was her doe-in-the-crosshairs eyes that got me yammering. "Well, I suppose I've seen my share of mean streets. Sure. And I've been in more than one place where staring wasn't just impolite, but hazardous to your health."

"I'd love to hear all about it. You'll have to tell me."

After that Kirsti regularly quizzed me about my private eye days each time she came to the room. Her grillings reminded me of an ex-landlady of mine who fancied herself a playwright hunting up background material.

With big eyes made even bigger, Kirsti asked, "Did you ever find a missing person? Or deal with a murder case? Did you ever have to … you know, kill anyone?"

"Well, I wasn't exactly Peter Gunn, but—"

"Who?"

"Skip it."

A few times she came by after her day ended and we talked for half an hour or so. I was glad to oblige. She was far easier on the eyes than most of the natives at Finecare. Plus, frankly, I was flattered by the attention. Granted, it was the attention a granddaughter might show her granddad, but still, it had been ages since an attractive young female had shown me any kind of interest. And I appreciated it. So much so, that at Kirsti's behest I began jotting down some of my recollections in a tablet—just a few words or phrases really, enough to remind me of a person, place, or thing. She got me prying into the undusted rooms of my mind. I was sweeping out memories from way back to just after the Second World War. Some were a hoot to recall, while others, well ….

By the third week of our acquaintance, she asked if she could visit on a Sunday to pick my brain.

"Don't you have a social life, Blue Eyes?"

"Don't you want a social life, Gunnar?"

I couldn't argue with her there.

"During our brief visits you've told me bits and pieces about your detective days, but I've been thinking that if we got together on a Sunday, maybe you'd be okay with telling me about one of your cases from start to finish. I mean, if you think you're up to it. *Talking* with me for several hours, that is …."

I made a dismissive wave with my hand. "Trading in ill winds as I did, *talking* was a big part of my business, Blue Eyes. And despite what some of the keepers here might think, I'm still no slouch at it." I gave her a level stare and smiled. "I can assure you, *my* ability to talk isn't the issue. It'll be *your* ability to listen."

"That's awesome. And besides, Gunnar, if it makes you feel any better, I'm being a little bit selfish. Who knows? With your permission, of course, I might be able to transform your memories into an extra credit paper when I return to school. You know, human interest, that sort of thing."

I told her she had my permission. "I'll even sign an official release form if you need me to," I said with a chuckle. And since she assured me the drive into Everett was a quick one for her, I was persuaded the extra visit would be no real imposition.

Come Sunday the 22nd, I refused to go the string-tie route, but I did wear a new flannel shirt. She said she'd come by around mid-morning. My note tablet sat on my lap. I kept up a steady *rat-a-tat-tat* with my fingers on the old Sucrets tin in my pants pocket that held my stash of cloves. I'd already sucked on five since about 8:00 a.m.

The corridor still smelled of assembly line pancakes when Kirsti finally showed up. She stood in the doorway, tote bag in hand and arms akimbo. I received a merry little look and a sorry-I'm-late. I countered with a nonchalant expression and an I-wasn't-going-anywhere-anyway. She wore a blue drawstring skirt that hugged her flanks and a white tank top that made her breasts look unusually abrupt.

"You're wearing sandals," I said as she went around behind me. "You paint your toes."

"It's nice out," she said. "And I sure do."

The distant sound of rattling dishes was dying down as she wheeled me through the corridor. My bumpy ride over the gravel and flagstone walk finally ended when we reached the outside courtyard.

She made chirping glad sounds as she parked my chariot and then planted herself on the wood bench facing me. Showing me her tote bag, she said, "Since you told me you like them, I made you a couple of pastrami sandwiches on rye for when you get hungry later."

Deeply touched doesn't begin to describe how that made me feel.

"I hope you don't mind, but I'd like to tape our conversation," she said, slamming a fresh cassette into the recorder she'd taken from the bag. "Just try to ignore the microphone and please be as candid as possible."

I smiled and fetched another clove.

"I'm not squeamish," she said, "and you should know by now I'm no prude."

"It's not as if I worked in a slaughterhouse, Blue Eyes."

She smiled, but her bright eyes narrowed. "Come on, Gunnar. You know what I mean. You started to tell me something the other day but then you shut right up. I saw the sparkle in your eyes. You said something about a dead body that led you into rooster paradise. I want you to tell me about that."

I looked from her to the mic she held in her hand.

"Like, what did you mean about the rooster thing?" she asked.

"You're positive you're not a prude?"

"For sure."

"A couple of ground rules," I said solemnly. "First off, I'm gonna need to take an occasional pee break."

"I'll wheel you over to the men's room whenever you say so."

"And second, I'm pretty sure I'll be all talked out at some point. So, figure on me having to finish this story in another installment. Maybe two."

"I think I can work with that," she said good-naturedly.

"Keep in mind that when I was young, a woman who smoked and wore pedal pushers was liberated, and if you spoke of 'feminism' you meant soft, ladylike, and sometimes sexy."

"Uh-huh."

"And Blue Eyes, you have to understand I'll be taking us back a ways to when being correct politically had to do with how you cast your ballot and not how you spoke."

"I'm with you."

I sighed.

"Kind of funny that it's June, because what I'm about to tell you happened during one week in June, back in 1950. Telephones then weren't like they are now, with all their beeps, hums, and tunes. Not hardly. No, most of them had a bell sound that was harsh and shrill. A call late at night, for instance—well, it was like a fireman's summons."

"Uh-huh," she said, clicking on the mic. "I'm all set."

I wasn't sure I was. But what the heck.

Chapter 2

—

Seattle, Washington
Wednesday evening, June 7, 1950

MY WIDOWED LANDLADY WAS an ex-fan dancer who wriggled and shimmied with the best of them. An exceptional talent, she always told me. Just past fifty, she was still a good-looking woman with a lithe pair of legs and most of her figure holding up. She was usually amiable and often on the flirtatious side. However, she regularly battled insomnia, and when she finally did drop off, there was blue hell to pay if she was yanked from slumberland. So at 11:30 p.m., when the walls began banging and the floors started thumping at my end of the boardinghouse, I sprang out of bed and pulled on my pants.

When the thumping reached my door, I opened it. Mrs. Berger stood there in a reddish-brown blanket looking like a frazzle-haired Geronimo at war council.

"Gunnar, if I don't get my sleep, what do I lose?" she asked, in a tone suggesting I'd better know the right answer.

"You lose your joy in life, Mrs. Berger."

"And when I lose my joy in life, what do those around me lose?" She was trembling, but not from cold.

"They also lose their joy."

I'd passed her test. A note with a hand attached to it poked out of the blanket.

"Cops want you," she growled.

I watched as the blanket-swathed form flounced down the hallway with just a hint of its onetime shimmy. I looked at the address scratched in pencil. Her handwriting was barely legible under normal conditions. What I saw resembled Sanskrit. Fortunately I'd grown up deciphering my grandfather's scrawl.

A light shimmered off the hardwood below the door across the hall. Mrs. Berger's thumping had awakened Walter Pangborn. His door opened.

"I couldn't help but overhear," Walter whispered. "Mind if I accompany you?"

"Come on."

My Longines said 11:35 when I got under the wheel of my car. I was the original owner of a '39 Chevy Coupe that had waited for me up on blocks till I returned from the war. The Chevy turned over as Walter hopped in next to me. He covered the right side of his face with a slouch hat with the practiced ease of an actor donning a familiar costume. Every piece of his outer ensemble was the color of a Hershey bar.

We headed for Ballard Avenue. Fifteenth Avenue and Market Street had robbed it of its commercial status during the Depression and then the war. Ballard Avenue had become a depressed neighborhood of thrift shops, taverns, cheap hotels and vacancies. It took us five minutes to get there.

A familiar white Lincoln-Zephyr approached as we neared our destination. The driver, clearly illuminated in the light of a street lamp, smiled and waved. Either she took me for a cop or recognized Walter. She was a local madam known as "Big Red," cheeks rosy with her usual rainbow rouge and decked out in a flamboyant, low-cut dress of the same color. Ballard was Seattle's Brooklyn, and Ballard Avenue was its tenderloin district.

I parked my Chevy thirty feet from a prowl car and an ambulance. Beams of light quivered in a passageway between two buildings. A small huddle of men examined a lumpy pile on the ground. Some distance beyond them, more flashlights bobbed and swayed as a search party spread out.

One of the uniformed cops spotted us and tapped the arm of a man lighting a cigarette. Detective Sergeant Frank Milland flagged me over with the first two fingers of his left hand. I approached and was met by expressions ranging from hostile to indifferent. Walter followed but held back a ways.

"Nice of you to join our little cotillion," Milland said, looking at and past me, "but who invited the freak show?"

"I invited him. And don't call him a freak."

Milland made an animal noise of acceptance. "Just as long as he keeps his distance. The stiff had your card. Take a look-see and tell us who we're looking at."

I stepped into the circle of men hovered over the body. During the war, I'd seen more than my share of the dead— enough to become inured and detached. But one of the things that continued to jangle my nerves was seeing the corpse of someone I'd visited with just the day before.

This was a nerve-jangler.

In combat, bodies are strewn about like damaged puppets with their strings cut. Sometimes a face looks at peace with its surroundings. The face on the body at my feet gave me a gut-tightening twinge. The strings had been cut, but the face didn't look at all peaceful.

"What's the verdict, Gunnar? Anyone you know?" Milland demanded.

"Yeah. But we'd met only once. Last night." I glanced at my Longines. It said 12:01. "Well, it's Thursday now, so make that *Tuesday* night when I met her."

Blood had run down the wall of the building, marking the

trail the body had made from its standing position to the pavement where it initially landed. A path of blood led farther into the alley where the body now lay. I took two cloves from my shirt pocket and slipped them in my mouth, sawing them in half with my teeth. I could see Walter flipping up the collar of his overcoat as he moved in closer, looking like a homogenized version of the Shadow and Phantom of the Opera.

Milland exhaled smoke and said, "So, you say you met this gal on Tuesday night. Tell us what else you know."

I had a fair idea as to *when* to begin. My tongue played with pieces of clove as my mind struggled with the who, what and why particulars that didn't make a whole lot of sense in the here and now.

"I CAN'T HELP BUT notice you're a bit jittery. Are you in some kind of trouble?" I'd asked.

"Well, it's certainly none of *your* business, buster," the slim brunette had said sharply.

That first little tête-à-tête of ours took place in the Ballard Theatre after the second feature had ended. But I'd first spotted this jittery one earlier in the lobby. Since the theater was just down the street from my office, I'd arrived during the middle of a color cartoon, well before the first feature began. So I'd waltzed back to the lobby for some popcorn—the extra buttery kind.

While I nibbled on a few kernels and waited for my change, I noticed Miss Jittery. She entered the movie house throwing looks over her shoulder and ignoring the pimply-faced usher who tore her ticket and gave her an appreciative once-over. If lust were a high note that kid would have shattered crystal.

I sympathized with the usher's appraisal. The girl *was* a looker, nicely wrapped in an olive green outfit made from tissue faille from no rack I'd seen lately. It was tailored to show every bump, dip, and half-moon to advantage. She stood about five-foot-four, not counting her cloche or her platform sandals with puff pastry nap that made them more art than footwear.

I finished eyeballing the girl and collected my change. As I started back toward the auditorium, I noticed her parallel with me but headed for the ladies' room. Before she ducked out of sight she turned around and scanned the lobby like a deer reconnoitering a salt lick. Our eyes met long enough for me to feel weighed in some balance and found harmless. I shrugged, popped a few more kernels in my mouth and went back to my seat.

I'd come to the movies to assuage a snubbed psyche. I'd rushed to my office to meet a client at the end of the day. He'd seemed iffy on the phone in the morning and rather loath to discuss fears of his wife's infidelity, so I wasn't exactly stunned when he was a no-show. But I didn't like being stood up any more than the next guy, so the movies it was.

I sat on the right, five rows from the front. Since it was a Tuesday night, and the crowd was small, I had a section all to myself. So I couldn't help but notice a few minutes later when the skittish brunette from the lobby plopped into my row just two seats away. We exchanged a quick glance. Even in dim light she had a face that caused double takes. I did one. She didn't.

She crossed a stunning pair of legs and started twitching her raised foot in a fascinating rhythm that distracted me through *Ticket to Tomahawk*. When not watching Anne Baxter, I stole peripheral glimpses at her face, toe, and calf. Miss Jittery didn't look at me once that I could tell, though every few minutes she glanced back up the aisle as if expecting an unwelcome guest.

After the first movie ended, she went back to the lobby. I thought I'd seen the last of her. But just as Howard Duff came on the screen, the girl dropped noisily into her seat again. She continued to toss glances up the aisle, and my attention was now divided between the fidgety brunette and Ida Lupino.

As *Woman in Hiding* ended, she stood up with the applause and looked up the aisle again. She seemed more at ease than when she'd sat down.

I stood and asked, "Did your assassin stand you up?" I was smiling a non-wolfish smile as her head snapped back toward me.

She half whispered, "*Excuse* me?"

It was then that I made my remark about her being jittery and she told me to mind my own business.

I put my hands up in surrender and pretended to be duly reprimanded. My role as Guardian of Womanhood had ended for the day. It was just as well. I was bushed.

"Suit yourself," I said as I inched toward her. "But do you mind?"

She hadn't moved from her spot and was blocking my way out, so I indicated for her to step aside.

She backed out of my way and stepped on the toes of a somber-looking dowager waddling up the aisle.

"Oh! I'm so sorry," she said to the woman as I slipped by unscathed.

I'd parked my Chevy near where Market Street meets Leary Avenue and was opening the door when I heard the clacking of heels on the sidewalk behind me. I turned to see the girl from the movie house approaching. She looked a little sheepish.

"Say, mister, please wait up a moment."

So, it was *please* now. And I'd gone from *buster* to *mister*. In the glare of the streetlight I gave her closer scrutiny. She looked to be in her early twenties and had a heart-shaped face and the high cheekbones that made Suzy Parker model of the decade. She nuzzled me with those lovely almond eyes some Scandinavians have—the epicanthic fold, they call it—one of the features Laplanders and Orientals have in common. Her mouth, free now of the strain of censure, was soft and childlike. Her lips had a cute, pouting quality that she used to full advantage.

"I want to apologize for being rude back there," she said.

"No problem. I'm in the habit of being a little nosy and have grown used to rudeness. Comes with the job."

Her head jerked slightly, and I might have dismissed it as a nervous twitch had her voice not risen an octave. "Are you a *policeman*?"

I quirked an eyebrow and smiled as I shook my head. "No. I'm a private detective. I work out of an office here in Ballard."

"Oh." She was relieved.

"My name's Gunnar Nilson." I extended my hand but intentionally did not move toward her. She took the two steps needed to reach me and gave my paw a gentle squeeze.

"Christine Johanson. Happy to make your acquaintance." She said it with a sugarplum voice and a fondant smile that put me in the mood for bonbons. Up close, her *eau de cologne* was a faint mix of sandalwood and cigarettes. "You were right, back there at the movie house."

"*Oh*?"

"I do think I might be in some kind of trouble," she said demurely.

"What seems to be the problem?"

"A man is following me—at least I think he is." As she spoke she gave a quick glance from left to right as if her words might conjure him up. I looked with her, but nothing was out of the ordinary—just moviegoers blending in with the few pedestrians about.

"Is this guy a masher?" I asked.

I WAS ABRUPTLY TAKEN from my story by Kirsti. "What's a *masher*?" she asked with a puzzled look in her eyes. "I mean, I know what a potato masher is, but you must mean something else here, right?"

"Yeah, I guess it's not a word that's used much anymore," I said wistfully. "At least not in the way I used it. A masher in those days was a man who made unwanted advances to a woman he didn't know."

Kirsti thought that over and nodded.

"But, Blue Eyes, maybe save up your questions as best you

can for when we take a break. Otherwise you might derail my already fragile concentration."

ANYWAY, I ASKED CHRISTINE if the guy following her was a masher. It was easy to imagine a lustful barfly chasing after this girl—whether in or out of his cups.

She shrugged, her brown curls flouncing on her shoulders. "Perhaps. I'm not sure. I think so. I had just parted with a friend and started walking down Market Street when I noticed him. He hasn't gotten close enough to talk to me. I've managed to keep distance between us. It's as if he's ... hunting me."

She seemed genuinely distressed. And I'd seen how she'd looked entering the Ballard Theatre. But, like Sam Goldwyn said, once an actor can fake being honest he's got it made.

"Do you think you lost the guy when you ducked into the movie house?"

"Perhaps ... I don't know. Frankly, I'm still a little shook up by it."

Her moment of uneasiness when she thought I was the law got me curious. Normally, a cop would be a welcome sight for a gal in her kind of difficulty.

"Would you like me to drive you to the police station?" the scamp in me asked.

But her earlier alarm must have been a rare lapse. No reaction this time. She just shook her head and touched my arm. Christine's voice had a seductive rumble to it as she said, "Would you mind dropping me off at home?" Hers was a siren's glance—half dare, half coy. The sparkle in her eyes hinted that she'd be a very grateful passenger.

I watched as she minced over to a nearby phone booth, green skirt flailing. "I'll phone my aunt to let her know I'm on my way. She's such a worrier."

After she'd made her call she gave me an address I placed about ten blocks up from us—west, over from Ballard High School. I headed us east on Market Street for Fifteenth Avenue.

It was soon apparent we were being tailed.

"Looks like your friend might be behind us," I said, fighting an urge to put more pressure on the gas.

Christine didn't spin her head around as I thought she would. Instead, she scooted over to where she was practically in my lap and peeked discreetly in the rearview mirror.

"What makes you think he's behind us?" she asked, not bothering to move once her look in the mirror was over.

"Educated hunch." But that was an understatement. Cruising down Market Street, I'd noticed a newer model Packard slipping smoothly into traffic a car length or so behind us. The driver maintained a consistent distance. What cinched it for me was his obvious attempt to keep pace as we moved north on Fifteenth—a four-lane main drag that runs through part of Ballard's business district. Even when I casually changed lanes, my pursuer dogged me. Whoever he was, he was either bad at tailing—or wanted the girl to know he was after her. My money was on the latter.

"Do you want me to stop and confront him? Scare him off?"

"No ... um ... he's probably just some drunk."

"He doesn't drive like a drunk."

"Can't you just lose him?" Christine asked, a plea in her eyes.

Not bothering to answer, I continued driving several blocks until a car finally nosed in front of our pursuer. I eased up on the gas a bit as we approached a traffic signal, hoping that the light would turn red by the time we reached it.

We came to the light and I braked at the first glint of yellow, causing the driver behind me to lay on his horn—the Packard snuggling up tight behind him.

"Brace yourself against the dash," I barked. When the light turned red I stepped on the gas, making a screeching left turn in front of an oncoming motorist that forced him to slam on his brakes. In my mirror I could see the Packard frozen in place. Christine was looking at the same scene—one hand gripping the dashboard, the other one squeezing my right thigh.

I sped along for three blocks in a residential area before making a hard right onto a side street with cars parked on both sides. I drove about thirty yards and pulled the Chevy in front of an older Willys I hoped would provide cover.

When I killed the motor, Christine scooted over to her side of the car. She was no modest damsel prying free from an hysterical clinch. More like a boxer returning to his corner at the end of a round.

"Do you think you lost him?" Christine asked, not bothering to look back.

"We'll see."

She started fumbling with the contents of her purse and asked, "Do you have a cigarette, Gunnar?"

I shook my head. "Sorry. Don't smoke. Quit." I reached into my shirt pocket.

"Care for a clove?"

She screwed up her face and shook her head slowly. I popped one of the dried flower buds into my mouth and began to casually crush it with my tongue against my teeth, releasing its numbing oil. Christine watched me.

"It's an old home remedy for toothache," I explained.

"Do you have a toothache?" she asked.

I shook my head and said, "Life's a toothache."

Her need for a smoke made her talkative.

"A girl I work with—her name's Meredith—she's always saying that a girl has to look out for herself because no one else will."

"She sounds hardboiled."

"*Mere*? Oh no. She's just very matter-of-fact. She's sensible. I really appreciate that about her. Meredith's a great friend."

Christine told me she was raised in Spokane, but had moved to Ballard to live with her aunt. She divided her time between classes at the University of Washington and part-time work at a boutique; but she eventually dropped the schooling and started selling fancy gifts and toilet water full-time.

After a polite listen, I gave her my business card and intended to ask her for her phone number. She anticipated me. I knew a discouraging remark when I heard one.

"Seattle's still such a hick town. I'm not setting down any roots. I won't be staying here much longer. I'm putting away some money. My dream is to live in a penthouse apartment on Park Avenue, in New York. It's good to have dreams, don't you think?"

"Yeah, sure. Dreams are good."

"Of course the best dreams cost lots of money," she said.

I didn't agree or disagree. At the time my dreams consisted of cutting a rug to music with a heartbeat at the Palladium, at least until I saw that hoped-for sparkle in the eyes of my date of the week. Or sometimes I just looked forward to quaffing a bottle of Pabst with my feet up and listening to pleasant mood music on KOL or KOMO—which at the time tended to be Hawaiian tunes.

We saw no Packard during our ten-minute palaver. At Christine's insistence I drove a zigzagging route south about ten blocks. Aunt Emelia's Victorian looked to have been built when Teddy Roosevelt was whacking away with his big stick. It was liberally decorated with fancy moldings, turrets, and bay windows, which gave it a false appearance of affluence.

I pulled in the driveway and Christine smothered a visit-ending yawn with a delicate fist—that universal way of saying, "Is it that time already?" I knew I wouldn't be meeting Aunt Emelia.

We faced each other and she took my right hand in hers. She squeezed my palm and playfully ran the index finger of her other hand up the front of my shirt—starting at my chest and ending at my chin. With a tug on my lapel, she pulled my face close to her pursed lips and gave me a full-mouthed kiss. She quickly pulled away and whispered, "Thank you," as she hopped out of the car.

I didn't surprise easy, but she shut the car door before I could even say, "You're welcome."

The stone footpath sloped upward. Christine walked in long climbing strides but with no urgency. Her faille skirt sculpted the back of each round and solid thigh as one leg shot in front of the other.

She disappeared inside the house. She didn't wave or look back. I didn't expect her to.

I'd struck out on getting her phone number, and though she had mine, I was certain she'd not be dialing it anytime soon. I wasn't the stuff her dreams were made of.

But it wasn't the last time I saw the girl. No, not hardly.

Chapter 3

———

I'D DRIVEN CHRISTINE HOME Tuesday night. A police summons rousted me from my bed in the middle of the night Wednesday. And now, in the wee hours of Thursday morning, I was seeing Christine once again. She was definitely slumming it. She wore her hair up this time. She didn't look so good. A summer dress of rayon crepe enshrouded the lumpy pile she'd become in the alley off Ballard Avenue. I was of no further use to her. The cops hoped otherwise.

A white-haired medical examiner squatted over her body. He shut his black bag, looked up, and said, "She died before she hit the ground."

"Dragged to this spot after she was shot," said Detective Sergeant Milland. "Killer wanted her back a ways. Out of sight." He was looking at Christine's foot as he pointed to the blood trail. One of her platform-soled sandals had fallen off, and the toe of her nylon was roughed up and torn. Her skirt was hiked up so that one of her thighs and the fringe of her underwear showed.

"Gal had a nice set of legs," Milland said. "A real shame to go

and break a dish like that." He didn't mean it to be funny, and
nobody laughed.

Cops in Seattle ran a gamut that included the crooked, slightly
bent, and those who mixed virtue with their dishonesty. Frank
Milland was not-so-crooked with honest leanings. Under his
fedora he wore short-cropped hair that was prematurely gray
and made him look well over forty. But I knew he was no more
than thirty-five, since he was only a couple years older than
me. He'd tried to enlist during the war despite a wife and kid,
but a severe case of hammertoes barred him from the army. He
became an embittered civilian and an even meaner cop who
waged his war on the many Seattle criminals unlucky enough
to get in his way before the defeat of the Axis powers. We'd first
met in the late '30s, when I was a neophyte detective working
for the Bristol Agency under the tutelage of Lou Boyd. Frank
and Lou didn't exactly get along. Lou's wit didn't meld well with
Frank's boorishness. But I respected Milland's expertise and
ignored his bad manners. We didn't really become anything
resembling friends until after the war.

Milland pointed to purse spillings near where Christine's
body had dropped.

"Your business card was bent double and crammed in
her compact. Looks to me like she wasn't too excited about
remembering you. Was she one of your *dissatisfied* clients?"
Milland asked me. "Something she tell you that might tie in
with this massacre?"

"No," I said, shaking my head. "No, to both questions."

"We didn't find no money or identification on the girl," said a
big-toothed uniformed cop standing off to the side. "Looks to
have been a robbery." He then added a "maybe," with a nervous
glance at the detectives.

Milland shook his head as he looked at the body. "A messy
robbery," he said. "If that's what it really was."

"Girl's name and address?" This question came at me from
Milland's partner, Bernie Hanson, a middle-aged man with a

weather-beaten face and a vacant stare. Hanson had the voice of a radio newscaster doing an ad for a funeral parlor. He held a pencil in one hand, a notepad in the other.

"Christine Johanson," I said. I could only remember the street number. "She lived with an Aunt Emelia. I didn't meet the aunt."

"So, how'd you happen to meet up with this gal?" Milland asked, pointing to the body.

I told them the story.

When I'd finished, Hanson asked, "Get a look at the driver of that Packard?"

"No. I just shook the guy for her."

"It seems he didn't stay shook," Milland murmured, giving me a level stare.

WALTER AND I RODE in mortuary silence back to Mrs. Berger's. We walked through the kitchen side door at one a.m. At least that was what the kitty-cat wall clock read—though it tended to run slow. The cat's moving eyes signaled each tick; its pendulum tail wagged like an inverted metronome. That and the refrigerator's hum were the only sounds to hail us. I shut and locked the door as quietly as I could.

A plate of inky black blobs sat on the drain board. Waxed paper sheltered them. It was Mrs. Berger's latest cookie experiment. She'd decided to call them Nightmare Drops. As volunteer guinea pigs, Walter and I each grabbed one.

We glided through the pantry and dining room and hopped, stepped, and tiptoed past Mrs. Berger's bedroom door. We were lucky. It was shut and she didn't stir—telltale signs she'd dosed herself with sleeping powder.

Light broke through the window at the bottom of the stairs, accenting my landlady's shrine to her bump and grind days. A display case of mahogany was mounted on the wall. It contained her prized fans, manufactured by the famous theatrical costumer Lawrence Sittenberg of New York City.

They were made from tail feathers wrenched from ostriches in Capetown, South Africa, then tinted and attached to celluloid handles. Alongside the case hung three framed photos linked like comic-strip panels. Each showed a younger Mrs. Berger working her fans in different stages of her act—billiard ball naked, save for rouge, high-heeled slippers and a G-string that was more thread than string. If she caught you looking at her pictures—which you couldn't help but do when mounting those stairs—she'd holler over something like, "Sally Rand was a piker next to me, am I right? If my Otto hadn't taken me from the life, I'd have been the big name," or, "I kept them spellbound and comin' back for more. Such verve and flourish I had. Those were good times. Good times."

We were still chewing our Nightmare Drops when we reached the top of the stairs.

"I'm afraid Nora's cookies deserve their sobriquet. I'll make us some coffee to wash them down, old top," Walter said in a whisper. "We'll chat. Plus, the first of the Napoleonics arrived. You'll have to see them."

I was easily persuaded. I needed more than burnt sweet bread to neutralize the images of a dead Christine.

Along one wall of Walter's room was his workbench—a wooden table, bar-high, three feet deep and ten feet wide. As a whole, the counter was unstained, but the area where he worked was peppered with dry paint droppings of every color. In the center crowding the wall were paint pots and worn brushes bunched in jars like mutant nosegays in small vases. In the far right corner sat a hot plate, an electric percolator, a can of Hills Brothers Coffee, a receptacle of Lipton's Tea bags, and a box of Ry-Krisp.

"Roughage is a must, Gunnar," Walter liked to say. "It's the key to the body's survival."

The man didn't know how right he was. His Remington typewriter was next to the Ry-Krisp, nestled up against a stack of paper anchored with an old railroad spike. That stack was

Walter's labor of love. He was helping the unlearned Mrs. Berger write a play she called *The Making of a Fan Dancer*. Walter struggled mightily to give it a philosophic twist. He wanted to rename it *The Gymnosophist*, but Mrs. Berger wasn't buying it.

Near his work stool, probably fifty lead soldiers on horseback stood on the bench in military columns. Each horseman's torso had been painted crimson, and a few of the horses were already white, black, or brown.

"British Heavy Dragoons," he said happily, handing me one. "This allotment came special delivery this afternoon."

I hefted it and studied the detail of the dragoon's drawn saber, pointed forward as if in a charge. After Walter got done with them you'd see the whites of their eyes.

"What's their destination?" I asked.

"A wealthy collector in Rhode Island. He's putting together a Waterloo diorama. It's the kind of order Perry salivates over. He intends for me to paint the whole lot for him. Consistency of style. That kind of thing."

Raymond Perry headed a family-run soldier-making business out of his home in Springfield, Massachusetts. He home-cast with lead, pewter, and rubber. Walter had worked on Civil War figurines the month previous, and had told me he was looking forward to his next assignment—toy soldiers from the Napoleonic era. I'd forgotten all about it.

"But Gunnar, here you stand all weak and weary, indulging an old friend's passion. Let me get that coffee going." Only the left side of his mouth lifted when he grinned. He pointed me to his channel-backed fireside chair, sans fireplace. He pulled the stool up closer for himself.

As Walter busied himself, he explained more about his latest assignment—the new paints he'd need, the research on the uniforms he'd be doing, the completion date he'd be shooting for.

"It's a classic testimony to vanity, Gunnar, that the whims

and idiosyncrasies of a regimental colonel often dictated the colors and patterns worn by an entire regiment—"

Walter had probably been quiet and reclusive long before his disfigurement. He futilely insisted he was of the bourgeoisie, but I pictured him in some upper-class Philadelphia playground, contentedly playing chess with his governess but graciously admitting anyone else who cared to play. The continuous gleam in his eyes went with a gift of making you feel his serenity. Likely it was due to the real interest he showed in people—their loves, hates, wants, needs, fears, and bugaboos. He rarely ventured out in daytime. But I joined him on nocturnal excursions and many times saw him console a lovelorn waitress, buck up a burly barge worker, and play shrink to a barkeep.

"… armies were costumed as if for a play. The Peninsular Wars were really a lethal grand pageantry …."

As the third Pangborn to attend Princeton, Walter absorbed its Gothic charms alongside a ripening F. Scott Fitzgerald. In Walter's junior year he infuriated his father, "The Judge," by rushing off to smash the Kaiser in World War One. He became a private in a Pennsylvania company. He fought in the Argonne and was badly burned when a fuel wagon he stood next to was shelled. He learned later that that very day his estranged father died of a heart attack.

"What do you make of it, Walter?" I asked as he got the percolator going. "What we saw tonight, I mean. My story about the girl."

Walter plopped gently on the work stool and said, "You realize, old socks, it's our respective perversities that take us down these roads."

"Sure. But we don't go screaming. And we like the scenery."

"Addicted to it, I fear."

After the war, Walter lived in a veterans' hospital in the Bronx—abandoned by his sole sibling, a grasping older sister who had power of attorney for their invalid mother. Walter was shut away in the kind of convalescent ward the public never sees, and he shared existence with men with no jaws, eyes, or ears. As he put it, "Each of us is in a valiant struggle to keep from going off his nut." After the big wars, society only saw the occasional man on crutches. Wouldn't want them to get the right idea, don't you know.

Walter's father had arranged a trust fund for him in his will. When this finally went into effect on his twenty-fifth birthday, it was the salvation of Walter's independent nature. Forsaking his blue-blood ties, he drifted out West and lived off an allowance that more than met his needs. Painting lead soldiers provided a supplemental income and occupied some of his time during the day. This, and the floor-to-ceiling bookcase that took up another wall of his room, played a big part in centering him.

"So what's the Walter Pangborn construct for what you saw and for the facts I fed to the cops?"

Walter had the fingers of his right hand to his chin, and cradled his elbow with his left hand. It was a definite Walterism. When he did that he'd knead his chin and look up and off to one side.

"Miss Johanson knew her pursuer," Walter said. "He didn't drive erratically, yet she suggested that he was drunk. She didn't want you to stop the car and confront him."

"Yeah. I figured it was a cock-and-bull story," I said.

"That phrase has a quaint origin, Gunnar. It comes from the renowned Aesop's stories of moralizing cocks and disputatious bulls. For that reason ...."

I raised a goading eyebrow.

"Yes ... sorry." He cleared his throat. "Of course, it was no coincidence that Miss Johanson sat so close to you in the movie house. She made you in the lobby as a man she could use, possibly lean on if there was trouble."

"I thought the same thing. I was to be her Galahad if her shadow-man entered the theater."

"Precisely, though not likely as gallant a role as you imagine. More like scraps to be thrown to her pursuing hound. Since the hound didn't enter the movie house, she could afford to be rude to you after the movie ended. But she miscalculated. My guess is that she saw the hound again when she stepped outside, and *that* is what accounts for her accosting you with her coy amends."

"Aw, Walter, you mean it wasn't my boyish charm?"

He laughed quietly. "You've still got appeal, old thing—so not to worry. No, the girl probably assumed you were just another lascivious chump she could manipulate."

"I'll take that as a backhanded compliment, Walter."

"By all means, Gunnar, you do that. Get them when you can. That's the way."

Walter could easily hide the hideous marks on his chest and right arm, but the ugly scars on his right cheek and throat, as well as his deformed right ear, gave him the profile of a vermilion monster. But he was a gentle beast. I never saw his injuries once I got to know him. In fact, I don't think anyone continued to see them once they truly began to experience his caring genius. Over the years he civilized an after-dark world of friends who wound up forgiving the repulsive, and seeing beauty in the grotesque.

"You say Miss Johanson was noticeably relieved to find you weren't a policeman?" Walter asked.

"Palpably relieved."

He stood up to get our coffee then resumed his perch. Walter reached under his workbench for a bottle of Black & White. It was his Scotch of choice, the one that featured a picture of black and white Scotty dogs on the back of each bottle. He held it up and gave me an inquiring look. My grin gave approval for him to dose my cup. He then gave his own coffee a healthy glug.

"Hmm, let's think on this, Gunnar. Miss Johanson spoke of costly dreams, had some money salted away, and was not attired like the common shop girl. Yet she lived in a working class neighborhood. In her case then, I'd say that her use of distaff allurements—while not an evil thing in itself, you understand—may suggest something shady, even sinister."

I agreed.

"She lived with her aunt, so she was not a kept woman. However, with the kind of beauty that transcends class distinction, she might well have had a wealthy suitor."

"I'm thinking that too. Yet she led me to believe she was leaving the Northwest soon."

"Ah, yes. Park Avenue."

"So what do you make of the Packard, Walter?"

"Well, given what has befallen Miss Johanson, I'm inclined to share Detective Milland's view that you'd not successfully lost the pursuing hound after all."

"Maybe she was in an affair gone bad. Her pursuer a spurned suitor."

"Perhaps. But if he were Miss Johanson's suitor, then he'd have known where she lived, and your efforts at losing him would have been a meaningless gesture. If so, she might simply have been trying to get rid of him for the evening. Possibly they'd just had a bad break-up."

"Something doesn't sound right," I said.

"I agree. But one thing is certain, whoever the hound is, tonight he turned vicious."

"And then he took her money and identification to make it look like robbery."

"Precisely. An old ruse. But shooting her near a dark alley sounds premeditated. Crimes of passion are generally more spontaneous—spur-of-the-moment."

"Yeah. More likely, a spurned lover would have conked her on the head with a fire poker or strangled her with his bare hands."

Walter nodded and took a sip from his cup.

We sat in silence a few seconds. I heard raindrops hit the roof. A wry smile appeared on the left side of Walter's face.

"What is it, Walter?"

"Oh, it's just that conceivably our speculations merely show that we're striking back at the encroachments of a humdrum existence."

"Life at Mrs. Berger's, *humdrum*? Walter, you shock me."

The raindrops now sounded like thimbles hitting the shingles. Walter got up to shut his window.

"Still Gunnar, perhaps we're making an Oriental tapestry out of a warp and woof throw rug. After all, there is the real possibility that Miss Johanson was simply robbed and this exercise has been nothing more than a grisly parlor game that hasn't been worth the candle."

Grisly? Yes.

Parlor game? Not hardly.

Chapter 4

—

Before Pearl Harbor I worked for a big detective agency in Seattle. After my discharge from the army I spent over a year furthering my education by means of the G.I. Bill. I toyed with becoming the teacher my grandfather had hoped I'd become. However, the temperament to learn but not teach led me back into detective work in the spring of '48—this time as a one-man show.

I dreamt about Christine Johanson just before sunrise on Thursday. We were waltzing in the lobby of the Ballard Theatre. Christine began to cough violently, so Mrs. Berger cut in. She wore high heels and a sequined G-string. She wanted to tango. Thankfully, I woke up. I always woke up when Mrs. Berger came to me in my dreams. I dreaded the night I didn't.

It was the eighth of June. I remember, because as I dressed that morning, I was thinking that my grandmother Agnette would have been another year older had she lived. So, by breakfast Thursday morning, Christine had become a cerebral footnote. By mid-morning she would have completely faded from caring memory had a telephone call not revived my concern.

My office was on the second floor of the two-story Hanstad Building. The owner was Dag Erickson, a local attorney I met the same month I hung up my sleuth shingle. We soon formed a working relationship that teetered on symbiotic.

Miss Olga Peterson came out of the Hanstad Building as I tried to enter. Miss Peterson was a spinster in her mid-fifties, and her "spinning" consisted of running a flower and knickknack shop when not playing mahjong, or reading romance novels and pulp magazines.

The envelopes in Miss Peterson's plump hand signaled she'd missed the mailman and was headed for the mailbox out by the curb.

"Mr. Vance," Miss Peterson said, as I sidestepped her rotundity. I was "Philo Vance" to her, and I'd stopped correcting her the first day we met. "I see that you've made a purchase, Mr. Vance."

I smiled and hugged my parcel close to my chest. Miss Peterson generously dosed herself with over-spiced perfume that caused my eyes to water and put my gag reflex to the proof.

She fanned her pudgy face with the envelopes and nodded at my parcel. "Shall I hazard a guess that your package has something to do with a case?" she asked. Hope was in her eyes.

I shook my head.

For a guy who made his living poking at underbellies, I never liked prying jabs at my own.

"Cold medicine," I said, and coughed to make the lie credible.

She looked disappointed. "My stars, but Mr. Vance, for a strapping young fellow you *are* a sickly one. It seems every time we meet you've come from the pharmacy with something remedial."

I made a mental note to come up with a better line.

"You're not one of those malaria-stricken veterans, are you? Some exotic disease from the Orient, perhaps?"

"No, Miss Peterson. I was in Europe."

She briefly pondered Anglo-Saxon and Celtic ailments and

was working her way to the Franks, when her face untwisted and brightened.

"We've missed Mr. Pangborn at our mahjong club. I trust he is well."

"Walter? All goes swimmingly. His is a rich and varied life."

"I must say, he's a most remarkable man. Most remarkable. Why, his everyday talk is simply bedizened with engaging insights that—"

"Are quite lost on the minds of lesser souls?" I asked, completing the familiar praise.

"Why … *yes*. Just so. You must please tell him that Olga misses those little crumbs of knowledge he lets fall as we stack our tiles. He's such a delightful east wind player. Why, sometimes that man's perceptiveness leaves me in an attentive state—"

"Bordering on the supernatural?" I said. "Uh-huh. Walter's been known to have that effect on *some*. I think it's part of his game strategy."

"*Really*? Oh … why, yes. Just so."

She gave my arm a squeeze. "Please be sure and give him a fresh greeting from Olga."

"No problem."

I entered the building.

"Why, a body would think you had the plague," Miss Peterson called after me. "My stars. It's not natural for a vibrant young man to be medicating so often. It's just not natural."

"No, Miss Peterson."

I tromped up the stairs. Behind and below I heard the thud and clap of her orthopedic shoes hitting the lobby floor on her return from the mailbox.

"Black strap molasses, Mr. Vance," she called up after me. "Remember to take two tablespoons every night. Do you hear?"

"Yes, Miss Peterson. Molasses. Every night," I shouted back.

My office adjoined Dag Erickson's. Dag had his suite enlarged during the war, reducing the remaining space I rented to two oversized pigeonholes he'd initially used for storage.

I snatched the morning mail from the slot and had my key in the lock when an attractive young woman stepped out of Dag's door. She'd doubtless seen me as I passed in front of the frosted glass. Miss Cissy Paget came with the pigeonholes.

What I mean is my rent included an additional telephone in Dag's office and Cissy as my answering service. Her filing skills were a negotiable extra. Her asking price for typing was out of my reach.

Cissy's heels clicked softly against the linoleum as each foot took its turn on an imaginary tightrope, causing her willowy figure to oscillate from midriff to toes. Hers was a gait a fashion model would envy, but knowing Cissy, she'd probably walked that way since she began to toddle.

A faint scent of violets came along with her.

"Any calls, Sweet Knees?" I said. I'd been gone only an hour.

"Just one," she replied, thrusting a small slip of yellow paper at me. "It came about fifteen minutes ago."

The note read, "Call Rikard Lundeen." I figured it meant a job, but it made me as ambivalent as a toothache victim facing a dentist's drill.

Cissy parked one hand on her hip and with the other removed a pair of round-lensed glasses that could have been stolen off of Winston Churchill or Mahatma Gandhi.

"Your caller sounded old, distinguished, and authoritative. He said it was important, but he didn't leave a number. He said you'd have it. Is he *the* Rikard Lundeen?"

"The very same," I replied, not telling her I was maybe one of five people who had special access to him on a very private telephone line.

She whistled softly. "Consorting with Seattle's upper crust now, are we?"

I smiled. "I helped him out with a family matter."

"*Family matter*. That's a rather droll euphemism, isn't it? It's right up there with *matters to attend to*."

I smiled. Ambivalence or not, I didn't want to jeopardize that special access, so I changed the subject.

"Curt Sykes and his orchestra will be at the Trianon," I said. "*And?*"

"Feel like dinner and dancing this Saturday night?"

"The Trianon, huh?"

I nodded.

"So, tough guy, you feel up to skipping and shuffling with me at Seattle's finest ballroom?"

"I'm sure."

"Do you think those gumshoes can take the strain?"

"Feet of steel, Miss Paget. Feet of steel."

She closed her eyes and put her fingertips to her eyebrows. "I'm getting a vision. I'm seeing you in a truck. You have a sheepish, desperate look on your face. You're hauling a load of typing that needs to be done."

"Cynical you. How do you know it's not your enchanting company I'm after?"

"Are you sure it's my company you're enchanted with?"

"Am I that transparent?"

"Like a display window at the Bon Marché."

Cissy was a brown-haired, narrow-lipped package of sweet-and-sour candy. She had those innocent chestnut eyes that crinkled when she beamed a smile that said the two of you were pulling a fast one on humanity. She'd been engaged in the fall of '44, and her fiancé was killed six months before V-J Day. When I met her she was in her early twenties and convinced the whole world had gone loony—which of course it had. She was amusing company if you liked pert and brassy, annoying if you didn't. She related to me with a fun-loving air. Slide this banister with me, tough guy. Lose the umbrella, Gunnar, can't you see it's raining? But like most of us walking wounded, she was assuaging pain. She failed miserably in trying to hide her empathy. She helped support her widowed mother with whom she lived in Magnolia. At a showing of *Bambi,* she led fellow patrons in a bawling jag. And more than once I caught her sniffling over some tragedy in the newspaper.

Cissy and I were buddies, but I was in no way immune to her feminine charms. I watched her taut rump slightly seesaw as she walked back to her workstation.

"Shouldn't you be examining your *mail*, Gunnar?" she asked without having to look back.

"You *are* a mind reader."

She shot me a glance before she went through the door. "In studying the orangutan's mating habits, I've learned telepathy is not a requirement."

I entered the inner pigeonhole before reading my mail. I stuffed my parcel in my desk drawer next to a paperback copy of Damon Runyon's *Take It Easy*. It was one of those specially printed for men in the armed forces during the war. It had helped me fend off many a boring moment. I kept it for reasons I still can't explain. An abandoned half-eaten éclair sat next to it. Its carapace was flaky but it still tasted okay.

Dag's remodeling project left me with a window. I raised it and took in my minuscule view of Market Street. It was the beginning of June, and mild out. Rain had pelted the city during the night, so the filtered air smelled fresh as garments dried on a clothesline. Only a couple of small clouds hung around the edges of an azure sky. The Italianate storefronts had the tint of a faded postcard—which reminded me I had two letters to read.

I chewed on my éclair as I opened the top letter. It was from the American Legion. They wanted me to join up. I sailed their letter and the last scrap of éclair into what my old partner used to call the "spilth receptacle."

The second item was a "Glad you ain't here," card from Honolulu, sent by an army buddy named Leahy. A color cartoon was on the front showing a goofy-looking tourist gyrating with three brown hula cuties. On the inside he'd written, "This beats huggin' trees in the Hurtgen any day."

The krauts taught us to be tree huggers in the Hurtgen Forest. Normally you'd kiss the earth when shelled. But in the Hurtgen, the krauts used shells with fuses set to blow in the treetops, showering the ground with hot steel and wood slivers. Being one with a tree lowered your odds in the old shrapnel lottery.

I stood Leahy's belated piece of gallows humor on the corner of my desk just above the spilth receptacle. I decided it could stay for awhile.

The mail was read, and there were no customers to delay the telephone call I had to make.

Rikard Lundeen was friendly, but our conversation was predictably brief. He insisted that we talk face to face. I agreed to meet him downtown for lunch.

"SURPRISED AT MY CHOICE of a bistro?" Rikard Lundeen asked, with a mock grin that caused his thin mustache to ripple.

"Should I be?" I said, after swallowing. "It's got ambiance, atmosphere, and a house specialty that makes it a subterranean paradise. Who am I to knock an institution?"

His grin remained.

Rikard Lundeen could easily have passed for under sixty instead of almost seventy, and he had those doted-on looks that money hires. But it was more than that. He was one of those incredibly lucky survivors of the genetic lottery. He'd inherited an amazingly lean physique that he aided and abetted with exercise and regular visits from a masseuse. His nails were precisely manicured and his full head of gray hair was carefully groomed and slicked straight back like those dandies you used to see on the covers of *The Saturday Evening Post*.

The lunch menu was easy. You either had the-gentleman-will-take-a-chance hash or the house specialty: corned beef and cabbage. We ordered the specialty. He picked at his. I wolfed mine down.

"I thought about having you as my guest at my club, but

I wasn't sure you'd be comfortable doing business there. I thought you'd feel out of place."

He knew that I knew I'd never see the inside of his club. Not as his guest anyway. I kept chewing.

"Besides, I decided I wanted the privacy this place provides me. I've eaten here at the Moonglow off and on for years. Getting among the people clears the mind. Mixing with the ordinary man renews the senses."

And it reassured him who was still on top, I thought but of course didn't voice. The ordinary man is an effusive back-slapper. Lundeen was calculatingly reserved and congenial only when it suited him. The ordinary man dreams big but is tormented by bugaboos. Lundeen bankrolled and profited from the dream factories and torture chambers. The ordinary man defies the luck of the draw at every turn and his entire life is an uphill battle. Rikard Lundeen was a hardboiled pragmatist who printed and sold the lottery tickets others had to buy and he lived on top of the hill they never scaled.

"It looks to me that for some of these customers, ordinary is a big step up," I said.

He laughed, but it didn't come from the belly. It was one of those social chortles going no farther down than the vocal cords.

Most of the caterers to good taste had moved up the hill some years before. The Moonglow Eats was an underground cavern on First Avenue—an old strip of real estate with neon-shingled stop-off spots for flesh peddlers, the fortune-twisted, and those who didn't give their right names. Fortunately, as you entered, the sharp aroma of corned beef and cabbage washed over all competing smells.

I'd arrived a couple minutes late. After making my way from the street down a dizzying flight of stairs that would never pass today's safety codes, I saw Mr. Lundeen reading the comics section of the *Seattle Times*. It made for an unusual opening. A Rikard Lundeen opening.

"Joe Palooka hasn't been in the ring lately. A real disappointment to a boxing fan like me. I like to see a good mix-up, even in the funny papers. But, Alley Oop never disappoints. What a hoot. He's being dogged by a persistent dinosaur and the old Grand Wizer is sorer than blazes at him. Cave men. Time travel. It stretches the imagination. Yes, indeed, a real hoot. Do *you* read the funnies, Gunnar?" he'd asked.

"Sure. I like Li'l Abner." I'd started reading it during the war in *Stars and Stripes*.

"Good for you. Good for you. To my way of thinking, a man who doesn't read the funnies lacks dimension. But I'd have taken you for a Dick Tracy man. What do you find appealing about Li'l Abner? Is it Al Capp's narrative technique? His political satire?"

I didn't usually give this much thought to the funnies.

"Gunnar, I'll bet you like the comprehensive lampoons—the social criticism. Is that it, son?"

I decided his questions weren't from curiosity but more likely an attempt to keep me in my place. I knew that Rikard Lundeen didn't want his common man setting his sights too high, and that included the average private eye. So, while I liked Abner Yokum's indestructible guilelessness, and how the big yokel brought out people's true colors like a human litmus test, instead I said, "Al Capp works wonders with paper and ink. Those pretty hillbilly girls in their skimpy little outfits practically prance off the page."

He beamed. "Why yes, son, I suppose they do at that. Yes, indeed, skimpy little outfits."

We'd snagged a spot in a corner and gave each other across-the-table scrutiny. I'd freshened the pomade in my hair and wore my mole-gray suit for the occasion. Mr. Lundeen wore a dark brown leisure jacket and khaki-colored slacks. On the table he'd placed the pilot's sunglasses I remembered he favored.

When he'd eaten a third of his meal he said, "Family." He watched me with shrewd eyes in a beatific face. "In the end, Gunnar, what else do we have?"

What else? If the man lived to be a hundred and used twenties for toilet paper, he wouldn't put a dent in his fortune. But I kept those thoughts to myself. I wasn't sure what my reaction was supposed to be, so I did my rendition of a sagacious nod.

He gave me what I took for a conspiratorial twinkle. "Come from a big family, son?"

I shook my head as I wiped my mouth with a paper napkin. "My folks were killed in an auto crash when I was six. I was raised by my grandparents."

"Ah, then you know something about enduring familial ties."

I didn't tell him that my grandparents had died when I was in my late teens. Instead, I gave an affirming smile.

"My beloved mother was one of the Mercer girls, did you know that?"

"Daughter of Asa Mercer?" I asked. Mercer was one of Seattle's founding fathers and first president of the University of Washington.

"No, no. I'm not related to that fool schoolteacher. The only smart thing he did was to bring a number of single women West after the Civil War to help balance out Seattle's man-to-woman ratio. I wouldn't be here otherwise. My father Guttorm married one of the girls from Mercer's second trip. I was the youngest of their five children—and their only boy."

Which made him heir apparent.

"You name it, my father did it. He showed the way in Seattle's early boom. Hell, he *was* the boom. He started off as a shopkeeper's helper, became a partner in a printing firm, a banker, a hotel-builder and an investor in land and local industry. And believe me, son, I could go on."

I believed him. Guttorm Lundeen was also an avaricious taskmaster, a strike-buster, and a payer of bribes and graft. And believe me, *I* could go on.

"Did you know that ours was one of the original families to move to First Hill?"

I confessed my ignorance.

"Well we were. Over the years I've merely enlarged upon and managed my father's holdings. Yet, I'm considered one of the barons of the Northwest. But it was my father's commitment to family that made it all possible. Do you know the maxim he lived by, son?" he asked solemnly.

Compound interest is your best friend seemed a reasonable guess, but I told him I didn't have a clue.

" 'Rikky,' my father would say, 'blood is tikker dan sweat. Work hard, boy, but stand by your family, or all the sweat is vert-less.'"

I had no idea where this conversation was headed. But he was paying for lunch, so I sipped my coffee and waited patiently for the punch line.

It was a short wait.

"I understand you knew Christine Johanson—the girl who was killed over in Ballard last night."

That surprised me. He noticed.

"Is my source wrong?"

"Yes and no," I said. "I met her briefly the night before last. But I didn't really know her. Was she related to you?"

"No, son. No relation. But the girl had a connection to my family. My godson was her boyfriend."

"I see."

"Not as clearly as I want you to, Gunnar. The murdered girl worked for one of my son's commercial brainchilds. It's an adjunct venture of Darlund Apparels. It's one of those projects where Rod can toy with being a businessman. Frankly, it's a dog. And it's a costly dog at that," he said, with a shake of his head. "But it keeps Rod occupied and provides us with a tax shelter. He doesn't even actually head the fiasco. One of his favor-begging college chums manages things for him."

Rod Lundeen's fame-claim had been his prowess as a

University of Washington athlete in the mid '20s. He'd turned into a flabby middle-aged man whose strengths lay more in the high life than in the life of commerce.

"And your concern is for *Rod*?" I asked.

"Not at all, son. At this moment Rod and wife number three are on a luxury liner mindlessly cruising the inland waters of Canada. As usual, I'm left to tend to business. This time, some rather unfortunate business. So much for semi-retirement."

I heard a complaint in there, but it was a hollow one. I knew that Rikard Lundeen would be ship captain till the day they carried his corpse from the pilothouse. And even then they'd have to pry his hands from the wheel. I continued to look at him between forkfuls of apple pie.

"But since young Dirk is involved—"

"Dirk?"

"My godson. Dirk Engstrom. I've known the family for years. His late grandfather was my best friend. And his father and I regularly go on fishing trips together. He's a local jeweler and a gem of a man. Pardon the pun."

I absolved him with a lift of one brow.

"And this jeweler's son is the Dirk who was romancing Christine Johanson?" I asked.

"Precisely. Dirk's learning the jewelry business from his father. Listen, son, if you haven't guessed it, I want to hire you to look into the girl's murder."

"Why not let the police handle it? I'm sure they'll be thorough." Especially for a man with your green, is what I thought.

"Maybe so. But I'd hate for them to get thorough in a troublesome way. The police are being discreet for now. But the murdered girl worked for a *Lundeen* company, and I view young Dirk and his father as my own family."

"And blood *is* thicker than sweat—"

"Exactly. You're tracking right with me, son. If the police should dig up something ugly, the scandal could hurt

Engstrom Jewelry. And I believe I'd even rather see Rod's costly enterprise die its own pathetic death than go down in some messy embarrassment. So, I want my own unofficial inquiry, and some effort made to contain anything disturbing that may come to light. It might be quite the task, but when it comes to discretion, you've definitely won my confidence, son."

I met his look of shared meaning.

"I noticed you kept it out of the papers," I said.

"An easy matter, once you helped me to spike her guns."

I shrugged. "Most people with larceny in their souls have something to hide. It's just a matter of discovery."

He sighed. "I've mellowed with age, son. That little tramp was lucky I only gave her walking papers."

Lundeen's inamorata had hoped to score big. For a B movie bit player, she was an A-1 actress. She threatened to play the part of an ill-used plaintiff in a paternity suit. I learned she had a record of just enough small-time forgery, petty theft, and bunco activity to lack proficiency. The trouble was I kind of liked her. It was not my finest hour.

Mr. Lundeen's hand disappeared inside the front of his jacket and came out with a checkbook. "Will five hundred dollars do as a retainer?"

I almost choked on a bite of pie. "That should cover it," I said.

"I thought it might. And you keep it as a bonus if everything goes well. What do you charge again, Gunnar?"

"Thirty dollars a day."

"Let's make it forty-five, and I'm assuming that your expenses are extra."

"Right."

"I've got some suggestions as to where you can start your investigation."

"I'm open." Hell, for what he was paying me I was downright pliable.

"Head on over to Fasciné Expressions. Talk to Leonard

Pearson. He heads the operation. I've told him to expect you."

He handed me a check that he'd made out ahead of time. I was a little irked at being presumed upon. But my wounded pride healed as soon as the check was in my wallet.

As I wrote down the address, Mr. Lundeen explained that Rod's "costly dog" was a two-year-old boutique with a parent company in New York. It was a local showcase for new product lines but with provincial flavorings.

"Frankly, the place is more than a bit excessive. I tried to tell Rod that we're not ready for such local sources of sophistication. The Eastern and European salons aren't likely to be forsaken by Seattle's toplofty. They're too chary and pompous to take up with Rod's enterprise. And all the others trying to scale the peaks are too pusillanimous not to follow their lead. No, the people of this city are still too wedded to the conventional to become his regular clientele."

I didn't disagree. Seattle wasn't exactly a trendsetter city. We were known for rain, Boeing, the movie star Francis Farmer, and more rain—and not necessarily in that order.

"Why, just the other day Frederick and Nelson was pushing some French perfume. They even shipped in a Parisian model to show it off."

"La Voodoo," I said.

"What's that, son?" His face was an incredulous mask.

"La Voodoo. It's the girl's stage name." I'd seen the ads with pictures of the gorgeous model. She took over where Bambi left off. The papers said it was she who'd inspired the "doe-eyed look" that season.

"Hoodoo, schmoo-doo. It makes my point. Rod's little venture hasn't been sanctioned and isn't traditional enough to become a big success. Still, I stop in from time to time to take its pulse. Rod spends a bundle on advertising. And I have to admit it, son, Len Pearson's lovely band of salesgirls have done remarkably well. At the very least, they've managed to charm a percentage of the pretentious. Especially among the male segment of society." He winked. "You know the sort. Mainly local and visiting businessmen. Guilt-motivated gift hunters out to pacify wives and mistresses, but not minding some beautiful scenery in the process."

Mr. Lundeen put a dollar on the table and anchored it with the napkin dispenser. I popped a clove in my mouth.

"Still chewing on those twigs, eh, son?"

"Still. Ever since a good friend convinced me to quit smoking."

He seemed mildly impressed. But it was hard to know with him.

"Anyway, Gunnar, go poke around. Stir the pot if you have to. But take care, son. As I said, I want to avoid the kind of fanfare that would be bad for business and hurt my family."

I told him I understood.

"Go talk to Len. In the meantime I'll grease the skids for you down at the police station."

"Police station?"

"Yes. I'll have it all arranged so that when you've finished talking with Len and his stable of lovely *Fräuleins*, you can talk to Dirk. I'll tell them you're a hireling of his lawyer."

"He *needs* a lawyer?"

"Definitely. For now, Dirk's simply being questioned. But if I know that hothead, he'll soon talk himself into being a full-fledged suspect."

Chapter 5

—

"WHAT WAS SEATTLE LIKE—JUST after the Second World War, I mean?" Kirsti asked. That hopeful gleam of the idealist in her eyes met the realist's flicker in mine.

"Well, Blue Eyes, think of the population of New York City as an apple pie," I said. I'd just eased back down into my wheelchair after a solo limp to and from the men's room, and was looking up at Kirsti's pretty face. "In 1950 the citizenry of Seattle was about the size of a one-sixteenth sliver of that pie. Now mind you, the financial and high-priced shopping districts were on a lot smaller scale, but I'd say they were as defined and striking as in Manhattan, and the Hudson River definitely had a kid brother in the Duwamish."

"What do you mean by 'kid brother'?" she asked as she turned my chair around and began to roll me back to the outside courtyard.

I went on, "Well, in those days from West Seattle the tide flats at Duwamish Head stunk up the Spokane Street corridor like a backed-up outhouse in summer. Then it wafted over the railroad tracks to gag the tipsy denizens of the Skid

Road flophouses—and anyone else who got within whiffing distance."

"Yuck."

I almost laughed out loud. "Sure. The view of Seattle's skyline from across Elliott Bay might have suggested Manhattan Island, but it was as awe-inspiring as a sink full of dirty pie tins and almost as colorful. Closer yet, you saw the pigeon poop garnishing the cornices of many a low-rise building from the base of Queen Anne Hill down south to King Street and the markets of Chinatown."

"Gross."

"Sure. But nobody noticed, girl, and nobody cared. Not in those days. The beauty of Puget Sound was a different story … and still is. It was awe-inspiringly scenic, especially as seen from one of the tallest buildings west of the Mississippi."

"The Space Needle?"

"No. Bless your heart. That wasn't built till '62. No, the pigeon droppings had a negligible effect on our very own forty-two-story high rise—The Smith Tower."

"But that's so puny now—"

"Uh-huh. And in those days Seattle's downtown was distinguished from its uptown solely by the slope of the streets."

I was headed uptown.

Fifth and Pine was where the larger retail establishments were cozying up in those days. It was considered a fashion metropolis. While searching for a parking space I spotted Engstrom's Jewelry. It was on the first floor of the building cattycorner across the street from the one I was bound for—the Atherton Building.

I sauntered through the mezzanine entrance past a coffee shop that had just beaten back a lunch-crowd assault. I loped down a broad staircase to the main floor devoted to fine clothing for the fair sex—an annex of the downtown Darlund Apparels. I made my way to the elevators and saw my ride would be a brief one. Fasciné Expressions utilized the entire second floor.

Rikard Lundeen had told me his son's venture was a costly one, so I wasn't too surprised when I stepped from the elevator into what looked like a sitting room from Maison le Swank. I think it was the chairs not meant for sitting that put me off. They were two of those brocade-covered jobs with knuckle arms made from dark wood native only to the Himalayas—or someplace equally remote. These flanked an ornate table that was pedestal to a stack of tasteful-looking business cards. But nothing was roped off and there were no signs reading "Do not touch."

Right and left of me were arched doorways. Inside were the display rooms where a salesgirl adjusted shelves of high-class gewgaws as two others parleyed with customers. Rikard Lundeen's "lovely *Fräuleins*" appraisal was no exaggeration, judging by these three.

I picked up one of the business cards from the table. The printed slogan read: "Exceptional Offerings for that Extraordinary Someone in Your Life." As I pocketed the card, the girl who'd been fiddling with the stock came over to me. She was a redhead of medium height and wore a tawny outfit that had that "French air" you used to read about in the rotogravure pictorial section of the Sunday fashion pages. Her face was long and angular. She was slim but wore a shirtwaist that strained to contain a bust clearly meant for nursing quite a brood.

"Good afternoon, sir. Welcome to Fasciné Expressions. My name is Meredith," she said in a lazy-toned way.

Meredith's full lips enclosed an albescent smile that warmed and gladly received. Her come-on scent ensnared my olfactory receptors.

"How may I help you today?" It was more an assurance than a question, and her pixie twinkle implied a delectable competency at being both naughty and nice.

"My name is Gunnar Nilson. I have an appointment to see Mr. Pearson."

"One moment please," said Meredith. As she walked over to the doorway on my right, her hips kept time to a melody that evoked wolf-whistle accompaniment.

Meredith switched on a wall intercom and said, "A Mr. Nilson to see Mr. Pearson."

She came back over to me and said, "Miss Anderson will be here momentarily. She'll take you to Mr. Pearson."

I'd been sent to nose around in a veneer world of "may I," "shall we," "momentarily," "perchance," and "not at all." It was a gracious environment of "oughts" and "ought nots" held together by such niceties the way stitches do a coat. Abolish the niceties and the whole thing unravels.

I decided to pluck at a stitch.

"Christine mentioned she worked with a girl named Meredith," I said.

Her smile disappeared and her lips formed a brownish-red oh. "You … you knew Christine?"

"Just briefly. Such a nice girl. A real shame what happened to her."

"Yes … yes, it was," she said. Her grimace showed a small fissure in her face powder.

Immediately I saw that Meredith was a counterfeit beauty. She had one of those faces that would wear pretty until about thirty, maybe a little longer—but only with the help of makeup, and only if you didn't look close. Chances were good she only vaguely suspected she'd lose her war against time sooner rather than later.

As Meredith attempted to reconstruct her composure, I felt a twinge of shame for rattling her, but was soon distracted by the appearance of another woman in the doorway next to the intercom. She was a Junoesque blonde who looked at me and said, "Mister Nilson?"

I went over. She introduced herself as Britt Anderson. I

couldn't place her scent, but my name for it would be *Come Ravage Me*.

Beautiful understates it. Miss Anderson had to be one of the most striking beauties I've ever seen. Wire-rimmed pince-nez glasses hung around her neck on a delicate gold chain. She wore a square-shouldered jacket of navy blue with a box-pleated skirt that ended somewhere between knees and ankles. She had skin like fresh cream, and while her thin-lipped smile didn't welcome like Meredith's, her teal blue eyes proffered their own kind of invitation. Her face *would* wear well for many years and I was pretty sure she knew it.

I reached for her extended hand. It was soft and just the right temperature. I felt body heat sufficient to keep two people warm in an igloo for several hours. She was probably in her mid-twenties. Christine and Meredith belonged to the same league, but Britt Anderson was definitely group leader. I'd been sweetened and stirred, but she was too busy studying Meredith to take notice.

"Meredith, are you all right?"

"Yes … I'll be fine. We were just talking about Christine."

Miss Anderson went to Meredith and began patting her arm. I could imagine the feel of that pat as well as the sound of the whispered "there, there" that went with it.

The women were hugging now, and their heads touched. I found it a bit moving.

After a minute they parted with what looked to be mutual reassurances. Miss Anderson rejoined me and said, "Please follow me, Mr. Nilson."

I never obeyed so easily.

Her trim calves tightened as her legs went striding. She moved with effortless grace, and had a gentle shuttle to her hips—just enough to pluck intriguing crosswise stretches in the fabric of her skirt that gave pleasant inklings of a firm but globular behind.

"Call me Gunnar," I said as I caught up with her.

"If you like. Please call me Britt."

As we walked beside each other Britt said in a solemn voice, "We've been expecting your visit, Mr. Nilson—I mean, *Gunnar*."

Coming from that mouth, my name sounded regal.

"The police have come and gone already. Routine questions, they said. We're all so distraught over what happened to our dear Christine," she continued. "Meredith took it particularly hard. They were close. They often worked together."

"It's a difficult time I'm sure."

It sounded lame, I know. But the snappy-rejoinder part of my brain was still a bit neutralized by its initial encounter with Britt's charms.

She led me to a windowless door with neat gold lettering that read:

LEONARD L. PEARSON
MANAGER

Britt gave the door two quick raps and opened it.

Leonard Pearson was talking on the telephone when we entered. With his free hand he was working a yellow Life Saver loose from a half-eaten roll. The walls of his office were flat white, offset by maroon draperies and a maroon rug. Pearson pointed an index finger straight up and greeted me with lifted eyebrows. Using his raised finger as a pointer he indicated for me to take a chair with maroon upholstery. I sat as his eyes busily mapped Britt's hemispheres.

Pearson's ogling was met with neither a prim frown of reproof nor an averted glance of disdain. Britt didn't even look at her boss. She seemed oblivious to what I suspected was his chronic leering.

Britt moved around Pearson's desk with poise and dignity, picked up a few papers and straightened a disordered stack. Afterward she emptied a glass ashtray into the trash and slid it closer to him. When she circled back she adjusted the angle of a framed photograph of Pearson's wife and kids. The door made no noise when it closed behind her. The execution of these little maneuvers comprised a seamless performance. But by then I was already biased.

I took Pearson's measure as he continued his phone conversation. He had ears that stuck out like Clark Gable's, but he definitely lacked Gable's he-manship. He looked to be in his mid-forties and wore a blue two-piece suit that transformed big-shouldered portliness into utter beefiness. His fair hair was thinning, his face was florid, and his chatter was energetic and cheerful.

He hung up the phone and we stood for a formal greeting. He gave me a virility-proving handshake. He was an inch or two shorter than my own six one, and showed an automatic smile and goodwill that I thought might actually be genuine.

"Sorry about that," he said, meaning the phone call. "An old college chum. He's in town. Wants to get together. Wants me to show him a good time. You understand."

I said that I did.

Within the first minute we were Gunnar and Len. The Life Saver he chewed didn't even begin to mask his bourbon breath. He pulled out a pack of Camels from his drawer and lit one.

"You've met our Miss Anderson, I see."

I nodded.

"Couldn't function without her. Assistant, secretary and general factotum. Irreplaceable. Easy on the eyes too," he said, giving me a mischievous grin. "But don't bother getting any ideas about her, Gunnar. She's unassailable."

"A real talent for putting on the chill, eh?"

"Exactly. And if she's pushed, she has these cute little emasculating stares. More than one of my friends has made a pass at her, only to be left feeling like he'd been gelded."

"The charms of the withheld charms."

"Exactly that."

"Well, she's certainly in good company in the looks department," I said. "From what I've seen, your entire sales staff seems to have stepped right out of *Vogue*."

"That's Miss Anderson's idea. Hire pretty girls and dress them up to fit the image we're projecting. Make the personnel exemplify the product.

"Listen, Gunnar, I want you to know you've got our total cooperation. The sooner this matter can be put to rest, the better."

"What matter is that, Len?" I asked.

"Why ... Dirk Engstrom's innocence, of course. I understand he might have been involved. I mean ... his tie with Christine and all ... well, Mr. Lundeen said ...."

He had that look like he'd volunteered more than he should.

"Len, I'm just here to ask a few questions."

He blanched. "Of course. Yes, of course. Mr. Lundeen speaks very highly of you." Pearson was the tense sort who needed to keep his gums moving. He talked of his friendship with Rod Lundeen, his concerns for the company's reputation and its growing patronage. I let him yammer on.

"It's a shame that Dirk Engstrom is involved even a little bit. It sort of complicates matters. I mean, it would have been so much simpler if the police could just have signed off on the whole thing. You *do* think it was a robber that killed Christine, don't you?"

I didn't answer him. I just cocked my head and watched as he flicked ash in the ashtray.

"I ... I just don't think the company can endure any bad publicity, is all. We're still in a fledgling state, you understand. But Mr. Lundeen is confident in your abilities. I'm sure you'll find out *something* that will ...." He closed his eyes and pinched the bridge of his nose. "Damn. It better have been a robbery."

Pearson snuffed out his cigarette and pulled another from his pack. He looked at me hopefully. Old Rikard must have told Len that I was brother to Mandrake the Magician. I popped a clove in my mouth as he took a big drag on a freshly lit Camel.

"I knew that Dirk and Christine were an item, of course. But I'm afraid I won't be of much assistance to you. I didn't seem to be too much help to the police. I don't pry into the girls' personal lives, and I leave their duties strictly to Miss Anderson. Now *she* may be of some help. But you'll really want to talk with Meredith Lane. I understand she and Christine were good friends."

He stood up and made a rolling adjustment of his upper arms to rejuvenate the padded shoulders of his suit. "Come with me. I'll have Miss Anderson arrange a brief conference."

He led me out of his office to a neighboring door. He knocked and we were told to come in.

We entered a storage closet transformed into a dwarfish version of Len's office. Britt sat at her desk going through some papers. She wore her pince-nez and resembled a very classy schoolmistress. Dorothy Parker might have been right about women's glasses deterring men's passes, but I'd discovered the premier exception to her witticism.

Pearson seemed to stand an inch taller in Britt's presence. "Would you get Meredith in here, please? Mr. Nilson would like to ask her a few questions," he said with a honeyed voice. Pearson's manner was courtly and he displayed enamel so bright you could read by it.

"Certainly," Britt replied. She used the intercom and told Meredith to take an early break.

"Poor Meredith," Britt explained, looking at me. "According to one of her neighbors she became hysterical when she learned the news about Christine. Another tenant gave her something to help her sleep. I told her to take some time off, but she wouldn't hear of it. I really fear she's overdoing it."

In less than two minutes Meredith joined us with purse in hand. Britt walked over and had her sit down.

"Meredith, you met Mr. Nilson out front. What you don't know is that he's been hired by Mr. Lundeen to investigate Christine's murder."

"I see," she said softly, giving a feeble smile. Some of the confidence she'd shown me when we first met had returned, but I could tell discovering my role flustered her a little.

Britt stood by with a box of Kleenex, and I noticed Pearson aping her, as he fumbled with his breast pocket in search of his handkerchief. Meredith didn't look like she was going to cry to me. She seemed more uneasy than sorrowful.

"How can I help?" Meredith said.

"Anyone you know who might want to harm Christine?"

She looked at Britt and Pearson. "No …. Christine was a sweet kid. I … I don't know why anyone would want to hurt her."

Britt's concern for Meredith was palpable, her eyes portals of empathy and compassion. Pearson's sympathies jumped out at you too. He held his handkerchief at the ready with one hand while the fingertips of his other lightly touched Britt's shoulder in solidarity. If he'd stood any closer to her they'd have been Siamese twins.

Meredith plucked a couple of Kleenexes from the box Britt offered, but I still didn't see any tears. I turned to Britt and Pearson. "Do you mind if I talk with Meredith alone? I think she'll be all right."

Britt nodded and smiled, giving Meredith a squeeze of the shoulder as she passed. Pearson seemed relieved at a chance to go, and looked libidinously eager to follow his factotum into a hurricane's eye if necessary.

I figured Meredith might find it easier to say some things about Christine to a stranger. Easier still, if Britt and Pearson weren't around.

I leaned against Britt's desk and said, "This is quite an establishment. A regular smorgasbord, especially for the affluent gift hunter. How do you like working here?"

That gave her renewed focus. She started talking about scents. Those she liked, loved and hated, and how she preferred selling perfume over cosmetics. Next the shifts. Then the work and the time spent on her feet.

Meredith opened her purse and took out a pack of Pall Malls. "Britt won't mind. Do you?" she asked.

I told her I didn't mind.

"Join me?"

I shook my head as I lit her cigarette for her. A glass ashtray sat on Britt's desk. I handed it to her.

After drawing deeply, she turned her head aside and exhaled a gray column.

I asked about Britt and Pearson.

She characterized Pearson as a phantom. The girls saw little of him. She made a joke about Britt being the power behind Pearson's throne, but gave no indication that anything romantic was going on between them. It was plain Meredith respected Britt Anderson. As she told it, Britt was fair to all the girls and acted as sort of a big sister to some of them.

"But she ain't ... *isn't* nosy."

According to Meredith, Britt saw to their clothes and she even had them regularly groomed by a drama coach—an older woman who lived over in Laurelhurst.

"Mrs. Arnot helps us with things like grammar and poise. Britt wants us to come across polished for the customers," she explained.

When she seemed more comfortable talking with me, I asked, "Do you think Dirk Engstrom killed Christine?"

She hesitated. "Do the police think he did it?"

"They're questioning him. Do *you* think he killed your friend?"

"He ... he might have. He's a jealous one, that's for sure. Christine complained about it all the time. A real jerk in my opinion. But I don't know ... Dirk had it for Christine in a bad way. It's hard to see him as her killer."

"Jealousy and homicide are frequent bedfellows."

"Sure. I know. Like I said, he might have done it."

"But you have another theory," I said.

My suggestion surprised her.

"Do you think it was a customer?" I asked.

She gave the closed door a quick glance before slowly dipping her chin once.

"This customer got a name?" I asked.

"No. I mean I wouldn't know who it might be. It could be any number of the repeat customers."

"You monitor them?"

"Uh-huh. It was Britt's idea. You know, a list of who referred who, and who waits on them. That kind of thing. A way to keep track."

"Track of the repeat customers."

"Uh-huh. *Men* customers. You know how it is. They flirt with you or you flirt a bit with them to make a sale. The next thing you know, some of them come in the store just to see you, but then feel a need to buy something." She laughed nervously. "Before you know it some of them think they own you."

She stopped suddenly, hearing herself talk too much.

"*Own* you?"

"Well, not really, I guess."

She took a last drag on her cigarette, held her breath and then exhaled a mouthful of smoke and then inhaled it through her nose. Teenagers called it the French-inhale. Only they would believe it was chic.

"So you think Christine may have gotten a little too involved with a particular customer—one who thought he owned her? Is that it?"

"Something like that. Listen, I'm not accusing anyone of anything. All I'm saying is that it wouldn't hurt to check in that direction."

"Meredith, why do I think you're working with more than just a feeling?"

She looked down and away from me and then stole a quick glance at the door. "At the end of the day yesterday," she said, "Christine made a phone call. I overheard her say something about meeting later in Ballard."

"Over where she was killed."

"Yes." She was looking at me again.

"Did she say whom she was speaking to? Or where they were to meet?"

She shook her head. "But I'm pretty sure it wasn't Dirk."

"Why not?"

"Because I've overheard her talking to Dirk plenty of times to know. She didn't sound yesterday like she does with him."

"How did she sound?"

She thought for a moment. "She was a little bit nervous. Maybe scared. But the funny thing was, she was also angry. Like she'd been cheated or something."

Meredith said she couldn't make out what the conversation was about. We talked a little more about Christine and their friendship. I could see she'd told me all she was going to, but I got the impression that she had more to say.

I thanked her and gave her my card. She tore off a page from one of Britt's notepads and wrote something on it. As she opened the door to leave she handed the note to me.

"That's my address and telephone number," she said. "I'd appreciate knowing anything you might learn."

Outside the door I could hear Meredith and Britt whispering, but their words were an unintelligible buzz. When it ended Britt came back in. Her glasses were hanging around her neck again.

"Where's the boss man?" I'd almost said *your devoted follower*.

"Len received a long distance telephone call. It sounded urgent."

"It must have pained him to tear himself away from you."

She loyally ignored my sarcasm, but didn't offer excuses for her boss like an unquestioning employee might. She merely smiled. I didn't see Pearson as her type—in this venue or in any other. He was just a hopeful base-stealer a long, long way from home plate.

"May I offer you some refreshments? Some coffee or tea, perhaps?"

I told her coffee black would be great. I watched her at her task.

Walter Pangborn owned a book on medieval architecture. One phrase had gotten forever burned into my brain: *Seldom has splendor of form been so well harmonized with subtlety of detail.* Britt Anderson was a Gothic edifice in the Nordic style. She was well conceived and skillfully made—every element a slice of pure perfection. She looked over at me through lovely ornate windows as she poured our coffee. Britt definitely had unity of design and harmony of substance and line. I found her well-proportioned buttresses breathtaking. I was extremely moved by her elegant curving vault, and I shamelessly surveyed her jutting pinnacles of natural grandeur.

She brought me my cup. I plopped in the chair Meredith had warmed. Britt leaned against a corner of her desk, one ankle crossed over the other. She made a casual pose look like enticing pageantry.

I almost told her that I envied the coffee cup she held to her lips. But I let it go. She'd probably heard all the lines in triplicate. And that one stunk. For the moment I stuck with chasing facts instead of skirts.

Britt had known Christine for about two years, but had never witnessed anything unusual about her. She told me that when she hired girls her initial screening process was fairly stringent. Christine was capable and wanted to juggle part-time employment with the classes she was taking at the U. Eventually she stopped juggling and began to work full-time. Britt didn't know much about Dirk Engstrom.

"I'm friendly with the girls, but I have to draw a line somewhere."

"And what keeps the power behind Pearson's throne from moving on to bigger and better?" I asked.

She smirked. "Did Meredith call me that?"

"Pearson himself said as much. So what keeps you here?"

She sighed. "It's changing, but it's still a man's world," she said, setting her cup on the desk. "I'll admit that I've thought about finding a throne of my own a few times, to use your phrase."

"I'm sure you'd make a great king."

She laughed. "I'll take that as a compliment."

I made a courtly bow from my seated position.

"Like I said, it's still a man's world. I was going to move to New York City to follow through on my plans, but I've been kind of tethered to Seattle."

"Tethered? How's that?"

"When my mother died, I moved here to live with her youngest sister. I was a teenager at the time. My aunt was only in her mid-twenties then, but of course she seemed so much older and sophisticated to a girl who'd lived her whole life on an apple farm in Wenatchee. I idolized her. She started out taking care of me. I ended up taking care of her."

She saw my puzzled expression.

"My aunt was highly sensitive. She had a romance go bad and I'm afraid it shattered her. She never recovered. I saw to her needs. I tried my best to take care of her for several years. But she got progressively worse. Three years ago I finally had to commit her. She died after a year in Steilacoom. The ravages of alcoholic dementia, they said. But I say it was a broken heart."

"I'm sorry." Putting a loved one in a mental hospital had to be rough. Having them die there had to be a nightmare.

"Thank you. It's probably for the best. She's no longer suffering. Some people don't snap back."

I said I understood. I knew a few guys who came back from the war but never really returned. Not everyone has the resilience of a Walter Pangborn.

We talked a little longer, and then I stood up and handed her my cup. Our fingers bumped. Gunnar the Smitten. Had she purposely touched me?

Gunnar the Gonadal, more like it.

"I may be back to talk with one or two of the other girls. I understand you keep a list of regular customers—males anyway."

She smiled. "I see Meredith told you of our little attempt at psychological merchandising."

"Whatever works, I say. Would you mind putting together a list of Christine's regulars?"

"Not at all. Does this mean I'll see you again?"

"You sound as if you like the idea."

"Maybe I do."

Chapter 6

—

Kirsti looked speculatively at me and said, "That Britt Anderson had the hots for you."

"Well, you know, Blue Eyes, I wasn't always a wizened wheelchair jockey."

With a teasing smile and a knowing look, she said, "Yeah, you were probably a real hottie. And it's pretty obvious that that boutique was the rooster paradise you'd referred to."

"Yes, but it wasn't me who coined that term for it."

"Who did, then?"

"All in good time, young lady. I'll not be rushed. Besides, you're supposed to save up your questions, remember?"

"Sorry," she said. But she wasn't in the least.

It was probably Rikard Lundeen's retainer along with Britt Anderson's bantam hint of interest that made me feel like splurging. I put two dollars worth of regular in the Chevy before I headed back downtown.

Everyday speech can be contradictory. Have you ever noticed how "fat chance" and "slim chance" mean the same thing? The word "choice" gets similar treatment. I'd rented my choice out for the day. I rarely entered a police station by choice. I chose to do so now because I had no choice.

Detective Sergeant Frank Milland's working milieu was a chaotic medley of desks, filing cabinets, ancient typewriters and overflowing ashtrays. The real human touches were the smell of perspiration and the mishmash of forsaken food scraps that looked to have been grown in petri dishes—and would surely have led to fantastic discoveries if analyzed under a microscope. But it wasn't my mission to bemoan this tragic loss to science. I was looking for my friend.

I took in scenes that reminded me that a cop's job deals largely with policies, procedures, complaints, and irksome details. Only a tiny fraction of their work is connected to bloodshed and murder.

The squad room was buzzing with cops and Seattle citizenry. I worked my way to the back, where Milland's partner, Bernie Hanson, sat at his hardwood desk beating out a concerto on his typewriter. To my right was a plump, middle-aged woman who wore a summer dress that had already seen way too many seasons. She sobbed and beseeched two cops who had mouths that looked sutured shut and who were about as open and friendly as that allows. To my left was an old colored man in a drab suit who earnestly told his story to another officer. The cop nodded as he hunted and pecked at his typewriter.

An old Scandinavian fellow in alpaca trousers, a flannel shirt, and a string tie remonstrated with the desk sergeant.

"*Ja*, but how can you go *back* before you been *forth*?" he argued. The desk sergeant shook his head and tried again. But it's hard arguing with that kind of logic. I know. My grandpa Sven was doggedly puzzled at how people got "in" an automobile but got "on" a train.

Milland stood talking with Lieutenant Archibald Lister. I slipped a clove under my tongue and walked over to them. Lister was about forty-five, sleepy-eyed, and balding. His deceased parents had named him Archibald, but apparently

they were the only humans who called him that. He refused
to be called Archie. And no one in his right mind called him
Baldy. Not to his face anyway. So it was either "Lieutenant" or
"Lister." I can only imagine what his wife and kids did when
they wanted his attention.

Lieutenant Lister favored funereal suits of gray blue or inky
black that helped to define him. Since he wore a perpetual
sneer, you looked for other clues as to his emotional state. At
that moment his face was the color of a toreador's cape, which
went well with his words and gestures.

"I don't go for this special consideration bullshit," he said as
he thrust his face within a few inches of mine. His lip quivered
and I could count his nose hairs. He looked back at Milland
and said, "Give him ten minutes. Tops. Then you kick his
privileged candy ass out of here."

The sobbing woman broke off her story to gawk at us. In
fact, everyone looked our way. Everyone, that is, but the old
Swede. He knew where the universe centered and nothing was
about to disturb the confidence he felt about it.

After Lieutenant Lister stomped off, I said to Milland,
"What's his beef? Is his wife dosing his coffee with saltpeter
again?"

"Ah, cut the guy some slack, Gunnar. It's been a pressure-
cooker week. You getting your well-heeled client to start
pulling strings hasn't helped. You know the lieutenant doesn't
like citizen interference. I figured you for smarter than that."

"I didn't ask for strings to be pulled, Frank."

"Well, strings have been downright jerked in your favor.
How is it you happen to know Rikard Lundeen, anyway?"

"I worked for him once. Is it my fault he likes me?"

Milland scowled. "You want to talk to the Engstrom kid?"

"Yeah. Lundeen was afraid he'd talk himself into the role of
prime suspect."

"He did more than talk himself there."

"Does he look that good?"

Milland picked up on the surprise in my voice. "Damn good," he said smiling. "Double damn good."

He explained that quite a few people witnessed the scene and overheard the noise the day before when Dirk Engstrom stormed in on Christine Johanson while she was working. However, only three people were close enough to the fracas to see that Dirk was enraged, and one of these three said he heard Dirk threaten to kill Christine.

"It doesn't sound good," I said.

"No, it gets better than that. We found drops of blood on a pair of shoes in Engstrom's apartment. We're checking on a match."

"It sounds *real* bad."

"It gets even worse. We found a gun in the kid's apartment that had been recently fired. His prints were lifted from it and the ballistics boys are checking to see if it's the gun that killed the Johanson dame."

"Double damn good is right." So ended forty-five dollars a day.

Milland nodded. "The Engstrom kid is on the brink of being charged, booked, sealed, and delivered. So get your chat in while you can, Gunnar. Lundeen's pull has got us taking things nice and slow for now. And we're also keeping the kid from the press as long as possible. Lundeen must have leverage with both the *Times* and *P.I.*, because I've seen no crime reporters sniffing around. But I'm not rooting for you on this one, Gunnar. Not if you aim to prove the kid innocent."

"Look, Frank, the Engstrom kid is Lundeen's godson. I'm rented for the day to nose into things. That's it. I'm not on some bleeding-heart mission, and I'm not out to undo your hard work. Besides, it sounds to me like the kid deserves to trade pinstripes for prison stripes."

"We like to think so."

I took out a pad and pencil from my coat pocket. "Let me at least earn my salt. It wouldn't hurt if I talked to the three bystanders of that fight." My plan, if you could call it that, was to talk to them and get some kind of reading off what they saw and heard. I needed at least something to put in a final report to Rikard Lundeen. "How about giving me the names?"

"The first one has quite the moniker. He's a fella named Guy de Carter. He's got a kisser that sort of reminds me of Smilin' Jack from the funny papers. Mustache and all."

Again with the funny papers. Smilin' Jack was a debonair-looking comic strip character that was a caricature of the movie star Errol Flynn—or vice versa.

"This de Carter works for an ad agency in the same building where the murdered girl worked. He says his company handles their ad work. The second witness is one Addison Darcy. He's a longtime local about as well-heeled as Lundeen. Darcy was a customer in the store when the lover's spat broke out. The third onlooker is the widow of a Dr. Henry Arnot. Gal's name is Blanche. She was there on business. Hell, it's not enough for 'em to hawk fancy toilet water. This Blanche Arnot says she teaches the salesgirls to walk and talk straight while they do it. Probably teaches them to piss and flush straight too."

Milland shook his head. "I'll put addresses and phone numbers to two of these names for you before you leave."

"What about the third?"

"Addison Darcy lives in The Highlands."

"Oh, *rally*?"

"Yes, *rally*. He made his statement and referred us to his lawyer. Like I say, I'll get you the dope on the other two. Good luck on reaching Darcy."

"Thanks, Frank. I owe you one."

"You owe me two. And I'm keeping track. You just missed the Engstrom kid's old man, but his lawyer's still with him."

He led me away from the clamor of the squad room over to a nook used for conferences.

"He's all yours," said Milland.

I heard arguing on the other side of the door. I knocked

and opened. Two men stared at me with expressions that said *altercatio interruptus*. I entered and the older of the two stood up and refreshed the crease in his pants. His crisp charcoal suit gave him a prim aspect that went with a genteel demeanor. He seemed to know who I was and why I was there. He introduced himself as Hiram Pender, attorney for Bern Engstrom and ipso facto for Dirk Engstrom.

"He insists on talking to you alone," Pender said to me. He gave his client a parting look that could pass for pity or disgust. "I'll be waiting outside."

I closed the door behind Pender. He was polite enough, but I consider lawyers guilty until proven innocent. So far as I knew he was just another highbrow thimble-rigger in an intellectual shell game, with truth as the pea. Now you see it—now you don't. Even if they do sink their chops into some meaty issue, truth isn't usually their objective. I see them as modern wizards who conjure for cash and celebrity.

I told Dirk my name. He stayed motionless and ignored my extended hand. I sat down in the chair behind the solitary desk in the room.

"I'm working for Rikard Lundeen, which means I'm working for you, Dirk."

"Don't call me Dirk. Only my friends call me Dirk." His complexion had crimson patches. His lower lip curled slightly to one side and uncurled only when he spoke.

"Okay, then. How's *kid* suit you?"

He gave me a glacial stare. Kid it was.

Dirk was a good-looking kid in his early twenties. His white slacks and Anzac-blue windbreaker told me he wasn't working at the jewelry store when the cops scooped him up. He had sandy-colored hair with an unruly forelock that matched his present disposition.

"I didn't kill her. Nobody here believes me, of course. Not even that pettifogging shyster of my father's."

"Your father and Rikard Lundeen are behind you. And if I can help, I will."

"I don't hear a very confident tone. You think I killed her too, don't you?"

"What the police have on you *is* pretty compelling."

"I didn't threaten to kill Christine! That guy is lying," he said throatily.

"What about the blood on your shoes?"

"I don't wear two-toned wingtips. Those aren't my shoes."

"And the gun the cops found?"

"It's not mine. No one believes me. It was after nine this morning when I felt it while I was reaching for underwear. I was shocked to find the thing in my drawer. I put it down on the bed when I heard the police knocking on the door. I don't even like guns."

"You *gave* the gun to the cops?"

"One of them spotted it on the bed. I told them I just found it in the dresser."

"You *let* them search your place?"

"How was I to know I had something to hide?"

"What kind of car do you drive?"

"What's that got to do with anything?"

"Humor me. What kind of car?"

"A Chrysler Windsor coupe—a '47. Why? What's it matter?"

I told him how I'd met Christine the night before she was killed. I told him the masher story she'd given me and about the Packard that followed us. That shook him up a bit.

"Any of your friends drive a fairly new Packard?" I asked.

"No ... I don't think so. No." His hostility began to fade. "Christine and I ... we were together that night. Just before you say you met her. I was taking her home. We'd had a bite to eat. She made me pull over on Market Street to let her out. We'd had a big fight."

"Sounds like you've had a lot of those lately."

He didn't hear me, or pretended not to.

"Do you think it *was* a masher following her that night you met her?" he asked.

"Beats me. What about last night? You don't have an alibi for the time she was killed, do you?"

"No. I argued with her in the store earlier yesterday like they say. I lost my head. I do that sometimes. I suppose I shouted some. But I didn't threaten to kill her. I swear it. And afterward I went back to work and finished the day. When work was through I went straight home and downed a six pack of beer and half a bottle of bourbon."

I asked him to tell me about his relationship with the Johanson girl.

He explained that he'd graduated from the University of Washington the year before. He'd met Christine the first month he started working for his father.

"She'd come in to buy a pair of earrings," he said softly. "Prettiest girl I've ever seen. Meeting her was the best thing that ever happened to me." He paused for a minute or so to struggle with his emotions. Finally he took a deep breath and continued.

He told me how he hated the jewelry business, but started seeing a future in it when he met Christine. She gave him the incentive he lacked.

"My dad could tell the difference in my attitude. I was whistling coming in the door in the mornings."

Soon he'd also become one of those repeat customers at Fasciné Expressions Meredith had told me about. Christine and he started dating. She was reluctant at first, but he was persistent. Everything was going well. At least Dirk thought so. And in the last couple of months, things had started to get serious. On his part, anyway.

"I wanted her to quit her job and go back to school. I said I'd help her with money. That place wasn't good for Christine."

"Not good *how*?"

"I could see what it was doing to her. The attention from male customers was starting to turn her head. More than once I walked in to find a customer standing a little too close, or maybe holding her hand. I'd gone in there yesterday to apologize for the night before. I wanted to patch things up. Do you know what I mean?"

I nodded.

"But when I walked in and saw that old lecher Addison Darcy sniffing the nape of her neck, I exploded. That geezer's old enough to be her grandfather!"

Dirk spoke of Christine in the present tense. It may not have meant much, but the blood that rushed to his face sure did.

"Is that what the fights were about? Your jealousy?"

He gave me a sour look. "I had good reason. You didn't see what I saw."

Dirk told me he'd recently raised the topic of their future together. He'd brought up marriage. His serious talk had started to upset Christine.

"She had ideas in her head about moving to New York. But I don't think that was what made my marriage talk upset her."

"What do you mean?"

"I don't really know what I mean. I just saw little changes in her when I started to get serious. She'd get upset real easily. She'd burst into tears a lot. Cry on my shoulder. Do you know what I mean?"

I said I knew what he meant.

"She kept telling me that she wasn't good enough for me. Like she was tainted or something. That kind of nonsense. But I couldn't get her to see reason. That night you met her at the movie house, she'd just broke up with me. It didn't make sense. It still doesn't."

He stared through me. I mulled over what he'd said.

"Any sign of a break-in at your place this morning?"

"Wha … why? Oh, you mean someone might have planted the shoes and gun?"

"Anything's possible."

"It's what I told the police. I told them someone had to have planted that stuff."

"Any sign of break-in?"

He thought about it. "No. My apartment is on the first floor. I was dead to the world after the booze. I'm not much of a drinker. I suppose someone could have sneaked in. I'd left the window open. But … who would want to set me up? *Who*?"

"Got any enemies, kid?"

He shook his head. It must have been nice being so well-liked.

"Clearly your girlfriend did."

Dirk had a bad case of calf love, bull lust, and green-eyed monster. Such a combination of symptoms has been known to lead to murder. But I sensed something wasn't right.

I stood up, and he did too.

"Does … does this mean you believe I didn't kill Christine?"

"Like I said, kid, anything's possible. Let's just say I'm believing the proof stacked against you a little less." I showed him my right thumb and index finger separated by an eighth of an inch.

"Oh."

It wasn't very encouraging, but it wasn't meant to be. Good cheer wasn't my normal stock-in-trade. I turned to leave.

"Mr. Nilson," he said, his voice an octave higher than it had been.

I looked back at him. "Yeah, kid?"

"Thanks for helping Christine out the other night."

"Don't mention it."

"No, I mean it. Some other guy might have taken advantage of her."

Gunnar the Gallant. I liked the sound of that. I preferred it to Gunnar the Randy. I figured there was no sense spoiling matters by mentioning Christine's titillating kiss, the stirring effects of her sex appeal, or the moves I was willing to make had she been amenable.

"And, Mr. Nilson, one more thing. You go ahead and call me Dirk."

In those days, Seattle wanted to be San Francisco in the worst way. But probably the most obvious testament to the city's uninspired humdrumness was its lack of A-1 restaurants; the kind long known to San Franciscans. The closest thing to fine eating was found in the better hotels. Fortunately for my pocket book and stomach, there were a number of decent eateries scattered around town, however humble.

Mrs. Berger was an excellent cook, but she held dinner for no man. If you weren't promptly seated at 5:00 p.m., your plate was removed and the food was served. Your absence was noted, but mourned only when liver was on the menu. My Longines said 5:05, so I headed for Market Street.

Holger's Café couldn't match the grill at the Hotel Sorrento and its Ballard location didn't offer the scenic view atop the Camlin Hotel, but Holger Lindgren served up a mean chicken-fried steak, and I'd take an eyeful of Verna Vordahl over Elliott Bay any day of the week.

Customers were parked on all stools but one. Holger's clientele were chiefly single men—mill workers, mechanics, and tradesmen. Holger chatted with regulars as he worked at the grill, his cook's hat down to his eyebrows at its usual rakish angle. He was the proud conductor of a hungry orchestra— the din of their conversation mixed with rattling stone- and silverware as they chowed down. It was the mealtime version of ruffles and flourishes. The familiar sounds and smells gave me a kind of serenity.

Verna Vordahl waited tables. She was a big girl but lean. Five eleven, and 36-23-34 was my best guess. Holger called her "My lovely Amazon." She had a pallid complexion with hair the color and texture of an Irish setter. A thin aquiline nose, heavy brows, and a broad face were kept from grimness by a lively disposition and a sort of alchemy she did with vivid brown eyes and lush lips that curved into a sweet smile.

Verna never slouched, and her sturdy hips always moved in easy rhythm with the nimble flex of a pair of Betty Grable legs. As I sat down I noticed that her movements seemed more frenetic than usual. I looked around at some of the other customers. I could tell I wasn't the only one preoccupied with the supple shape encased in a blue waitress uniform that on her was transformed into erotic body armor.

Lustful eyes might mentally disrobe her, but as Hank Vordahl's wife she was off limits to the male patrons of Holger's. Verna was accustomed to being gazed at, and while she probably even liked what she took for speculative appreciation, I doubt she fully realized just what a star performer she was in many a private fantasy, and how feverishly customers ate to sublimate. Holger knew exactly what was going on, and he wisely paid Verna top wages for her marquee value.

Verna's hash-slinging was a foreign and violent ceremony that day. Plates slammed when they should have landed gently. Silverware clashed and clanged instead of being scooped up with a thuffing noise. I had reason to suspect she was redirecting her own sexual tension and conflict. It was the first time I'd seen her since learning the news. I counted Verna as a good friend, so I faced one of those uncomfortable crossroads that comes with the obligations of friendship. I knew I had to bring up the subject sometime if I wanted to keep coming to Holger's. But it had all the charms of broaching funeral arrangements to an aged parent.

"Sorry to hear about you and Hank."

I was suddenly one of Hitler's generals, Verna was the *Führer*, and the Russians were storming Berlin.

"What's a girl supposed to do, Gunnar?" she asked in her throaty contralto voice. "I could deal with his nightmares from the war. And who don't need a good belt now and again? I understand that. And I been workin' since I was six years old, so I didn't mind helpin' out with expenses till Hank settled on somethin' steady. But comin' home in the middle of the day to find him and some B-girl in the very bed I picked out and am still payin' for …. Well, a girl's gotta draw the line somewheres. Am I right?"

I told her she was right.

She took in a deep breath that lifted her breasts like hillocks in a seismic upheaval. After a heavy sigh the trembler stopped. The seismologist seated next to me put a big tip on the counter and left.

"I mean, what's a girl supposed to do?"

"I understand."

"I got me a place over in Greenwood. Moved my things out. Let Hank stew in his juices."

"What else could you do?"

"That's right. He keeps beggin' me to come back. He tells me things are gonna be different and that he's a *new* man."

And how about a purpose in life to go with that new man? I thought but did not say. No point in it. She'd have become instant snow-girl and I'd have to forget about those timely and cheery refills.

Hank Vordahl was a big, rock-jawed man with shoulders that could double as a warehouse's main support beam. Unfortunately for Verna, Hank's decisions and actions were those of a ne'er-do-well. A dreamer of big dreams was Hank Vordahl. The only successful thing he ever did was to get Verna to believe in his dreams and marry him. The year before, the owner of an appliance store downtown needed a delivery man. The guy knew me, so I recommended Hank for the job as a favor to Verna. The first two days went okay. On the third day Hank was so sauced he drove that truck with his lips right through the front window of a café in West Seattle. Thankfully no one was hurt.

"So how's it going?" I asked.

"So far so good, Gunnar. But it's only been five days, so I figure it won't hurt for me to give it another week. Just to be sure. No sense rushin' things." She took in another deep breath and let it out slowly. "He's gonna have to start all over again. I told him I expect flowers, candy, wining and dining. The whole works. We got our first hot date Friday night. Need another refill, hon?"

When I finished my meal I put a clove in my mouth and an extra big tip on the counter before I went over and put a nickel in the payphone.

I called Rikard Lundeen.

"Things are bad for young Dirk," he said as soon as I said hello. "It looks like the hot-tempered fool might have killed her, son."

I agreed, but filled him in on what I'd done so far, only giving him the gist of what I'd learned.

"So *you* believe he's innocent," he said when I'd finished.

"What I believe is that something's fishy. Finding out what and why looks to be a Herculean task."

"You're the man for it, son."

I told him I wanted to talk with the onlookers to Dirk's scrap with Christine. "I can reach two of them with no problem. The third might be a little challenging." I gave him the name.

"Addison Darcy, that pompous windbag. We're old friends. *Old* friends."

I asked him what he was like.

Mr. Lundeen hesitated. "What do you need to know, son?"

"As much as I can. I never know what might be important going into an interview."

After a silent moment, he sighed and laughed a concessionary laugh. "Addison's a crafty sonofabitch. He's about my age—a few years younger. We're still partners in some interests, although he's become a fairly mute one in recent years. He's the 'Dar' in Darlund Apparels. But you probably already knew that, eh, son?"

I told him I didn't know that.

"Addison was always at home, whether in a boardroom or a bordello. He was a wild one when we were young. Always a cool businessman, but definitely a rounder who mixed pleasure with business. I liked the ladies myself, you understand, and still do, as you know. But when it came to womanizing, it was a rare one who could keep up with Addison Darcy in his youth. He married a gal from a New England family. Very old money dating back to the time of the Revolutionary War. They have two married daughters who live out of state, but they lost their son in the war. The boy's death changed old Addison. Heartache and getting older finally slowed him down in a way marriage never could. But he also lost his drive—a certain zest he once had. He's cut back on active management of his holdings, divested a bit, and rarely bothers with new ventures. That boy of his meant everything to him. Everything."

"I understand he's one of your neighbors in The Highlands."

"A distant neighbor, yes. We were partners and good friends from nonage to long past juvenescence. We made business trips and regularly raised hell together a long, long time ago. But we've drifted apart. I rarely see him. He lives in semi to near-total retirement and cultivates his garden without fanfare. He attends church most every Sunday now and has settled into the staid role of community pillar." Mr. Lundeen laughed. "What's the saying son? You wind up fulfilling your destiny in your desperate attempts to avoid it. When would you like to call on that boasting bundle of bones?"

"Any time tomorrow would be fine."

"Give me an hour, son. I'll set you up for a visit."

I thanked him and told him I'd get back to him.

I called Britt Anderson.

She was all business until she recognized my voice.

"My, but you have a very alluring voice on the telephone, did you know that?" she said.

I told her that I knew that, and that it was a curse, and that if it mattered to her, flattery made me extremely vulnerable.

She laughed. A genuine snicker, not a polite one.

The information I wanted from Britt could have waited until morning, but I felt like hearing her voice again. I asked how she was coming along with that list of repeat customers.

"It's waiting for you on my desk."

"Thanks. So very prompt, Miss Anderson."

"At Fasciné Expressions we specialize in prompt service with a gracious smile. Or haven't you noticed?"

"Oh, I've noticed. I'll be by for the list tomorrow. But tell me, is an Addison Darcy one of the names on it?"

After a half-second check she said that he certainly was. "Is it significant?" she asked.

"Probably not." I told her about the witnesses to Dirk and Christine's fight.

"I can help you out with two of them. I'll call Guy de Carter and see if I can set you up with a lunch appointment tomorrow."

"You're too kind, Miss Anderson."

I gave her my office phone number to call in the morning to confirm. "I was hoping to stop by Blanche Arnot's this evening."

"I'm sure that will be fine with Blanche," Britt said. "Let me telephone and tell her you're coming by. When exactly do you intend to go see her?"

My Longines said 5:40. I planned a stop home for a quick bath and change.

"Would seven o'clock tonight be too late?"

"I'm sure it will be fine. You're in luck in two ways. Blanche has become more of a homebody since her husband died, and she's always been a bit of a night owl."

"You sound like you know her pretty well."

"Oh yes. She and my aunt were very close despite the difference in their ages. They shared the same passion: they performed with a local theater group. Blanche helped me a great deal with my aunt during her decline. I think seeing Alexis fall apart was as hard on her as it was on me. When Blanche's husband passed away shortly afterwards, it was extremely unsettling for her. It was as though she'd been cut from her moorings. It's one of the reasons I asked her to work

for us. I thought a new focus in life would be a good distraction
for her."

Britt told me a few snippets from Blanche Arnot's theatrical
past. "I think you'll like her. But be warned, she's ... *quaint*."

We bantered a bit and then I thanked her and hung up.

"You two were sure getting cozy with each other, weren't
you?" Kirsti yelped with delight.

I pretended to ignore her question as I swallowed the last of
the pastrami sandwiches she'd brought me. I then took a sip of
the bottled water she handed me and decided to shift her mind
in a different direction.

"My friend Walter Pangborn had a high regard for our
landlady. Actually, Walter was in love with the woman."

"Really?"

"Yes, *really*. But Mrs. Berger didn't seem to have the slightest
clue as to Walter's true feelings."

"Oh, come on, Gunnar, a woman knows."

"Well, it sure didn't show."

"Trust me."

"Walter had been a boarder at the Berger's for years. From
a few remarks he let slip, his feelings had developed after Otto
Berger died. Hell, it took Sten Larson and me months to make
sense of the obvious indications."

"Who's Sten Larson?"

"Mrs. Berger's nephew. He was a boarder too."

"And so what were these obvious indications?"

"Little things. Walter's agreeing to write Mrs. Berger's
play—which meant spending an hour or more every Sunday
brainstorming with her as she reminisced and created;
his siding with her in discussions at mealtimes, however
ludicrous her opinion; his chuckling at her idiotic anecdotes;
his despondent retreats to his room when she went out on the
occasional date. Why she didn't see it was beyond me."

"Trust me. She saw it."

"Well, eventually … yes."

"What do you mean?"

"I'll get there, Blue Eyes. Be patient."

She stuck out her lower lip in a playful pout of resignation.

"Walter and Mrs. Berger were close in age, and I fully understood his physical attraction to her, She had a handsome, angular face, with those classic planes and hollows. She had long slim legs with taut calves, and though the sand was in mid-drain at that time, her hourglass proportions were still suited for a passable fan dance."

"It sounds like you made quite the study of her yourself. Why am I not surprised?"

"Well, I'll confess to my own disturbing moments of lusty curiosity when it came to Mrs. Berger. In my dreams she was often making a play for me or trying to lure me into bed."

Kirsti looked horrified. "She had to be twenty years older than you."

"I'll admit to some ambivalence, Blue Eyes. But, age disparity sometimes has a way of disappearing in amorous half-light."

Her eyes eluded me for a few moments of puzzled silence. I finally interrupted.

"But what I didn't understand was why a learned and sophisticated man like Walter so ardently adored a crass and poorly educated ex-stripper."

"Oh, come on, Gunnar. I think it's sweet. That whole 'opposites attract' thing."

"Maybe so. But I filed the whole thing somewhere between Sweet Mysteries of Life and Riddles of the Orient."

Chapter 7

—

BEFORE THE WAR MY home had been a fifth floor studio apartment on Eighth Avenue, north of Seneca. I worked a lot of out-of-town jobs for the Bristol Agency, so my tiny little flat was literally a place to hang my hat and flop between assignments. It was Walter Pangborn who steered me to Mrs. Berger's boardinghouse after my discharge.

I met Walter in 1939. Actually I *found* him. His estranged sister had hired a Philadelphia detective firm that had arranged assistance from the Bristol Agency. We'd been told Walter was badly burned on one side of his face and body, so I was braced for how he'd look. What I wasn't prepared for was his reaction when I called at the Berger's house in Ballard.

At that time Otto Berger—the man who'd deprived the burlesque world of its bump and grind queen—was still alive. After Otto relayed to Walter my name and mission, he returned to the front door and said in his faint German accent, "Walter thanks you, but he wishes to stay lost."

I was not deterred. I figured Walter for a twilight trekker. He proved to be an after-dark ambler.

I followed him to The Moonglow Eats on First Avenue,

where I'd had my conference with Rikard Lundeen. After he'd ordered, I sat on a stool beside him, asked for coffee I didn't need, and struck up a conversation. Walter wasn't embittered or unsociable, as I'd expected. I explained to him that his sister had become infirm and simply wanted to make amends. He listened graciously, thanked me for my efforts, and told me the matter now rested with him—a polite way of saying "butt out." I never bothered to ask what he did about his sibling, but I'd made a good friend that night.

Walter embodied the wisdom of not judging a book by its cover. Thereafter, every week or two, I'd pop in at the Bergers' or at one of Walter's nighttime lairs to visit with him. At his suggestion, I came to live at the Bergers' after the war.

Mrs. Berger's house was what they call the Classic Box style—a two-story gabled-roof affair originally built by a prosperous shingle mill owner around the time Teddy Roosevelt led the Rough Riders. Otto Berger enclosed the porch and painted the place forest green to set it apart from the blander hues of its immediate neighbors.

As senior boarder, Walter Pangborn parked his DeSoto in the driveway. It was a '36 Airflow coupe—that ill-fated, nontraditional model, so ahead of its time that time never did catch up.

I hadn't seen Sten Larson's Buick outside, but the blast of cigarette smoke that greeted me told me he was home. Sten was one of those match-conserving smokers who lit his next cigarette with his last one. I pictured him getting out of bed in the morning and pressing the end of a fresh smoke up against a light bulb. His *raison d'être* seemed to be keeping that flame going till bedtime. He was a glowing success if you'll pardon the pun.

Sten was sprawled on the porch sofa with an ashtray on his stomach, the never-ending cigarette in one hand and a gin and bitters in the other. I recognized one of Walter Pangborn's special tumblers. Gin and bitters was Walter's spring and summer drink come Saturday night. "The secret is to get gin of the first chop," Walter would say. "Distilled *London* Dry."

"Walter's serving drinks on a *Thursday*?" I asked Sten. "What's the occasion?"

"When dinner broke up Aunt Nora was in one of her antic moods and Walter was bit by the artistic bug."

"So, what's keeping the young and unsettled housebound?"

"Kenny's got my car. He's picking me up in a bit and we're heading to the 211 for some pinochle. But no reason not to be sociable first," he said, holding up his tumbler. "This sucker's good."

Sten's homes away from home were downtown. He was a devotee of the noisy and dimly lit world of card playing and billiards, either at the 211 Club or at Ben Paris. Usually it was the former since it had first-class pool tables, all the better for a penniless shooter with a little talent to eat and drink to his heart's content just for sinking more balls than the other guy. As Sten put it, "Sinking shots on one of those babies ruins you. Anything less is like dropping marbles down a drainpipe." When he was at his hangouts, heaven was not on his mind.

Sten was in his late twenties and the only son of Lena Larson, sister to the late Otto Berger. Otto was a plastering and painting contractor, and before Uncle Sam sent Sten off to fight in the Pacific, he'd worked with his uncle. Otto died of a heart attack just after the war. So Sten was working for Otto's old partner Sully and boarding at his aunt's house in one of the rooms in the basement. The basement entrance suited his comings and goings.

"Aunt Nora's got a kind of hybrid divinity percolating on the stove."

"Hybrid?"

"No nuts. Cornflakes."

As I made a move to leave the porch, Sten said in a subdued voice, "Walter thinks he's got that *eye* thing finally figured out."

Sten and I edged into the living room-turned-studio.

"Shall I concoct a refreshing libation to gladden your heart, old top?" Walter asked, palette in one hand, brush in the other.

"No thanks, Walter."

"Sten, be a dear," said Mrs. Berger. "Go and see how the candy's doing on the stove. I'm going to call them Snow Flakes." She sat in her Boston rocker, posing solemnly for Walter, a drink balanced precariously on her lap.

Walter was a fair caricaturist and a dabbler at painting still lifes. But Mrs. Berger was convinced that he was the ideal person to paint a life-size, posthumous portrait of her departed Otto sitting beside her. Frankly, if it hadn't been Nora Berger who made the request, Walter wouldn't even have considered the project.

"Can I take a quick sip, Walter?" Mrs. Berger asked.

Walter nodded as he brushed.

The past week Mrs. Berger had been trying to stop biting her fingernails. She'd put Band-Aids on all her fingertips as deterrents, most of which looked a bit gnawed on and frayed.

"I think it's hardening now, Aunt Nora," Sten hollered from the kitchen.

"Take care of it, Sten. And on your return voyage from the kitchen, go ahead and feed Popeye. He's looking like he's about to eat the shredded newspaper again." Popeye was Mrs. Berger's hamster, which had one eye in a perpetual squint.

Anyway, progress on the portrait dragged at first, because Walter agreed to paint only when the mood struck him. And it didn't strike often. However, recently this had changed.

"Not to rush you, Walter, but the sooner we finish this picture, the sooner we can start the showpiece," said Mrs. Berger.

"Showpiece? What showpiece is that?" I asked, though Walter had already told me.

"I've decided I want a full-length picture of me for the shrine. When this picture is done, Walter and me are gonna rummage through my old valises to hunt up all my promotion stills of me at my best. You know, to help come up with the right motive."

"That's *motif*, Nora," said Walter.

"Whatever."

"Sounds thorough and even professional," I said.

"Uh-huh. I'm gonna pose in just my G-string and my fans. You know, to make it … to guarantee more …. What was that word you used, Walter?"

"Verisimilitude," Walter said.

"Yeah. To make it more that," said Mrs. Berger. "We want it to ring true. Me posing in costume was Walter's idea."

"I'm sure it was," I said, with my back to my landlady. Walter ignored me. His brush strokes had seemed to quicken lately and his artistic moods had noticeably become more frequent. Artists get inspiration where they can find it. It was the "eye thing"—as Sten called it—that was the rub. Mrs. Berger's right eye tended to wander, especially when she was tired, stressed, or tipsy. I learned to look at the bridge of her nose when we talked.

I walked over to Walter's side of the easel and took a look. Walter had finished the Otto Berger portion months earlier. I stared at the middle-aged, bald-headed, bespectacled Otto.

"You've definitely captured him," I said. "The rascal comes through loud and clear, despite the puritanical grimace. I think it must be the shine in the eyes. Well done, Walter."

"Why, thank you, Gunnar," he said.

When completed, the picture would resemble a cartoonish version of American Gothic, sans pitchfork. But Mrs. Berger loved it so far and her belief in Walter's talents was unshaken. But the "eye thing" was a real obstacle. It stood between Walter and the coveted showpiece project.

"That eye is driving me crazy," Walter would confide to me. "I don't know where to leave it. And she insists the painting should look life-like."

"Maybe she'd agree to pose wearing sun goggles," I'd

suggested once. Mrs. Berger wore dark glasses when she had a killer migraine. "It would add realism. You could call the painting, *The Dead and the Dying*."

Walter didn't laugh. He was a bit touchy on the subject and remained inconsolable.

"I really think the nightmare is finally over," he whispered to me, the left side of his mouth lifted high to form a big grin.

I told Walter I had a question for him in private, and if he'd ask Mrs. Berger to take five. Over near the stairs I said to him, "I'm curious about a local nabob."

"Ah yes, 'nabob.' A Hindu word referring to a provincial governor of the Mogul empire of India. It's come to mean a man of great wealth or—"

"Ever hear of an Addison Darcy?"

Walter nodded. "A Seattle haberdasher. *Very* successful. He's part of Darlund Apparels. His name and picture appear in the newspapers from time to time for charity events—things of that nature. He resembles C. Aubrey Smith."

The craggy features of the elderly British actor came readily to mind. "Know anything about this Darcy? Anything of a personal nature?"

He shook his head. "Are you considering him for a client, or making inquiries on behalf of one?"

"Sort of the latter. I'll fill you in later. By the way, fresh greetings from Olga Peterson."

"Duly noted," he said graciously.

"She misses those mesmerizing crumbs of knowledge you're so generous with."

He nodded, but I knew my message left him in a state of indifference bordering on the narcoleptic.

Mrs. Berger's back was to the stairs. So, before ascending, I sneaked a sidelong glance at her three cheesecake photos. I tried to find my own solution to Walter's dilemma—maybe detect what the photographer had done with her straying peeper.

"There was no one quite like me," Mrs. Berger yelled over to me, causing my spine to tingle. "I did a fair muscle dance but an exquisite hootchie-cootchie. I worked hot and did *all* the kicks. The muscle, the hitch, *and* the fan kick. Those were good times. Good times."

I vaulted up those stairs.

I grabbed the new Silvertone portable radio I'd just bought at Sears. I placed it on a shelf in the upstairs bathroom next to a couple of porcelain swans. The bathroom had lately taken on a swan theme. It was a veritable swandom, as Walter put it. There was a swan soap dish, swan-shaped soap, and towels and dishcloths with interwoven swans. The latest purchase by Mrs. Berger was a plastic set of shower and window curtains with swans printed all over them. In our Northwest climate, I rightly suspected they'd become great mold and mildew-makers.

I ran my bathwater and soaped up with Barbasol as I listened to the news. As I scraped at my face, the announcer updated me. Pilfered document case put on hold in 1945 by F.B.I. finally investigated by Senate committee. Loss of U.S. Navy Privateer plane in Baltic called "first air victory" by vodka-sodden Soviet fighter pilot. Shady postage stamp plan probed by Federal grand jury. Australian minister recalled from Moscow. Legal secretary in L.A. murdered by employer's wife.

I'd had enough. My work put enough strain on my nervous system without me having to borrow the experience. I tuned to KOL, and heard Hawaiian melodies playing. I let them play. I usually took showers, but I felt like a nerve-settling soak in Epsom salts, and I figured a little ukulele and slack key guitar might help to settle my jitters.

Downstairs again, I saw the empty porch and knew that Sten's chariot had swept him away to his hustler's paradise. The art studio was still open, but Walter the Sanguine had become Pangborn of the Dashed Hopes.

Mrs. Berger had ceased modeling and stood smoking one of her Chesterfields inserted in an ivory holder. Her eye was beginning to take a drink-induced meander. I got close enough to her this time to get a whiff of one of her five-and-dime frangipanis. She was loyal to two fragrances. I called them *Essence of Tawdry* and *Spent Lust*. I envisioned atomizer instructions that read: "Squirt profusely."

"You'd better not be taking out a girl wearing that suit," said my landlady.

"Why? What's wrong with it?" I was wearing my new seersucker.

"It's a horrible color, Gunnar. Pathetic. It looks about as cheerful as an overcast day the morning after."

"It's mottled indigo. I think it's sharp."

"Hell's bells and whistles. Whoever sold you that suit should be drawn and quartered and the parts hung up by toes and thumbs."

"What do you think, Walter?" I asked, wanting support.

Walter gave me a quick glance and said without smiling, "Gunnar, you're a veritable coxcomb. A regular popinjay."

Mrs. Berger was pleased. She didn't understand Walter's words. It was his tone and knit brow that convinced her he was taking her side.

"What do you think about a profile, Nora?" Walter asked her. "How would it be if I paint you *facing* Otto? You know, a serene pose of wifely adoration?"

Mrs. Berger wasn't buying Walter's nice try. "It just wouldn't be true to life, Walter. You should know that. I never looked adoringly at Otto. *He* was always *my* audience." She walked over to scrutinize the canvas.

I left them.

My phone chat with Britt Anderson about Blanche Arnot got me a little curious. I'd never met an ex-Ziegfeld girl before. By 6:50 I was in the Chevy headed over to Laurelhurst. About 7:10 I reached the address Frank Milland had given me.

LAURELHURST RESTS ON A peninsula jutting out into Lake

Washington. It was what Mrs. Berger called a "snitzy area." I suppose it still is.

I negotiated the Chevy through the winding streets that dissected Mrs. Arnot's community of junior mansions. Laurelhurst has its share of waterfront plots. Mrs. Arnot's wasn't one of them. Her house sat inland a bit on a lot tightly linked to others like squares of a patchwork quilt. Still, it compared to Mrs. Berger's place like caviar to pastrami—which is all a matter of taste.

Hers was a house built of burnished brick and just enough plaster facing in spots to qualify it as a Tudor. I looked up at a roof with three high peaks of different heights—the two in back covered gabled windows, the shorter one in the foreground sheltered the front door and foyer.

I passed through a wrought-iron front gate with a thin metal silhouette of a fleur-de-lis ensconced about chest level. The front door was of solid wood except for a peephole with one of those little grated windows that opened from the inside and reminded me of a speakeasy I'd finagled my way into as a teenager.

The buzzer was a pearl-colored button that triggered ornate chimes at a touch.

Inquiring eyes gave me a quick glimpse through the grated peephole. When the door opened she gave me a straightforward feminine assessment.

"Come in, Mr. Nilson, come in," she said, smiling. Her voice was that of a woman half her age.

For some reason I was expecting to meet a doddering, white-headed septuagenarian. Instead, I faced a stately woman, at most in her mid-fifties, with silver-streaked brown hair worn up in one of those French twists. Still fetching, she had the high cheekbones and classic features of a once-great beauty, and the glimmer in her eyes signaled me that she was pleased I could tell. She wore a russet dress and a cream-colored sweater.

I was led in to her living room. She reached over to turn off the radio. She'd been listening to *Counterspy*.

"May I get you something to drink?"

"No thanks. I'm just fine," I said, planting myself on the sofa she pointed to.

"Nonsense. I have tea already made. No point wasting it. I'll get us both a cup."

As she quietly strolled back to the kitchen, I scanned the room. I was expecting décor from the 1910s and 1920s. While her reading lamp looked ancient enough, and there were a few mementos and a number of pictures from earlier in the century, surprisingly most of her furnishings were circa 1940s. Mrs. Arnot had memories, but she didn't seem overly anchored in the land of the bygone.

She served me my tea and then eased into a Morris chair with a cup of her own.

"I'll not take up much of your time, Mrs. Arnot," I said.

"Nonsense. It's rare when I receive callers, and rarer still when they happen to be handsome young men. Take all the time you need."

"The police talked with you earlier today about the quarrel you overheard when you were in Fasciné Expressions yesterday."

She laughed. "That's correct, but it was no quarrel, young man. I'd call it more of a harsh scolding. Christine hardly said boo. Her boyfriend didn't give her much of an opportunity."

"I'd like to know what you saw and heard, please."

"As I told the police, I didn't see or hear much at all," said Mrs. Arnot. She got up to adjust the wide louvers of her Venetian blinds to beat back the sun's departing encroachments. "I had finished talking to one of the girls and was just leaving when Mr. Engstrom started shouting. Naturally, I turned to look."

"Naturally."

She sat down again.

"Did you hear Dirk Engstrom threaten to kill Christine?"

"Dear, no. And what I did hear were mere fragments.

Nothing that made sense, you understand. Mr. Engstrom was wildly waving his arms in the air and Christine wasn't saying much at all. She simply looked upset. Had the girl not been killed, I'm morally certain that her relationship with that *boy* would have soon been over anyway."

She reflected a moment and continued, "It looked as though Christine had been talking with Addison Darcy before her boyfriend arrived. But that's merely my impression. Now, Mr. Darcy may have heard something that might interest you. Also, there was a young man about your age standing next to Mr. Darcy. I've seen him in the store many times. He looks to be what in my day we called a drugstore cowboy."

"Drugstore cowboy?" I asked, as I slipped a clove in my mouth. Britt was right about Mrs. Arnot being quaint.

She laughed again—some of her youthful beauty peering through for a moment.

"I'll explain. I worked in Hollywood well over twenty years ago. Some of the Western movie extras used to loaf in front of drugstores between pictures trying to impress the ladies. That young man standing next to Mr. Darcy projected that same kind of attitude and carriage. A harmless lothario. It's merely an impression, you understand."

"Miss Anderson tells me you were in the *Ziegfeld Follies*," I put in.

"That's correct." She stood up and crossed the room to retrieve a silver-framed photograph that sat on an end table with several others. She showed it to me. She laughed when I gave a low wolf whistle.

It was a full-length picture of a very young, very beautiful and very shapely Blanche Arnot. She was wearing an elaborate feathered headdress, a scanty top with a low-cut neckline, and pleated bloomers with what looked like a bridal train trailing behind her. Two similarly dressed beauties stood on each side of her but a few feet behind.

"Delicious times. This was taken on stage at the New

Amsterdam Theatre. We thought we were *something*," she said, amusement in her voice. "And I guess, in a way, we were."

"How'd you come to be a Ziegfeld girl?"

She told me she was born and raised in Springfield, Massachusetts. She got her notions of life on the stage from an aunt who was a teacher of elocution and singing. At sixteen she ran away from home, worked as a shop girl and a waitress before eventually getting her first break.

She laughed. "I became a cigarette girl in a Broadway nightclub. I thought I'd *arrived*."

Someone connected to the *Ziegfeld Follies* must have thought so too, because he invited her to audition, and that led to her being in the *Follies* of 1915-1921. After that she moved out to Los Angeles, did some stage acting, and had some bit parts in silent films before becoming a drama coach.

"I realized early on that I wasn't going to become a screen star. But like the saying goes, those who can, *do*. And those who can't, *teach*. So, I taught," she said a bit wistfully. "But I have no complaints, as it led to my life here. I met and married the older brother of one of my female students—a doctor from Seattle."

"And so those who teach make do," I said.

She laughed.

"Britt Anderson tells me you were quite close to her aunt."

"That's correct. We were very close. I loved Alexis. She was such a deliciously sweet person before her tragic deterioration. My heart ached when she died. She was extremely talented."

Mrs. Arnot explained that she'd groomed Alexis. "I worked with both Alexis and Britt. Britt has talent, but not like her aunt did."

She'd encouraged Alexis to become a professional performer. "I offered to put her in touch with some people I still knew in Hollywood. Few people really succeed in the arts, but she could have made it. Of that I have no doubt."

"So, why didn't she make the move?"

Mrs. Arnot sighed. "Two reasons. She felt a strong family obligation as Britt's guardian—though I told her that Britt was welcome to live with me. Then, there was also a romantic attachment that kept her in Seattle."

"The one that went sour?"

"I see Britt's told you the story."

I nodded. I asked about her job with Fasciné Expressions.

"I agreed to it originally as a favor to Britt. She insisted on paying me for my work with the girls. I objected at first. Henry—my late husband—left me very comfortable, so I don't need the money. But I conceded to her wishes and do accept a pittance. However, the money really is irrelevant, as I genuinely enjoy helping out."

"What exactly are your duties?"

She laughed softly. "I suppose I'm part drama coach and part finishing school teacher. The first few weeks after a new girl is hired, I give her a crash course in poise, speech, and civilities—that sort of thing. Thereafter I simply monitor progress and advise when necessary."

"I've never heard of a retail outfit going to such lengths."

"Granted. It's one of Britt's ideas. She's blended an artistic flare with her business school training. She's a very innovative and determined young woman. She insists on creating a certain image and atmosphere. And as far as the salesgirls are concerned, I'd say she's been deliciously successful."

I agreed. From what I could tell, Mrs. Arnot had done a great job of helping the girls attain enough polish and bearing to mask their origins—with a dash of Ziegfeld girl in the bargain.

Blanche Arnot didn't have anything helpful to add about Christine. Not at first anyway.

I asked a little more about her days in the *Ziegfeld Follies*. She'd known and worked with the likes of Fanny Brice, Eddie Cantor, and Will Rogers.

"Everyone loved Will Rogers. He was my personal favorite of the starring performers. He'd say the funniest things. For instance, he wisely advised to never miss a good opportunity to stop talking—which is what I think I should do right now. I'm probably beginning to bore you."

I told her not at all, and assured her that I was enjoying our visit very much. I decided that part of Mrs. Arnot's quaintness was a certain air she projected. There was something otherworldly about her. I couldn't put my finger on it exactly. I figured it was a carry-over from having lived and worked in a fantasy world populated by show people.

We talked a little more about her past, and then something brought her back to the present. "It's too bad about poor Christine. No one deserves to die that way—let alone one so young and lovely. However, I have a feeling that, had she lived, her life would have been a stormy one."

"Why so?"

"Oh, take it from an old chorus girl, well-versed in the ways of young coquettes and their aging admirers. I've grown older, but I'm not senile—not yet anyway. Nor am I naïve. I see things. It's pretty plain that some of the girls working for Leonard Pearson are after more than just sales commissions. Christine was one of them. But she didn't strike me as a girl with good judgment in the matter."

"Could you enlighten this babe in the woods?"

"You don't look like such a babe to me," she said with a pert smile. "Still, let me be a little bit delicate. I'm not talking about sex and lost virtue. That was often a rite of passage for a chorine—generally a foregone occurrence for girls in a revue. Florenz Ziegfeld himself was a flagrant philanderer who often sampled the merchandise. No, Christine was a big girl, as are the others working at the store. I have no prudish illusions about their chastity. I'm sure some of those girls carry on quite a *full* social life with the occasional client—especially the more affluent ones. In my day a girl flirted, trifled, and even granted her favors for good times and whatever gifts they would garner. Some became mistresses. And sometimes a lucky one would land a wealthy husband. Things aren't all that different today, Mr. Nilson."

"Props change; people don't," I said.

"That's correct. Definitely. But some fail to grasp it."

"You say Christine lacked good judgment. Could you explain?"

She shrugged her shoulders. "A mere impression. I hope you realize, young man, I was referring to the significance attached to the cat-and-mouse games adults play—the expectations created, the demands made, the unspoken but implied boundaries. Some girls know how far to carry a dalliance. Others don't, and carry it way too far. At the very least a heart is broken or someone's pride is wounded. At the very worst …." She thought for a moment, head cocked to one side, "well … you certainly look astute enough to figure it out."

"You think Christine was killed as an act of revenge or spite?"

"Or perhaps self-protection."

She picked up the photo of her as a Ziegfeld beauty. She pointed to the girl behind her on the right—a lovely and busty specimen.

"That was my good friend, Sally Miller. "Sal," we called her. Sal started off flirting with a married businessman who stayed in the city weeks at a time. He'd come see her regularly. Sal and I went out on the town a time or two with this man and one of his friends. They even took us to Jersey City, to watch Jack Dempsey bludgeon that poor Frenchman …. Oh, what *was* his name?"

"Carpentier."

"You had to have been in rompers at that time. I take it you're a boxing aficionado."

"Call it the tutelage of an impassioned grandfather."

"I enjoyed that particular bout. We sat ringside. Fifty-dollars a seat. Sal and I rooted for Carpentier in what little French we knew. A delicious event, really. But still, by then I'd had quite enough of our escorts. They were a good fifteen years older than we were and they were moneyed, overbearing, and extremely self-important. I'm afraid that even then, I had little patience with blades of their stripe. But not Sal. She eventually fell in love with her suitor. She fell hard. I tried to warn her. But Sal wouldn't listen. She believed him when he said he'd divorce his wife and marry her. You know the old story. Sal believed so hard, she even made plans to leave the show. But like I suspected, he was stringing her along. It was a game to him. It broke her heart when she finally realized it, and it ate her up."

I asked her what became of Sal.

"It was worse than a tragedy. Sal refused to cut her losses and move on. She foolishly threatened to make trouble for the man. She said she'd tell his wife—expose him publicly. His friend—the man I'd been paired with at the fight—had powerful friends in the city. Sal's lover and his crony had her jailed on trumped up charges. They railroaded her and had her sentenced to prison for two years."

"How was she when she got out?"

"She didn't. The poor girl couldn't take it. It crushed her. She died in prison."

I told her I was sorry.

"There's a deliciously cruel humor to all of this, when you think about it."

I asked her to explain.

"Well, after all, such things as secrecy and trust are usually implicit in an *illicit* amour. Ironic, isn't it?"

I grinned and agreed.

"Let me make myself clear, Mr. Nilson. I know nothing for certain. I've simply witnessed many times what goes on between older men and the young women they chase after. I'm spouting mere speculation, mind you. Having said that, let me say that if Mr. Engstrom is *not* Christine's murderer, then it wouldn't surprise me one whit if the foolish girl took things too far and somehow crossed the wrong man of means. It's the type of thing that's happened many times before, and to girls far more clever than Christine would ever have been had she lived to see thirty."

Mrs. Arnot walked me to the door.

"Britt didn't exaggerate about you," she said.

"How's that?"

She smiled. "Well, now that I've had a chance to talk with you awhile, I do see that there is indeed a bit of Cary Grant's charm about you—and like him, you've also mastered a certain relaxed breeziness."

"Breezy I can do. It's the dimpled chin and carefree saunter that need work."

I gave her my card.

"I'm sorry I couldn't be of more help to you, young man. I wish you luck."

It was 9:15 when I left. I stopped at The Twin TeePees off Highway 99 across from Green Lake. As the name suggests, it was a roadside diner built in the shape of two large adjoining teepees—one of those oddball monuments to advertising boosterism.

I used the payphone to call Rikard Lundeen. He told me that Addison Darcy would be staying around home the next day and that I was welcome to stop by at any time. I put a clove in my mouth and took a table looking out at the highway.

I ordered a cup of coffee and a piece of pecan pie. After the waitress brought my order I watched the pavement strain with night traffic. I let the cars mesmerize me for a while as I chewed and mulled over what the aging and seasoned Ziegfeld girl had told me.

Before the war, Lou Boyd and I came to the rescue of a lawyer named Grant Lincoln Presswell. He'd come to the Bristol Agency with a recurring problem. A crazed weakness, really. Presswell was a whimsical old reprobate who seemed unable to restrain himself around the pretty office girls who worked for his firm. He'd never touch the current focus of his adoration. Not so much as a grope, pinch, or a wink. Instead he'd write her love songs. Love lyrics. *Lewd* lyrics. Pages and pages of them. Lucky for Presswell, the girls never took him to court. They were usually too embarrassed or intimidated to do anything. Presswell generally exhausted his emotions or ran out of paper and ink—I never knew which. It was our job to try and retrieve the love songs amicably, or simply buy them outright—if the girl hadn't already burned them, that is. Eventually, one of the girls did turn adventurous and tried to get hush money from our client. He came to us in a four-alarm panic. Before we could do anything, he died of a heart attack. The girl had obviously carried things a little too far. But, then again, so had Presswell.

I parked the Chevy in its usual spot in front of Mrs. Berger's. I'd thrown my coat on the passenger side and remembered it only after I stepped into the street. Normally I'd have left it to rumple overnight. But the suit was new. Plus, I planned to wear it the next day when I saw Britt Anderson again. So, I turned and stepped back toward the car.

That move saved my life.

I heard the tires squeal as the car shot past me. I don't know if I leaped or was propelled, but I slammed into the side of my Chevy. As I slid to the ground I cursed the driver and all his forebears, and hoped he'd stop and apologize so I could curse him to his face. But when I looked in his direction I saw the dark outline of a sedan hurtling down the street like a rocket.

"Are you all right, Gunnar?"

It was Walter Pangborn, a little winded from running out of the shadows.

"I … I think so," I said as he helped me stand. "That idiot could have killed me."

"I think that was his intention, old socks. I think that was his intention."

Walter had been sitting on the front steps with the porch light switched off when he saw me drive up.

"I'd just tamped and re-lit my pipe. I thought it peculiar that the driver of that sedan didn't turn his lights on when he pulled away from the curb. He was waiting for you, Gunnar. He meant to kill you."

"Did you get a look at him?" I asked.

"Sorry. Not a clear one."

It figured. I was parked too far from the streetlight.

"Was it a Packard?"

"As for that, I can only say that it might have been. I can say for sure only that it was a very dark sedan. I must admit, old thing, as the lyricists might say, my eyes saw only you."

"I'm touched, Walter."

Walter's assessment got me to drop the idiot-driver theory. I'd angered plenty of people and racked up my share of enemies over the years. The driver could easily have been somebody out to settle an old score. But my profession made me wary of coincidences. Given the timing, it was just as likely that my close call had something to do with my nosing into Christine's murder.

We went inside. Sten was still out. Mrs. Berger was making Zs, her insomnia being no match for several of Walter's gin and bitters.

Walter poured us each a shot of Black & White as I went over the details of my day with him.

"I'd like to meet this Blanche Arnot," Walter said. "She sounds enchanting. I'll wager she has quite the photo album to go with those reminiscences."

"Overall, Walter, what do you make of this pretty kettle of fish?"

"Ah, yes, a reference to the salmon and trout Scottish picnickers cooked in kettles for their picnic meals. Arguably, not a pretty sight. A mucky, jumbled mix. And when you also consider how chaotic a picnic can often be …."

I held up a hand. "Walter. Please. Your thoughts about what I've told you so far. What's your take on Dirk Engstrom?"

Walter held his shot glass to his nose and sniffed the whiskey. "Prisons are filled with people who insist on their innocence, of course. Still, the way you characterize the lad and his story, I'm inclined to think he's being framed. That near hit-and-run outside would seem to confirm it."

I agreed.

"Gunnar, if we combine some of the details you've gleaned, I'd say it's fairly safe to assume that Christine Johanson was involved in an *affaire de coeur* with an older man—presumably one of her customers."

"Sure looks that way. It would explain why she told the Engstrom kid she wasn't good enough for him. She was a two-timer with a grain or two of conscience."

Walter nodded and suddenly drained his glass. "The eavesdropping Meredith Lane said Christine sounded nervous and angry when talking on the phone. What was that other word she used to describe how Christine felt?"

"She said Christine sounded like she'd been cheated."

"*Cheated*? You're sure that was the word? Not deceived or betrayed?"

"I'm sure. She said 'cheated.' What's the difference, Walter? Maybe she'd been a sucker to the old routine. 'I'll marry you, cupcake, after I divorce my wife.' The whole sleazy nine yards. Only, her lover boy didn't mean a word of it and Christine found out she'd been played for a sap."

"Perhaps. However, I'm certain Miss Lane would have put a different word to it had Christine been the victim of a lover's broken promises. In such a case, I see her using a word like betrayed or duped."

"Walter, I know these girls are getting groomed by Mrs. Arnot, but Meredith didn't exactly strike me as a budding lexicographer."

"You'd be surprised, old top, how exacting people can be when it comes to labeling the emotional state of another."

"So you're thinking *cheated* as in *money*?" I said.

"That makes more sense to me, although I admit I don't quite see how it all fits together."

"Well, you're in good company, Walter. Christine's behavior with me the other night may have hinted at something shady, but I pegged her as a sweet kid overall, just self-involved. You make her out to be a shakedown artist."

"Possibly she was all of that. You must admit, old socks, you were taken with her looks. You were in one of your ... *drooling* moods. No one—especially a libidinous male—wants to think the worst of a beautiful face. But, it's likely that poor Christine wasn't as sweet as you might like to think. It would also fit with Mrs. Arnot's excellent theory about the murderer acting to protect himself."

KIRSTI HAD HER LOWER lip between her teeth and was staring at me with rapt attention, as if I was the wise old man of the mountain. She got up off the wood bench and came around behind my wheelchair.

"After a few more minutes of conversation, I told Walter goodnight and went to my room," I told Kirsti casually, as she pushed me toward the cafeteria. She and I had decided a cup of coffee was in order.

It was between feedings, but since it was Sunday, pockets of visitors and Finecare inmates loitered here and there in the cafeteria dining hall, glibly talking about old times and ditheringly passing on what might be new. A few kitchen ladies were robotically preparing meals. Another one of their number was going around bussing recently abandoned tables and being dogged all the while by a grizzled golden-ager, younger than me, who was trying to get her to listen to a letter he clutched in his hand. There were printed signs on a couple of walls about not sharing food, and not taking your trays and silverware with you, and not sitting on tables, and keeping hands, feet, and objects to yourself. If you weren't careful, it was the kind of place that could make you forget there was anything right with the world.

As sensitive and perceptive as Kirsti was, I wondered if she saw Finecare as I did. I decided probably not. After all, this was her time for defining moments and not for grappling with moments trying to define her.

Kirsti found us a private spot, looked at me with the expression of a veteran waitress, and said, "*Black*, right?"

I said "Right."

Kirsti got us our coffee and then positioned a chair across from me and sat down, placing one of her dimpled knees over the other. She held her cup in both hands and perched its edge on her top knee.

"That Walter sure read you right," Kirsti said, after a few moments of silence. "About you drooling over beautiful women."

I laughed. "I was young."

"You were … *horny*," she said with a shrewd glitter in her eyes. "And all the time, it sounds like to me." Suddenly she had a pink tint on each cheek that ran to the temples and was not completely hidden by the crescent-shaped locks of her pageboy.

I coughed, and then took a big swallow of coffee. "I admit to having had a full array of youthful impulses," I said defensively.

"For sure," she said, the flush on her face deepening. She raised her cup to her lips to take a sip.

"How about we let this old jaw of mine rest up a bit while we soak up the ambiance," I said as I waved my left hand at our surroundings and brought my cup to my mouth with my right.

She nodded and we finished our coffee in silence.

Kirsti brought our empty cups over to the gal doing the bussing, and then she wheeled me back to the outer courtyard. She continued to keep quiet, so I said nothing as we bumped and jolted across the gravel and flagstone walk.

"So, you were in danger. Someone tried to run you over.

Someone was out to get you," she said when we reached the wood bench and she'd turned her recorder back on.

"Looking back, I'd say that's putting it mildly."

I KEPT MY SNUB-NOSED .38 in my desk drawer when it wasn't riding on my torso. I pulled it out of its hiding spot and placed it on the little nightstand near my bed. It became anchor for a *Pep Comics* magazine starring Archie Andrews as well as a tattered copy of Spinoza's *Ethics* that I'd recently picked up at Shorey's Bookstore downtown.

Setting my gun out in the open was the only precaution I took, but I knew I was going to sleep like a guilty baby. Or was that a selfish rock? Whatever. For, no matter what I said to dissuade him, Walter insisted on standing guard all night. He planned to paint toy soldiers until the wee hours. Nearby on his workbench he'd have one of his few souvenirs from France that a buddy smuggled home for him after he'd been wounded. It was an 8mm Lebel revolver, popular among French troops during the First Great War. I fluffed my pillow and pitied anyone foolish enough to break in the house on Walter Pangborn's watch.

I dreamt I was running in a Sadie Hawkins Day race with Dirk Engstrom. We'd looked over our shoulders but couldn't see the girls chasing us. But we could hear them. They were gaining on us, and we were worried. Dirk tripped and a shell exploded near him. The dream shifted and I was with a buddy named Mike. I banged away with a carbine as Mike blasted the air with his BAR.

I woke up wet and clammy with a tom-tom thumping in my chest.

Mike was killed in the Hurtgen. He was a state-the-obvious pragmatist who didn't mind the sleet. We were running through a creek when a kraut machine gun started stuttering. I didn't know Mike before the war, but he'd come to us from Seattle via the replacement depot. It was one of those "Repple

Depple" flukes that put him in my platoon. More a chocolate fiend than a nicotine addict, he traded cigarettes for Hershey bars. I liked him. He was dead before his knees hit the water.

I reached over to the nightstand and broke open my revolver to make sure all the chambers of the cylinder were loaded.

I decided it would be keeping me company for a few days.

Chapter 8

———

MISS PETERSON WASN'T WITH a customer when I entered the Hanstad Building on Friday, June 9th. I made sure to keep moving and met her beckoning look with a vigorous wave that bordered on frenetic.

I found Cissy Paget alone in the anteroom of Dag Erickson's suite. Only her left leg was showing in the kneehole of her desk, the other comfortably tucked under her left haunch. This told me no clients were in the offing. She had the telephone cradled in the nape of her neck as she rolled fresh paper and carbon into her machine. Whoever she was talking with was jabbering away, because Cissy was repeating a litany of yes, uh-huh, I know, and I won't. We exchanged waves and I sat down across from her in the waiting area.

I picked up a stale copy of the *Seattle Times*. The heading told me that the Park Board had approved the $235,000 Aqua Theater. The headline below announced that an oil tanker was grounded by an ebb tide in nearby Shilshole Bay. A picture accompanied the story. I hadn't been paying attention to local events and was wondering what happened when Cissy hung up the phone.

I looked up and saw exasperation on her face and heard the sigh that went with it. I put the paper down.

"And how's Mother, Sweet Knees?" I asked to be cordial, deducing the source of her aggravation.

"Oh, Mom's fine. Just fine. She's off visiting her sister in Bellingham for a few days. The one I told you was recently widowed. When they get together they bake and cook up a storm. It'll help to distract my aunt from her loss."

"Well, that's good."

"Yes, but then they both put on weight and get depressed and start to bicker."

"Oh, well, that's not good."

"No, but it does give me a needed break for a few days."

"And that *is* good."

"Uh-huh, except Mom worries about picayune details. So of course she's got to make sure I'm feeding this, and watering that, and that I'm buttoning up my overcoat when the wind blows free. The usual. I have to tell you, her little departures might renew *her* spirit, but they take their toll on *my* nervous system."

I rolled sympathetic eyes.

"But say, tough guy, that's also a good thing. It means I'll have the place to myself tomorrow night, if that matters to you."

"Sounds like it's got possibilities." I'd almost forgotten our date for Saturday night. "Am I hearing an offer to cook dinner before we hit the Trianon?"

"Not on your life. Dinner's still on you. My idea is that if you behave yourself, I might invite you in later for a nightcap."

I promised to be a regular Eagle Scout.

"How's his nibs this morning?" I asked, nodding at the door to Dag's office.

"He's in court all day today," she said, a slight lilt in her voice.

"Sort of cuts into your combat pay, doesn't it?" I said, reaching in my pocket for a clove.

"Be nice," she said, giving me a glare over the tops of spectacles that rode precariously on the end of her cute nose.

Then she grinned. Cissy had let it slip more than once that spending all day with Dag gave her a headache. She liked and respected her boss, but he emitted nervous energy and passed on stress like a runner in a relay race, hands off the baton.

"I'm surprised you're in so early," she said. "I thought you'd be sleeping one off after your little reunion."

"And what little reunion is that?"

"Didn't your army buddy get in touch with you?"

"What army buddy?"

She looked puzzled. "Yesterday afternoon some guy called. He told me he was in the same gang or troop or squad—or whatever it was you were in together. He wanted to surprise you and begged me for your address." She took her glasses off and studied my face. "He seemed okay, so ... I gave it .... It *wasn't* okay, was it?"

I shook my head and told her about the near hit-and-run.

"Gunnar, I'm so sorry."

"Forget it. I'd have done the same thing. Anything distinctive about this guy's voice?"

"Uh-uh. Sorry. He sounded like the average Joe. That's why his story convinced me. Again, I'm so sorry."

"He missed me. That's what matters."

"Are you still in danger? Maybe he'll try again."

I was touched by her concern, but was determined not to show it. "I'm on the look-out this time. Not to worry."

Gunnar the Brave. Gunnar the Vigilant.

I asked if she had any messages for me.

"Just one," she said, picking up a slip of paper. "The phone started ringing this morning before I even had my coat off. A *Miss* Britt Anderson called."

The name piqued my interest and Cissy noticed.

"At least I think she said it was *Miss*. She sounded very officious in a sensual sort of way. Is she pretty?"

"Yes. I'd say she is. Pretty in an officious sort of way." I thought it was a clever comeback.

Cissy didn't. She handed me my message and started pounding out a funeral march on her Smith and Corona. It sounded like *Requiem to a Gumshoe*, and it left me wondering if our friendship had developed a new wrinkle when I wasn't looking. Gunnar the Clever-by-half.

I read the message from Britt as I ducked inside my two pigeonholes. I made a call to Frank Milland, who answered on the second ring.

"A driver of a dark sedan tried to run me down last night."

"No shit."

"Shit yes."

Walter once talked for fifteen minutes straight on the Anglo-Saxon word for diarrhea, and how amazed they'd be to know that it now outperformed a wild card.

"Where'd this happen?"

"Right in front of my boardinghouse. Walter Pangborn saw the whole thing."

"Any idea who'd want you dead?"

"A handful of people come to mind, most of them with overripe grievances from before the war. I'm guessing this maniac has a newly acquired grudge."

"Meaning?"

"I think someone's not happy about me nosing into the Johanson girl's murder."

"Uh-huh. And you know how that'll go over with Lieutenant Lister, don't you?"

"I've got a fair idea."

"Well, fair idea this. He'll accuse you and the Engstrom kid's lawyer of fabricating a red herring to divert suspicion. And just how do I know that isn't the case?"

"Walter was there. He saw the whole thing."

"And who'd believe that freak?"

"Don't call him a freak." I said it slowly, pausing between each word. I was mad. Milland knew it. "Walter got that face fighting Huns when you were still in knickers. If you ever bothered to talk *with* him instead of just *at* him, you'd find he's completely human and quite credible."

Frank was silent for a moment longer.

"So what am I supposed to do about this info? Did your war hero happen to get a license number?"

I told him the details, and what we saw and didn't.

"Gunnar, what happened to you not screwing up our investigation? That gun we found in the Engstrom kid's place *is* the one that killed that Johanson dame."

"Frank, Dirk Engstrom could still be your killer. I just thought you'd want to know what happened. That's all."

"Yeah, well, so now I know."

"Yeah, well, so now you do."

We hung up.

I reread the message from Britt. It told me that Guy de Carter had a mid-morning appointment near Woodland Park, and he wondered if I could meet him there about 12:30 for a duck dinner—he'd bring the duck. He said he'd look for me near the fountain in the rose garden.

It was okay by me. It gave me plenty of time to go see Addison Darcy in The Highlands.

SOME COMPARE SEATTLE TO Rome because it's built on a series of hills. By the 1890s wealthier families had built their homes on three of them: First Hill, Capitol Hill, and Queen Anne Hill. In the early 1900s the well-to-do started to shift their location to exclusive suburbs like Broadmoor and The Highlands. Both Addison Darcy and Rikard Lundeen lived in the latter.

The Highlands wasn't really a part of Seattle. It was sort of an enclave outside the city limits.

I headed the Chevy north. I checked now and then to see if I was being followed, occasionally caressing my .38.

I shot a quick glance in my rearview mirror as I pulled up to the small gatehouse. So far I hadn't grown a shadow.

The gatehouse guard came out and circled the front of

my car to get to the driver's side. He was a burly, bandy-legged hombre. He had an ex-bouncer look in his eyes that telegraphed a residual itch to French walk all trespassers and troublemakers. I rolled the window down and showed him as many teeth as I could.

"Good morning. Welcome to The Highlands," said the guard, droning like a bored museum tour guide. His lapel badge read "Charlie." Charlie glanced from me to the clipboard in his hand, then back at me again. It was his way of goading me to give my credentials.

"Addison Darcy is expecting me," I said.

"Your name, sir?"

"Gunnar Nilson."

When he discovered my name on his list, his mouth twitched into what resembled a smile and froze that way. I took it as a good sign. Charlie came across like one of those people who believe that the only thing they can be sure of is their own existence, because when he said, "Yes, sir, there you are," he said it in a way that made me feel I didn't really exist to him until I made my appearance on his list.

Charlie gave me directions. When he said "the Darcy *residence*," it sounded like he was struggling with a second language.

I spotted a lead pencil in the grass near his feet.

"You really should check into that and find out who the guy was who was holding that pencil," I said, pointing to it. "At the very least, you should let the police know. That's got to be the worst case of human spontaneous combustion I've ever seen."

I drove off. In my mirror I saw Charlie bend over to pick up the pencil. I liked to think that small discovery would lead him to start a solipsist splinter group with him as its leader.

The Highlands is still situated above a massive bluff, with spectacular views of Puget Sound. My route was mostly shaded and flanked by shrubbery, oaks, maples, and tall evergreen trees. I left my window down to take in the smells of fir and pine and to better catch the breeze coming up off the water. At points where the sun peeked through, I got glimpses of the bay, and beyond it the majestic mountain range of the Olympics.

Addison Darcy's neighbors had long driveways. Their homes reflected the taste of the owner or the fad of the decade in which it was built. Tudor-style, early American colonial, opulent gingerbread cottages, and even a few Spanish haciendas dotted the remote acreage.

I saw a modest little sign that said "Darcy." I pulled into the driveway and took a right past three outbuildings. I reached a sweeping space where I whirled the Chevy around and parked. Nearby sat four automobiles in or around a huge garage.

The main building on the Darcy estate was a three-story brick and stucco Tudor that made Blanche Arnot's place look Lilliputian. Each floor of this manor home looked to have four times the square footage of Mrs. Berger's entire house.

The door opened and there stood a lean woman in a dress the color of a coal miner's face. She was on the far side of middle age and was long immune to the very best in disarming smiles.

Our chins would have been level without the threshold. But as it was, I had to stare up at the close-set peas that passed for her eyes. Her hair was pulled straight back into a bun the size of a man's fist. Each strand of hair was stretched so tight it left her face strained and juiceless. It went well with the tightly drawn horizontal line that did duty as both a frown and a smile. She was the kind of female house servant you'd absolutely insist on if your husband had roving eyes. One word summed her up.

Scary.

"You are?" she said, in a voice that sounded like it was piped in.

"Gunnar Nilson. I'm here to see Mr. Darcy."

"Come."

I obeyed. As I stepped inside, my eyes were immediately drawn to the foyer's vaulted ceiling. It made me feel tiny and prepared me for what came next. She quick-marched me into a first-floor parlor large enough to hold congress. A wizened finger pointed to a glazed, calico-covered armchair.

"Sit," said the piped-in voice.

I sat.

"Wait."

I did.

She gave me an abrupt nod. When she was out of sight I put a clove under my tongue. I looked around. The room had modern furniture and felt comfortable enough. The décor had the feminine touch—though definitely not by the talons of the she-goon who'd just greeted me. The place was festooned with foreign and exotic curios, highly valued little knickknacks, and rare and strange art, the sheer volume of which only the moneyed could afford and wish for. All was arranged with the care and devotion of a person not fettered by the workaday world.

On the table next to me were several framed photographs. I picked up one of them. It was of a nice-looking man in his mid to late twenties and dressed in a naval officer's uniform. The inscription read, *To Mother and Dad, with all my love, Addie.*

"That *was* my son."

I put the picture down and stood up to face the voice. It came from a man wearing an ink-black velvet jacket and beige trousers. He walked over to me. He was a rugged old war-horse, the kind who told tall tales of the Crimean War—at least by Hollywood standards. Time had not been kind to him. From what Rikard Lundeen had said, Addison Darcy had to be somewhere in his late-sixties. He looked far older. His thinning top hair was more than offset by hirsute eyebrows and a bristly mustache no wax could conquer. Walter was right. He *did* look like C. Aubrey Smith.

He clamped my hand in his. It was more of a hand-wrench than a shake. He was baronial. He might have become more withdrawn in his old age, but he still projected a manly carriage, a residual sureness from past achievements. After introductions we sat down, and Addison Darcy pointed to the photo of his son.

"He was killed in the Pacific. Damnable kamikaze plowed right into his ship. Not very sporting of those Japs. Not very sporting at all."

I agreed, but chose not to mention the two atom bombs we finally dropped on Japan. The timing wasn't right. Talking about his son, Addison Darcy had a familiar look about him. He had that injured-spirit glaze to the eyes. I'd seen it in many a dogface, including the one in my shaving mirror.

"Addie would have gone far. Groomed him myself. He had a rare business savvy. He'd have gone far and done exceedingly well."

He was quiet for a moment.

"Can I offer you anything, son? Coffee? I know it's early, but I can trouble Hildy to get you something stronger."

I told him no thanks. I guessed that Hildy was his scary receptionist, and I didn't care to trouble her whatsoever.

Addison Darcy went on, "I've given up alcohol, myself. Doctor said my liver would explode if I didn't. But I sneak a drink now and again. Hell, what's life without a few guilty pleasures?"

I gave a commiserating smirk.

"As it happens, I received a telephone call not half an hour ago that summons me away before noon. So I'm glad you came early. I was just about to take a quick steam bath. Would you care to join me, son? We could talk while we sweat."

Hot and murky had no appeal. I preferred to sweat where we were, so I declined and told him I wouldn't keep him long.

"I'm not really clear as to why you want to talk with me. I've told the police what little there is to tell."

"Maybe you've given things more thought, and you'll tell me something you didn't tell the police. I just have a few questions," I said.

"Well, old Rik speaks highly of you, son. If it weren't for him we wouldn't even be having this little parley, of that you can be certain. I'd just as soon keep my nose and name out of anything connected to that salesgirl's murder."

I told him I understood. "You saw Christine Johanson squabbling with Dirk Engstrom the day of the homicide."

"Yes, that's true. Only the girl didn't say much. The Engstrom lad did all the shouting. He's hot-tempered like his mother. But I suppose you could call it a quarrel. The girl was none too happy to see him, of that you can be certain."

"The police said that one of you bystanders heard Dirk Engstrom threaten to kill Christine."

"No. That wasn't me, son. Although he might have done so at that. His conduct was abominable."

"Tell me what you saw and heard."

Mr. Darcy told me he was buying perfume for his wife and Christine was letting him smell samples when Dirk Engstrom grabbed her by the elbow and jerked her aside.

"He told her to take a good look at how she was behaving— something like that. She tried to speak but he kept at her. I started backing away. I've never been one to borrow trouble. I haven't lived as long as I have for nothing. I did hear the Engstrom lad say he didn't want a floozie for a wife. I do remember that."

"Dirk told me that when he walked in the place you were smelling the nape of Christine's neck. He said that's what set him off."

He glared at me. "And what's that supposed to mean?" he asked coldly, leading to a hot question, "Is *my* behavior on trial now?"

I didn't want Hildy getting me my hat just yet.

"Frankly, I'm finding Dirk is the overly jealous type. He's got a temper that goes with rash and wild remarks. He probably misinterpreted or exaggerated what he saw. What's your version?"

Mr. Darcy was straining with his anger, driving it off, packing it away. A small frown remained a moment then disappeared.

"Well, perhaps the young woman gave the lad just cause."

"Do you think Christine Johanson was a floozie?" I asked.

He gave me a crafty grin. "It was she who controlled the atomizer. She chose where to spray the perfume. *She* invited me to take a whiff. You know how some girls of the common variety can be, son."

I smiled and raised an eyebrow that said I knew the ways of common variety girls.

"When I was a young buck," he continued, "it was mainly actresses and showgirls who were looking for a good time. The age of bobbed-hair, flappers, and bootleg changed all that. Now a man can find willing girls most everywhere he turns. The kind you have fun with but don't take seriously, of course. I think that's a big part of the Engstrom lad's problem. Of that you can be certain."

"What do you mean, sir?"

"Dirk was getting serious with the wrong type of girl. Anyone could see that she had round heels. What did he expect from a salesgirl?"

"The common variety," I said.

"Exactly." He pointed to his son's photo. "My Addie was heading down the same path. He was going to make the same foolish mistake."

"Foolish mistake?"

"Addie was getting serious about some trollop. A dancer. He carried on with her to the point where he was talking marriage. Fortunately, the boy listened to reason and I was able to put a stop to it. You sow your oats with that kind. You don't marry them. A man would have to be insane to do so."

He insisted that he had nothing more to add and steered the conversation briefly to politics and then to business. He did a little of that boasting Rikard Lundeen had warned me about. He talked of real estate holdings, the structure of companies, trusts, securities portfolios, and corporate investment entities.

But he spoke more in terms of past battles fought and won. I sensed detachment behind what passed for eager prattle. Rikard Lundeen was right. Addison Darcy made a remark here and there that told me he'd personally taken a fairly static position toward the management of his holdings ever since his son was killed.

The talk grew tedious. I went along for the ride awhile before telling him it was time for me to go and for him to take his quick steam bath.

As he escorted me to the door I asked him if he'd ever been to the New Amsterdam Theatre in New York.

He laughed and gave his thigh a slap. "Many times, son. The New Amsterdam, the Manhattan, the Palace, the Majestic— you name it. When I was a younger man I made regular business trips to New York. At one point, I practically lived in that city six months out of the year. I always made a point of taking in a show or two."

And a showgirl or two as well, I thought. Of that I could be certain.

MY VISIT WITH ADDISON Darcy was a dead end as far as I was concerned. But I had to be onto something or someone wouldn't have tried to grind me into roadbed. It was a perverse form of encouragement.

I'd purposely given myself a little time to kill before meeting Guy de Carter. I headed over to the Atherton Building. I planned to pick up that list of customers from Britt Anderson and question Meredith one more time.

It was 11:00 when I sauntered in the Maison le Swank sitting room of Fasciné Expressions. Another gorgeous female of the fashion plate persuasion pranced up to me.

She was a little taller than the other girls, had a broad face, skin like porcelain, and hair the color of charcoal briquettes. She was wearing an imperial purple suit and told me her name was Peggy in a sultry speech that made the name sound original and its bearer as enchanting as she looked. Her engaging scent was distinctly overstated. Before she could ask me how she might be of help, I gave my name and purpose in calling.

"Oh, yes. You're the private eye," she said, giving me a top-to-bottom reappraisal. "Miss Anderson said if you were to stop by we were to tell you to go on back." Her voice went from sultry to soothing nasal. "She said you'd know how to find her."

Peggy was turning to leave when I said, "I understand Guy de Carter comes in the store quite a bit. Do you know him?"

She frowned, tried to smile, but the frown stuck. "I know him a little. More than I care to."

"Sounds like he made an impression."

"Not with me," she said. "When he's on one side of the room, I manage to be on the other." I could see she was debating over what to say next. "A friend of mine went out with him a few times."

"Happy times?"

"If you call getting smacked around a happy time."

"Rough customer?"

"That's putting it mildly, buster."

"Was it one of the girls who work here?"

She shook her head.

"You didn't make Guy's date book I'm guessing."

"You'd be guessing right," she said, pleased with her answer. "But I *do* think I'd like to make *yours*." She was instantly in a better humor, her sultry voice returned. "You already know where you can find me."

I watched as Peggy flounced back to her station. She was definitely one of the team and out after more than just sales commissions. An exquisite pair of legs flexed smoothly while round hips swung and derrière jiggled under her rayon skirt. She gave me a parting smile over her shoulder.

The Parisian model La Voodoo clearly had local competition in Peggy.

Britt Anderson was in her office and had only gotten more

beautiful since I'd seen her last. She stood up when I entered. She had a remote, besieged look that turned to one of lovely calm when she saw me. The pinze-nez fell to her neck. Her serene and faultless face was decorously framed by waves of gold hair that seemed somehow more abundant today. She was wearing a glossy, emerald-green dress, drawn tight to her slender waist.

Britt gave me a little grin and picked up a piece of paper from her desk. The rustling accordion pleats of her shiny outfit caused her to scintillate as she glided across the room toward me.

Gunnar the Bedazzled.

"That list of Christine's repeat customers you wanted," she said as she handed me the paper. Our fingers gently collided. "I presume that's what you came for."

Did she mean the touch or the list?

"I know you're meeting Guy de Carter, but can you stay and talk a little while?"

She smelled supernal. The fragrance was spellbinding. *Essence of Allure* is what I'd call it.

"Uh-huh." It was all my mesmerized brain cells could muster at the moment.

There were two chairs near the door. She motioned for me to take one as she pulled the other around to face me. She eased into her chair and crossed a pair of hosiery-ad legs that sent bumps goose-stepping up my backbone.

"When we talked on the phone yesterday, had I told you about poor Meredith?" she asked.

I said she hadn't told me, and I asked about poor Meredith.

"She became extremely agitated at the end of the day yesterday. It's like she had some sort of breakdown. We had to call a doctor. He gave her something to calm her nerves. I had one of the girls see her home."

It had looked to me like Meredith was keeping things together okay. But Britt and the others obviously knew her better. And Meredith *had* been chums with Christine. I figured she was more fragile than she appeared and finally snapped under the pressure of it all.

"She's lucky to have such good friends," I said. It sounded every bit like the trite solace it was. Britt didn't seem to notice.

"I phoned her later and told her to take a few days off. I made it an order."

I nodded.

"I didn't mean to rattle on so," she said suddenly and sighed. "You probably see things like this all the time in your line of work. Have you made any progress in your investigation?"

"I suppose. If you call almost getting killed progress."

Britt looked horrified.

"Who? Wha ... what took place?" she asked, uncrossing her legs and leaning closer to me.

"A driver of a dark sedan tried to run me down last night when I was getting out of my car. Fortunately I'd forgotten something. If I hadn't turned back to get it, I wouldn't be talking to you now."

Her mouth fell open. I told her about Walter coming to help me and what he'd witnessed. Her eyes grew wide.

"Who ... who could have done such a thing? Did your friend see the driver?"

I shook my head. "But my guess is that someone's not too happy about me looking into Christine's murder."

She put both of her hands on my knees. I liked that. I felt the tingle of a fly-fisher with one on his line. Time to do a little reeling in.

"I'm keeping a third eye open," I said. "Someone's obviously desperate, and I'm sure I'm not out of the woods yet."

Her eyes showed the empathy and compassion I'd seen the day before. It moved me. Well, it stirred me, anyway.

Her hands left my knees and gripped my fingers. "Did you call the police?" she asked.

"Yeah. It's all taken care of." I gently squeezed her hands in reassurance.

"Doesn't what happened to you prove Dirk Engstrom's innocence?"

"It could. But it's also possible someone is trying to sabotage an open-and-shut case. Dirk still has a mountain of evidence piled against him."

"I see," she said thoughtfully. "Can I be of any more assistance to you, Gunnar?" she asked, in almost a whisper. She moved her head closer to mine.

I cleared my throat. "There is one thing you could do," I said quietly. Actually I could think of several things, but none I could verbalize.

"Name it."

I suggested to her the possibility that Christine had been having a love affair with one of her customers.

"I suppose it's possible," she said. "So, what can I do?"

"I'd like you to chat up some of Christine's coworkers. Keep it cool and casual. See if any of the girls might know if she was seeing anyone special other than Dirk. These things are hard to keep from girlfriends."

"Meredith might know of someone. She was Christine's closest friend."

"Right. I'll talk to her again myself after she's had a chance to rest a bit. I have a feeling she had more to tell me yesterday but was holding back for some reason."

Britt gave me a puzzled look. I left her that way. She agreed to help me out and said she'd get started as soon as I left. Our faces were almost as close as a couple of Eskimos ready to rub noses. She gave me a quick peck on the lips.

"You watch out for yourself," she said.

"You can bet on it."

Chapter 9

—

"THE NEXT THING I knew I was staring at bare naked ladies. Nine of them."

"What?" Kirsti said in a puzzled tone, a deep blush to her face and eyebrows arched in surprise.

"Each of the ladies was in a different pose. Some were frolicking with scarves the size of drapes. They looked happy in a serene way and romping seemed to be their hobby. One of the gals held a small child and two deer were standing nearby. Across from them another child was riding what looked like a lioness."

"Wha … Where were you? A nudist colony? I thought you had to meet this de Carter guy."

"No, that's Guy de Carter. And I *was* meeting him."

"At some burlesque show? I thought you set it up to meet him at some garden."

"I did. What I was staring at was in the rose garden near Woodland Park Zoo. It's still there. I was facing a wall about my height, maybe a little taller. It's a relief made back in the '20s that gives credit to the Lion's Club for the garden's existence."

"Well, aren't you the tricky one." Kirsti said, trying unsuccessfully to act annoyed.

"But Blue Eyes, before I continue, let me catch my breath a moment, and maybe take a slug or two from that water bottle," I said, looking at her lazily.

GUY DE CARTER WAS not punctual.

It was 12:25 when I walked up to the small reflection pool to study the girlie show masquerading as art. The fountain where Guy de Carter wanted to meet sat thirty or forty yards behind me. Fifteen minutes went by. In that time I repeatedly fondled my .38 and had surveyed the garden four times.

I looked around again. The sun was out. Warm temperature hadn't joined it, but the chill in the air hadn't kept visitors away. Nearby a young man whispered sweet somethings in his girl's ear and got a smile for his honesty and an elbow in the ribs for his nerve. Beyond them, a middle-aged woman worked at an easel, desperately trying to capture a scene on canvas that was probably destined to grace a corner of a grandchild's attic. To my left a delighted mother was pushing a perambulator and leading a dull-faced boy and grim-faced girl on a forced march of appreciation.

I headed over to the fountain and saw a Fancy Dan approaching. He held a brown paper bag. It was a tough one to call. He was either my man carrying our promised duck dinner or some dandy out bootlegging smut. I walked over to him. Our eyes were about level. Milland was right. Guy de Carter did resemble Smilin' Jack—complete with solid jaw and pencil-thin mustache.

We shook hands. He was extraordinary and engaging. Within fifteen seconds he was Guy and I was "Sport." He had a strangely prim mouth that expanded to show perfect teeth that were possibly all his own. A toothpick that passed for a cigarette perched on his lip. He wore a Panama hat and a desert-toned gabardine suit. These went nicely with his tan

Koolie wingtips—the kind of shoes riddled with hundreds of little holes to cool off overworked feet. But though it wasn't hot out, Guy de Carter wore no socks, just to be on the safe side.

"Thanks for accommodating me, Sport," he said, leading us over to an empty bench. With the ease born of habit he took the saliva-laden toothpick from his mouth, bent it in half till it formed a V, and then flicked it on the nearby grass. He parked the paper bag between us and took out a couple of sandwiches and handed me one. "I had a meeting with the owner of the Chit-Chat Café over here on Forty-Fifth. It's a small potatoes account, but it has its upside. That's where I got this grub. On the house. I hope you like pastrami on rye."

"Love it," I said, and took a big bite as proof.

I gave him another look-over as he focused on his own sandwich. He was about my age. The dark hair showing under his hat was razor-cut and neatly combed. He had clean knuckles, manicured fingernails, and a deep tan that I'd have labeled asinine if I were any more jealous.

"The honcho lady over at Fasciné Expressions told me you wanted to ask me a few questions."

I smiled. "Is that what you call her? Honcho lady?"

He shrugged. "I call 'em as I see 'em. But mind you, I don't call her that to her face."

"I don't know. She seems to roll with the punches okay."

"Maybe so for you. But she doesn't like me very much. I go in that hoity-toity gift palace only when I have to, and that's not often. I know when I'm not welcome. Honcho lady is the chief hen in that rooster paradise—and believe you me she lets you know it. And with this rooster she's all business and no pleasure, if you take my meaning."

I took his meaning.

"You must like roses," I said, glancing at the plants around us.

"Not really, Sport. But *women* like roses. And I like women who like roses. This garden is just one of the spots I come to troll. And it brings back some good memories, if you take my meaning."

I did. He was a jaunty sort with a contagious grin and was loaded with that easy charm that made a woman feel appreciated, safe, and cared for. Until he got her in the sack, that is. Afterward she'd learn fast that she was no more than prey, or a commodity akin to a dishrag. And according to sultry Peggy, he played rough. Of course, some women like being quarry, and some think they deserve to be kitchen towels. And some put up with getting smacked around.

Still, I felt like one of those blind men of Indostan, touching only my part of the elephant.

"You strike me as someone who'd have no problems with the ladies," I said.

"I do all right. But then, I've had a lot of practice, Sport. I bet you've broken a few hearts yourself. We should hit the town together some night. It'd be a guaranteed hoot."

I laughed one of those social laughs I despise.

"Ever feel like ending it all by settling down and getting married to the right girl?" I asked him just to ask. "Maybe have a few nippers, a dog, a cat, and a mortgage?"

He shook his head. "Not this kid, Sport. It's not my style."

"Aren't you afraid the skirt-chasing will get old someday?"

"Perish the thought. I figure I'll just work on being more distinguished as I get older. A man can get away with it. A few flecks of gray at the temples will go well with the crows-feet that make an older man look the dasher. I'll just use a new kind of bait for a different school of female fishies; that's what I'll do. A man's got to revise and improvise, if you take my meaning."

"Revise and improvise. It sounds like you've thought through your future."

"You better believe it, Sport."

We ate in silence for a while. A couple of pretty bobby-soxers sauntered by. A real salt-and-pepper pair of teenagers that could easily play the movie parts for Archie's Betty and Veronica. They peeked back at us over their sweatered shoulders and tittered and chirped.

"Untouchables," de Carter muttered.

"Say again?"

He nodded toward the girls, his nostrils flaring like those of a satyr in rut. "San Quentin quail. Jail bait."

He watched the girls disappear while I studied him. His satyr's grin was pleasant. A friendly grin. A grin that told you he was harmless, companionable. The grin didn't go with the tiny glint of coldness in his eyes that hinted at those parts of the elephant I couldn't reach at the moment.

I asked him about his work at the ad agency.

He told me he was part idea man, part salesman for Sloane and Associates. "I've known Sloane for years. He gives me a pretty free rein. I come up with gimmicks and campaigns that sell the merchandise. I schmoose the clients. I wine 'em and dine 'em when needed. And believe you me, sport, I'm generous in pouring on the schmalz," he said, giving me a wink. "Basically I sell merchants on my ideas and try to keep them happy and writing those checks."

"Do you like the work?"

He shrugged. "I'd like to be rich, but who wouldn't? Working for Sloane keeps me in food, duds, and trolling money. I have no real complaints."

I took our sandwich wrappings and walked over to a trashcan to make a deposit. When I returned he pulled out two cartons of milk from the paper bag.

"Care for an after-lunch drink?" he asked, handing me one of the milks.

I thanked him.

"Is Guy de Carter the name you were born with?"

He shook his head. "No. My mother named me Buford. Buford Carston. I had it legally changed when I got out of the navy after the war. Felt I needed a little more flair than Buford, and a wee bit more pizzazz than Carston. And the ladies *do* love the name. Gives me a continental air, don't you know."

We slugged down our milk. I took the paper bag from him and crumpled it with our empties inside before saying, "About what you saw the day before yesterday …."

"Oh yes. The lover's spat. I'd popped by the store to pick up some product samples to study. But tell me, sport, what exactly do you want to know?"

"It sounds to me that when Dirk Engstrom started sounding off at his girlfriend, you were standing pretty close."

He nodded. "From about here to that geyser." The fountain he pointed to was about fifteen feet away from us. "I was just leaving when the kid exploded. His girlfriend was spraying perfume samples for an old timer. The old guy was giving the girl his imitation of Count Dracula when the boyfriend came in and started shouting. Believe you me, I noticed." He started to laugh. "The old timer and I practically bowled each other over trying to get out of the way."

"What all did you hear?"

"Only a little. And not all that clearly. Who wants to be part of a fracas? Gramps and I slowly retreated together with the kid's back to us the whole time. At that moment his girlfriend was the only one in the room as far as he was concerned. But I did hear the kid say 'Or I'll kill you.' That came through clear as day."

"You're sure of that?"

He crossed his heart and held his hand up.

De Carter reached in his shirt pocket and pulled out a fresh toothpick and hung it out of the corner of his mouth. I got myself an after-lunch clove.

He went on with his story. "I thought his threat was just one of those things people say in anger. Who knew he'd really do it? Kill her that is."

He stared at me with pure-hearted astonishment, but his surprise was just a wee bit too earnest.

"At the time the kid wasn't hitting his girlfriend or anything.

He was just beating his gums. So I got out of there after a minute or two. Like I said, I'm rarely in that place as it is. And besides, I was already late for an appointment."

He looked at his wristwatch. "Speaking of appointment, I'd better be on my way to my next one, Sport."

"One last question."

"Shoot."

"What kind of car do you drive?"

He gave me a curious look, a flicker of reappraisal in his eyes. "A '49 Ford convertible. Maroon. I bought it new. Risky in our wet city, I know. But what's life without a few risks. Am I right, Sport?"

I told him he was right.

"Why the interest in the make of my car?"

"Oh, I don't know. Given the swath you cut, I'd have pegged you as a Packard man."

He laughed a laugh that could spread like cholera.

"No. Not me. Packards are a little *too* conventional. Besides, the ladies like the open air. They like to feel the wind blowing through their hair. Candy's dandy, and liquor's quicker, but the open air makes 'em breezy and carefree. It's all part of the game, sport. All part of the game."

We stood and shook hands.

He handed me his business card and said, "Let me know if I can be of any further help."

I thanked him and studied his buoyant gait as he left the rose garden. I watched him get into his maroon ragtop. For Guy de Carter, the world wasn't simply his oyster. It was an oyster with a healthy dollop of cocktail sauce to be swallowed whole with a champagne chaser.

Sex has always been pretty high up on my pursuit of happiness list, but I liked to think I was a nobler cut of beefcake than Guy de Carter. At least I hoped so.

Dames were dames to Guy de Carter. They were useable and disposable. Like clothes put on and taken off, or money that quickly changes hands. Always a new suit to be bought. Always some new bills issued by the mint.

I couldn't see any reason why de Carter would lie about what he'd heard. No apparent motive. But either he *was* lying or Dirk did indeed threaten to kill Christine and was denying what he'd said to cover his butt. Or maybe Dirk said so many stupid things in anger that day, he simply didn't remember what all he said.

I thought of the term Blanche Arnot had used for Guy de Carter: drugstore cowboy. I suppose it fit him. But while there were no silver spurs on his Koolies, he was no ordinary cowpoke. And he was definitely no harmless lothario.

Mrs. Arnot said she'd seen de Carter in the store many times. De Carter told me he was seldom in the place. It could simply be a conflict of perception—one of them overstating the case. Or someone had just plain lied.

People I met in my line of work let you into their life a keyhole at a time. And, I was used to being lied to between those brief peeks. I was lied to all the time. People don't usually divulge very much unless they think you know something that might hurt them. Then they'll chat and jabber with the intent of persuading you that you're mistaken or that you've heard things wrong. They'll lie when they don't need to. And sometimes especially then. That's what usually trips them up.

I was still holding the paper bag containing our empty milk cartons. I uncrumpled it, dug around inside, and pulled out a small receipt from the Big Bite Café on Greenwood Avenue. It was proof of purchase for two milks and two sandwiches. Our lunch was no Chit-Chat Café freebie.

If de Carter had lied to me about something as trivial as where and how he'd gotten the lunch, what else had he lied about?

I'd left the Chevy in the zoo's nearby south gate parking lot. I scouted the area before I turned the motor over. All was quiet on the zoo's southern front.

I wended my way southeast then headed over toward the water and Ballard. I figured to stop in at my office. Spotting a phone booth, I pulled over.

Britt Anderson was delighted to be hearing from me again so soon. She didn't say those words exactly, but I like to think I'm a fair translator of female inflections.

I told her I'd just come from talking with Guy de Carter. "He says he seldom comes into the store. What say you?"

She thought for a moment. "I'll admit I've encouraged him to keep his visits strictly business."

"He thinks you don't like him very much."

She sighed and hesitated to answer. "I don't *dislike* him. Not really. It's just that … well, I guess I don't know him very well. But, he's been known to distract some of the girls when they should be working. I've talked with him about it. He seems to have gotten the point. But maybe he stops in when I'm not aware of it. After all, Sloane and Associates is just two floors up. It is rather convenient for him. *Why*? Is it important?"

"Just clearing up a small discrepancy. You started to say something about de Carter, but didn't. What were you going to say?"

"Oh, it's nothing really. It's just that there's a certain … menacing quality about him. I'm sure it's nothing. Please forget I even said it. Like I said, I don't know him well."

"Any luck with your staff?"

"I'm sorry, Gunnar. I've only had time to talk with Peggy. A minor emergency came up. A colossal mix-up with one of the orders. Peggy did say that as far as she knew, Dirk Engstrom was the only serious suitor Christine had. She emphasized the word 'serious,' and I was going to press her on it when I got called away. But before the day is through I'll be sure and get back to her, and to a couple of the other girls as well."

I said I appreciated it, and asked if she'd call me later. "Let me give you my home phone number," I said.

"Better still, are you busy tonight?" she asked.

I told her I wasn't particularly busy, so she invited me over to her place. "We've both got to eat. I'll just fix a little extra. We can talk over a meal."

I said it sounded good to me.

"Do you like Chianti with your macaroni and cheese?"

"Is this some kind of test?"

She laughed. "I'm teasing. I'm not too elaborate in the kitchen, but I've been told I'm actually a fair cook."

We agreed that 7:00 would be just ducky. She gave me the address to her apartment off Queen Anne Avenue.

Before we hung up, I remembered another reason why I'd called.

"Your girls probably won't know a Packard from a Studebaker, but when you're talking to them, ask if they know of any man they've come in contact with who drives a newer model Packard."

"Why, I do. I don't know makes or models, but I know that Len Pearson bought a Packard just last year. The reason I'm even remembering it is because that's all he seemed to talk about for probably two weeks straight."

We hung up and I called Pearson's office.

When he picked up I told him who was calling and said, "Do you mind telling me where you were between ten and ten thirty last night?"

"Why should I?" he asked.

"Someone driving a newer Packard tried to run me down around that time.

"And you think it was *me*?" He was clearly annoyed and flustered. He was also a bit drunk. I almost didn't catch it. But, his *was* came out as *wus*. "That's absurd. Why would I want to run you over?"

"You still haven't answered my first question."

"This is ridiculous. I resent what you're insinuating."

"Humor me."

He was silent for a moment.

"Why ... if you must know, I was with an old college buddy of mine. We were at my club. Afterward we went to dinner and a show."

I listened more attentively. He was making his statements like an expert drinker trying to show he's in control—carefully putting words together, despite the booze-induced limits.

"I was with him till well after midnight. He can vouch for me."

"What was the name of the show?"

"That's none of your business."

"I can make it my business."

"Just screw off," he shrieked, though he didn't hang up.

"Suit yourself, Len. But if I have to find out your whereabouts by digging around, there's no telling who else will find out. So, whatever you're trying to hide, is it really worth the possible ballyhoo?"

I heard him groan on his end. He was silent for a moment.

"We ... we were at the ... the Menagerie. But it's not what you think. And we'll both deny it if you make an issue of it."

It was my turn to be silent. When people tell you it's not what you think, it usually is. But I pegged Len as the unusual exception to that rule.

"Keep your shirt on, Len. Your secret's safe with me."

"But it's not *my* secret! You don't understand. It was strictly *Jack's* idea. He's always been somewhat of a skylarker. We went as a joke. A gag. I *do* have a wife and kids, after all. You ... you *do* believe me, don't you?"

"Yeah, Len, I believe you."

And I did believe him. He was too readily befuddled. He told the truth needlessly. He could just as easily have lied and told me he was simply at a girlie show. But he didn't. Plus, I was pretty sure I'd read him right at our first meeting. His unbridled gazes at Britt Anderson and his pathetic yearning for her were too oafish to be anything but genuine.

In San Francisco before the war, I'd gone once to see a drag show at Finocchio's. My youthful curiosity and wet earlaps didn't make me one of nature's misfires. But Len's pal Jack was no longer making his first grand tour. His salad days were long over. I wondered how well Len really knew his old buddy.

"Were you driving your Packard last night, Len?"

"The whole night. I swear it. Look. Jack is staying at the Meany Hotel. I'll give you his number if you like. He'll tell you the same story. Just be discreet about this. Swear you will."

I swore I would and hung up.

I wrote down the number Len gave me but scrunched up the note a minute after the phone was back in its cradle. Len was suited for the role of unwitting tour guide to a double-gaited pal, but he didn't strike me as a killer—at least not one nervy enough to kill on the fly. Too high strung. A guy like Len would need weeks, maybe months to plan. And I didn't think Christine's murder took that kind of calculation. But I'd been wrong before. So, I unscrunched the note and put it in my wallet.

"You have two messages," Cissy said when I opened the door to Dag's office. "One from Detective Sergeant Milland. The other is from Rikard Lundeen."

Cissy stood in front of a filing cabinet, her chest level with an open drawer. She turned and reached for some notes on her desk.

I took the slips of paper from her. I could feel her watching me as I read.

"When did Milland's come in?" I asked.

"About an hour ago."

It was 2:30 by my Longines.

"How about Lundeen's."

"Twenty minutes ago. Tops."

I thanked her and headed to my pigeonholes and telephone.

Cissy's note from Milland read, "Call. Urgent." Lundeen's message was simply, "Call me." You had to admire their economy of words if not their imaginations.

I rang Milland first.

"About time you called."

"Been busy. What's up?"

He told me someone took a shot at Addison Darcy.

"When? Did you catch the guy?"

"Not so fast. Me first. I want an account of your whereabouts. Darcy says you left his house around eleven. Where'd you go from there?"

"Straight to Fifth and Pine, and Fasciné Expressions. After I talked with Miss Anderson I went and talked with Guy de Carter. Made a couple of phone calls after that, and now I'm talking to you. So what happened to Darcy?"

"He says he left his place about thirty or forty minutes after you took off. He was no more than a hundred yards outside the front gate of The Highlands when someone put a bullet through his windshield."

"Was he hit?"

"Nah, but he wrapped his Lincoln around a telephone pole. He's all right, but the Lincoln needs major surgery. Lucky for him he wasn't going too fast. Guard on the gate phoned it in."

I recalled Darcy saying he'd received some kind of summons just before I'd arrived.

"Where did Darcy say he was headed?"

"To a hotel downtown. He said one of his son's war buddies had phoned him. The guy said he was going to be in town just overnight, and had a few things that belonged to Darcy's son. Wanted to know if Darcy would meet him."

I told Milland about Cissy's call from someone posing as one of my war pals.

"That army buddy ploy is no happenstance. It's got to link both attempted murders," I said.

"Damn." I took that for agreement. "A little *too* coincidental," Milland added.

"Just a tad."

"Any good ideas who'd want to kill both you and this Darcy?"

"Nary a one, Frank." It wasn't really a lie. He'd asked for *good* ideas. "But I have a suggestion for you we both might profit by."

"Spill it."

"Like I told you, the car that tailed the Johanson girl and me was a late model Packard. Walter said the car that nearly pulverized me could have been that model as well."

"I sense a hunt for a needle in a haystack coming my way," he said.

"Not really. Come up with the registrations for all Packards for the past couple of years in the greater Seattle area. Check the owners' names against the Johanson girl's repeat customer list. See if you come up with a match."

He let out with an animal noise of approval.

"You carrying?" he asked.

"Yep."

"Well, keep your powder dry and your eyes peeled, you dumb Swede."

"Why Frank, I'm touched. If people should overhear us, they'd think you care."

"Ah, shaddup."

I called Rikard Lundeen.

He'd heard the news about Addison Darcy. I told him about my own close call.

"Well son, it looks like a tiger's getting beat out of the brush. It also goes to help young Dirk's case, don't you think?"

"It's starting to look that way."

"So, what's your next move?"

Hell if I knew. But what I told him was that I'd look up Christine's repeat male customers and check on their whereabouts for the past couple of days.

"What's the connection to Addison Darcy? Any thoughts there, son?"

I told him I had none. At least none I wanted to share at the moment.

"DIDN'T YOU TRUST HIM? Was that it?" Kirsti asked. She had stopped her recorder and was flipping the cassette over.

"No that wasn't it," I said. "Oh, I'll admit I didn't care for the man, but I believed in doing a good job for someone whether I liked him or not."

"Been there, done that," she said, nodding.

"No, the thoughts I was mulling over just weren't ready to be passed on. That's all."

"Well, tell me. I want to know. What had you figured out by then?" She'd turned the recorder back on.

"Well, young lady, I hadn't figured out much of anything. It was plain Guy de Carter had lied to me. Greenwood Avenue was halfway between Woodland Park and The Highlands. So I knew he could easily have taken a shot at Addison Darcy and still made our rendezvous at the rose garden."

"But why? What was his motive?" she asked as she handed me a plastic water bottle.

"That's what I wondered. It didn't make sense."

"You make Guy de Carter out to be a real sex addict. Did you think maybe he had a thing going with Christine Johanson?"

"Oh, sure. At first it crossed my mind that they'd been lovers. I pictured Christine as the smitten nuisance who wouldn't let go till de Carter killed her. But I dismissed that pretty quickly. Too drastic. To a man like Guy de Carter, promises and hearts were meant to be broken. No, he didn't need to murder to end a relationship."

"Yeah. A little too way out there for a theory. And besides, how would that tie in with Addison Darcy?"

"Exactly. Either de Carter or Christine had to have had some tie to Darcy."

"Maybe they both did?"

I nodded. "Life is far less happenstance than we care to believe, Blue Eyes."

"How do you mean?"

I took a big swig from the water bottle she'd handed me. As

I screwed the cap back on I said, "What I mean is we're not hermits living in a vacuum. We're more like trailblazers in a vast wilderness."

"Sounds like happenstance to me," she said as she put the bottle back in her tote bag.

"Wrong. As we blaze our personal trail through life, paths cross and merge. It gets messy."

"Like the bumpersticker? Shit happens? Is that what you mean?"

"That'll work. Look, we all do stupid and selfish things at times. Some souls make it their career. Most of the time our actions play out to a rather harmless finale. As they say, we luck out."

I could see in her eyes she'd experienced just such luck.

"But like it or not, our actions touch others. Sometimes, the things people do are so half-witted or so self-seeking, they set events in motion that quietly start to percolate." I switched from a coffee metaphor to a weather one: "One day, a bolt strikes someone out of the blue. Except it's not out of the blue. All along the beanie they were wearing was a lightning rod."

Kirsti had a direct intent stare that bore right through me.

"A small thunderbolt you were hoping to dodge, Blue Eyes?"

She shook her head, and the brooding moment seemed to pass.

"Whether it's just plain reaping what was sown, or taking the consequences when someone from the past surfaces with a vendetta, the results are often unpleasant and sometimes disastrous."

"So what are you saying?"

"Well, Blue Eyes, at that point I wasn't saying much at all. And I'm not going to rush my story by telling you the end out of sequence."

She smiled.

"No, at the time an analysis of what little I knew didn't

provide me with a whole lot of answers. I had more nosing around to do. Let's see now, where was I?"

After I got off the phone with Rikard Lundeen, I grew extremely tired. I yawned a monster yawn. I fought to keep my eyes open.

I looked up at the picture hanging on the wall across the room. It was a short distance, so I could make out the details easily—although I knew them by heart. The picture showed nubile girls in a majestic outside setting. One was dressed and reclining. She was looking up at the other girl, who stood naked and was leaning over the first—her arms conveniently placed to cover up her pudenda. When I was a kid I'd make up conversations for them. I later learned that the girl on her feet was the artist's daughter and the other was William Jennings Bryan's granddaughter. The artist called the picture *Daybreak*. It was a favorite of my grandmother's. Agnette had been a fan of Maxfield Parrish. This particular print had hung above the fireplace in the home where I was raised.

Most of the time, looking at this picture gave me mixed feelings. At that moment it made me feel good. I needed to feel good.

I started to nod off till I quit fighting it and gave in to a catnap.

The clacking of Cissy's typewriter coming in through the transom woke me up. By my watch I must have dozed in my chair for ten minutes.

I pulled the Damon Runyon paperback out of my drawer. As Cissy pounded away on her machine, I spent fifteen minutes with good guys and nice Judys before I put the book back inside the desk.

Cissy's typing stopped. I pictured her getting ready to button things up and go home early. I decided to say goodnight and head for home myself. That would give me plenty of time to spiff up for my dinner date with Britt. It was the second time in a week that a spur-of-the-moment decision saved my life.

My Longines read 3:15 when I locked my outer door and went over to Dag's office, not bothering to knock as I entered. As I imagined, Cissy had her coat on and wasn't wearing her reading glasses—indicators that she was making moves to take off for the day.

"Clearing out early, eh?" I asked.

"Dag's still tied up in court. He phoned and told me that when I finished my filing I could pack it in if I wanted to. I want to."

"You've got my vote."

She smiled and said, "I meant to ask earlier—any luck on your investigation?"

I'd shut the door behind me when I came in. My body blocked Cissy's view of the door's frosted glass window; otherwise she might have seen someone walk by.

"I've come up with more questions. Problem is, the answers aren't keeping pace," I said.

She smiled broadly, causing her cheeks to dimple.

"You're still alive. That's a good sign. I'd hate to be without my date for tomorrow night."

"You're a cold one, Sweet Knees."

"Callous to the bone."

"Is that all I am to you? A warm body to drag around a dance floor?"

"When you put it that way, it sounds rather macabre," she said, frowning. "Pick me up at six, will you? And be sure your warm body's wearing a different suit. That one resembles used carbon paper, and I see enough of that each day already."

I was going to reply but didn't get the chance.

At first I thought it was an automobile backfiring down on Market Street. But the second, third, and fourth shot that immediately followed were unmistakable. Someone was blasting away at my end of the corridor.

I grabbed for Cissy and yanked her with me in a dive and

roll over her desk. I thumped to the floor with her piling down on top of me. We hit in a dizzying sprawl that formed a chaotic heap of legs, thighs, elbows, and torsos that normally I'd have found intriguing. We lay still for a moment.

Silence.

I felt Cissy's heart keeping time with mine as her breast-points nudged and pushed at my ribcage. She quickly broke the scissor lock her knees had on my waist. My hand sprouted my .38 as we disentangled. One of her nylons had a run from ankle to mid-haunch. She hitched at her coat and skirt, retrieving them from where they'd been hiked by our tumble. Her face was pale.

I whispered, "Stay put while I go check."

She grabbed my coat sleeve and said, "Don't, Gunnar." For a split second I heard a rare vulnerability in her voice. I liked it. "Whoever it is may still be out there."

"That's the idea," I said, breaking away from her.

I took three soft strides to the door, opened it, and dropped to my knees, pointing my .38 in the direction of my office. When I saw nothing, I quickly wheeled about and pointed my gun down the other way.

More nothing. The corridor was empty. The tenants across the way were either out or lying low.

I moved over to my office. The glass to my door's window was in shards on the linoleum. The inner door had suffered the same fate. The back wall was bullet-pocked and pieces of plaster littered the floor.

The shooter had scrambled.

I rang Milland again. A dispatcher contacted him by radio. He and Hanson came right over and took our brief statements. Downstairs, Olga Peterson had heard the commotion. She told them she thought some kids were celebrating the Fourth of July early. No one had seen anyone suspicious-looking come or go.

"He probably ran out the back way," Hanson said.

I was going to give Milland the list of customers Britt had given me.

"We got our own copy. I'll get back to you on any matches."

They told us we could go home.

Before I left I tugged from the wall the corkboard I used to tack up my notes. I jury-rigged a temporary cover with it for where my window had been. It didn't make my office secure exactly, but at least it would discourage an honest man.

Cissy waited around and watched me work. I sensed she wanted company. Normally, I'd have taken her out for a drink to help bring harmony to any nerves that were still ragged. But I was mindful of my date with Britt, and didn't want an awkward breakaway later. I told her I needed to stop off home before heading out to another interview.

"Have a good belt before you hit the hay tonight, Sweet Knees," I said as we parted. "We'll shake this incident off tomorrow night at the Trianon."

She told me to please be careful.

I told her I'd be incredibly careful. She was a little teary-eyed. I felt like shit served on stale shingle for leaving her, but managed to do it all the same.

I headed home.

As I ENTERED THE kitchen side door, I was hit with a hearty whiff of Musterole. Sten—the undying cigarette hanging from his lip—had just finished constructing a Dagwood sandwich at the kitchen table.

I gave the air two meaningful sniffs and asked, "Rough day?"

"Shoulder's acting up. I think the shrapnel is migrating. Rubbing Musterole on it seems to help," he said with a grin. At Bougainville, Sten had jumped out of an amphib right into what he called a Tojo surprise.

Sten had built a six-inch tower of bread, cold cuts, lettuce, tomatoes, pickles—all of which was probably held together with liberal amounts of mayonnaise and A-1 Sauce. It looked fantastic. My mouth watered. The kitty-cat wall clock read 4:40, which meant it was closer to 5:00.

"What? Not waiting for feeding time?"

"We're poor little lambs all on our own tonight."

"And why isn't the young and unsettled chowing down at one of his haunts?"

"Oh, I plan to," he said. "This sucker's just an appetizer to tide me over."

"Where's your aunt?"

"She just left. Some guy she met at the Shurfine Market is taking her out on the town."

"Does Walter know?"

"I'm pretty sure he does. He's been shut up in his room since I got home. Walter's no idiot," Sten added as he put his sandwich on a plate and poured himself a glass of milk.

I opened the door leading to the basement for him. He called his room the dungeon. I noticed his souvenir Jap bayonet sticking out of his back pocket.

"Why the bayonet?"

"Kenny's got a boil on his butt the size of a walnut. He wants me to lance it for him before we head over to the 211."

"My luck to Kenny."

With a ghoulish laugh, Sten said, "There's plenty of eats left in the fridge if you'd like one of these puppies." He lifted his plate, a self-satisfied look on his face.

"Thanks, but no thanks. I've got a dinner date myself."

"We talkin' about the dollface with the half-shimmy getalong?"

"*Who*?"

"That almost-receptionist of yours?"

"No."

"So, you'll put in a good word for *me*, then?"

"What happened to Claudia?"

"You mean Pin-Curlers? That beauty parlor in heels? I swear

that girl never finishes getting ready. She's last month's news. So, how about the endorsement?"

"I'll introduce you if you come by. But you're on your own after that."

"Fair enough. So, about tonight, are we talkin' Everett good-lookin' or Tacoma good-lookin'? Or *what*?"

"This one's off any scale you could ever hope to devise."

Sten whistled. "Don't do anything I wouldn't do," he said as he descended to the dungeon.

Things were quiet in Walter's room, but I knew he was still awake. I freshened up in the bathroom, swatted my face with a little cologne and changed into my dark brown suit. Britt didn't seem to be put off by my new seersucker, but maybe she was just being nice. If both Mrs. Berger and Cissy gave it a thumbs-down, I wasn't about to wear it to dinner.

I rapped lightly on Walter's door.

He told me to come in. A good sign.

He was seated on his work stool over near the window. The bottle of Black & White was on the sill alongside a full shot glass. His 8mm Lebel revolver was in its holster sitting on the end of the workbench nearest him. At the other end the British Dragoons were set up in a charge that looked formidable. They appeared to be finished. A package sat next to them postmarked Springfield, Massachusetts. It was from Raymond Perry. My guess was it had arrived that afternoon. It remained unopened.

Not a good sign.

"I'm glad to see you're still among the living. Care for a drink, old thing?"

"Can't right now, Walter. I'm heading out again to go talk to someone."

"You won't mind if I drink in front of you, I trust," he said, downing his glass. "Did you know that the Arabic word *al-kuhul* originally referred to the powdered antimony used to paint eyelids?"

I let him expound. It was the least I could do. He was maudlin but still lucid.

I sometimes pondered the Walter that might have been. I wondered what he'd have made of himself if he hadn't been so close to that fuel wagon in the Argonne.

Usually, my musings about Walter were self-indicting. My own life hadn't been molded by physical scars, but I suspect something caused me to settle for an addiction to conundrums and a fascination with the twists and folds of human makeup. Family life in the suburbs might have cured the addiction, and a more genteel career may have blunted the fascination, but I never put this theory to the proof. So I was in no position to judge Walter Pangborn. Somewhere along the way I'd stood close to my own version of Walter's fuel wagon. Not the *tangible* kind. One far more insidious.

I told Walter what had happened at the office.

It didn't pull him out of his mood, but I could see concern in his eyes.

"Any ideas yet as to who would want to kill you?"

"Nothing fixed. Just some free-floating notions."

I told him Len Pearson drove a Packard and related my phone conversation with him.

"Hmm. Levantine mischiefs or not, he sounds rather harmless, Gunnar. Like the rest of us, he doubtless plays many parts, depending on what the occasion demands."

I agreed. "But I figure the real Pearson is probably a frightened understudy hiding offstage."

Walter smiled a tortured smile. "Like all of us, old top. Like all of us."

Walter poured himself another shot of whiskey. He drank in an elegant, almost lordly manner. His speech was never slurred and he never got surly.

I told him about the attempt on Addison Darcy's life. I also told him about Guy de Carter.

"He calls Miss Anderson 'honcho lady,' eh?" He smiled as

expansively as his ruined face would allow. "A term from the Japanese word *hancho*, meaning squad leader ...."

I interrupted and told him how de Carter had lied to me about where he'd gotten our lunch.

"And you think this de Carter might have taken a potshot at Mr. Darcy?" he said.

"Yeah. But I don't know why yet. I might be looking at the wrong person entirely."

"A fellow with Guy de Carter's proclivities may well have just come from a tryst with a married woman. That could account for his lying. Besides, he didn't poison your sandwich."

"I thought about that. We ate in too public a place for him to kill me in that fashion. Too many good citizens eyeballing us. Plus, he might have decided just to find out all what I knew."

I described Guy de Carter to him, and told him what we'd talked about.

"You're a student of human nature, Walter. What do you make of this guy?"

"What do I make of a *guy* named *Guy*? I forgive your pun," he said, taking a drink of his Scotch. "I'm no more than a dime-store analyst, Gunnar. A dabbler, really. So remember, you're getting just what you've paid for."

He belched.

"Excuse me, old socks. I seem to have an upset stomach that has gotten the mastery of my manners."

I popped a fresh clove between teeth and jowl and watched as Walter pondered.

"All of us, Gunnar, have pursuits that help us escape life's tedium—activities we enjoy to change or modify our dispositions, our moods. Mr. Guy de Carter has merely carried things to an extreme. He's on a neurotic treadmill. Actually, more like that little wheel in Popeye's cage downstairs. Your Mr. de Carter is on one of those wheels."

"A hamster wheel."

"Yes. Just so. He's running. Some people become booze

hounds." Walter lifted up his shot glass a few inches. "Some—like our fellow boarder Sten—turn to gambling. Others chase after money, eat too much, or are consumed with their employment."

Walter paused for a moment's thought as he warmed to his topic.

"Mr. Guy de Carter is what the hoi polloi commonly call a ladies' man, a lady-killer, or even a sex fiend. Whereas the psychiatric mandarins and alienists speak in terms of complexes, compulsions, neuroses, aberrations—"

"A sex fiend, eh?"

"Siding with the hoi polloi, I see. Doubtless a wise choice."

"Sex fiend is a pretty severe label, don't you think, Walter?"

"Perhaps. But Mr. de Carter *is* a fiend of sorts, at least in the sense that his devotion to sex is *excessive*. For him sex is like an opiate. He's running, running, constantly running—just like the caged Popeye on his little wheel. An analyst might tell you that some childhood need of Mr. de Carter's went unfulfilled. Whatever the case, he's running from feelings like loneliness, bereavement, hurt. He's on a flight from a tormenting reality. He's trying to flee his personal hell."

"I get the picture."

"The tragic thing about it is that Mr. de Carter probably is actually desirous of—is actually seeking—a close, deep connection, but he never gets it, and he never will. Not the way he's currently going about it."

He was silent for a long moment.

"With each woman Mr. de Carter sleeps with he makes things worse—he adds to the very mishmash of troubled and tormenting feelings he's running from. He's on a madman's run. Again, he's like Popeye on his little wheel. But when you think about it, our hamster downstairs is really better off."

"What do you mean, Walter?"

He lifted the left side of his mouth in a smile. "Because the lowly Popeye lives for the present moment. And while Mr. de

Carter does so as well, he's also dogged by his memories of the past, and uncomfortably aware of the approaching future."

I'd never seen Walter quite this passionate in his comments on human behavior. As he sliced, diced, and shredded de Carter's ego, id, and superego, I have to admit I grew increasingly uncomfortable.

"My guess is that at some level he can't stand himself or what he does. But he keeps on doing it, over and over and over again."

My head swam with clear images of de Carter bedding woman after woman like some sexual jackhammer.

"You might say that women are Mr. de Carter's way of chastising an already injured psyche."

"You mean like self-flagellation?"

"In effect, but certainly minus any religious aspect."

"Punishing himself with *sex*?"

"Yes."

"Well, I suppose there's worse fates."

Walter ignored me. "He'll probably die a pathetic, miserable, unmourned womanizer. It's one of many ailments in this life that few seek to cure."

"I get the idea," I said quietly. His verbal barrage got my own psyche running for cover. "Is it possible that *self*-loathing could turn *outward*?"

"You mean, could Mr. de Carter objectify his feelings and violently turn on the women in his life? Actually kill them?"

I nodded.

"Anything's possible. I'm sure it's happened before, old thing. That's the construction some place on those Jack the Ripper killings back around the turn of the century. So yes, anything's possible."

"Maybe he and Christine Johanson had something going. He killed her. Then he framed the Engstrom kid. Then he tried to kill me because he's afraid I'll figure it out and expose him."

"It sounds a little too pat, Gunnar. It doesn't account for his trying to kill Mr. Darcy, if indeed that was also his handiwork."

I told him about getting Milland to hunt up registrations for Packards.

Walter nodded his approval.

"I'd be interested in any match Detective Milland might come up with. It may just be the puzzle piece you're looking for. And by all means, please let me know if you learn anything more from Miss Meredith Lane."

Mrs. Berger's social life was just a trigger. I empathized with Walter. I had my own triggers. I also knew the kind of soul-piercing pain that gets a man looking for his own brand of mind-numbing relief.

So I felt a little guilty when I got up to leave. Walter would probably have enjoyed the company. I know I would have. But I just couldn't bring myself to cancel on Britt Anderson. I had my own frailties to consider. As I shut Walter's door I watched him pour another shot of "the Scotch with character." Or so the advertisements claimed.

Chapter 10

—

VISTA COURT APARTMENTS WAS a misnomer in at least two ways. First, it wasn't really a court at all. More like a long hairpin. Secondly, though situated on a hill, there was no vista. To my mind the only gorgeous view was the tenant I was there to see.

I parked on Queen Anne Avenue. I hadn't been tailed, but I still looked around to be sure before leaving the Chevy.

I entered one end of the hairpin and was flanked by nicely maintained adobe-style bungalows connected one to the next. They looked to have been built in the early '30s. Each was terraced in ascending progression to conform to the slope they were built on. So I didn't exactly gambol along. I'd say it was more like a brisk climb.

Britt's apartment sat on the outside of the bend in the hairpin, affording a little more privacy than most of her neighbors'. Given where she lived on the grade, I had to scale two sets of concrete steps to get to her porch. The porch was a small, enclosed affair decorated with several hanging flower baskets. Most contained blooming fuchsias that gave her doorway a cheery appearance. They went with the peppy music that was playing inside.

I looked at my Longines. It was 6:40. I was early. All right, I was shamefully ahead of schedule. I knocked anyway.

The music stopped.

When the door swung open I surveyed a stunning but stunned Britt Anderson. She'd pulled her hair back with a headband, her face was a bit flushed, and she wore a glossy blue leotard from her throat to her bare feet.

"You're early," she said, sounding a little winded. She wasn't angry, but she wasn't exactly happy either.

Gunnar the Ill-Timed.

"Sorry. I was hoping for a before-dinner drink. Someone tried to kill me again."

It was a cheap trick, but it had the desired effect. Her eyes immediately showed the concern I'd seen earlier in the day.

She took my brown fedora and ushered me in. The shiny parquetry floor of her living room was fully exposed. An Oriental rug sat rolled up over to one side.

I quickly gave her a two-sentence report of what happened.

"That's dreadful," she said with a small shudder. "How distressing for you." Her voice practically reached out and hugged me.

I stole Rikard Lundeen's line. "It looks like a tiger's getting beaten out of the brush."

"It truly does. It's just horrible."

Britt daubed her face with a towel. Residual makeup and perfume fragrances were now blended with another scent, not at all unpleasing—the feral brininess of vigorous exertion.

"I'll want more details, of course. But let me get cleaned up first." Then, feeling an apparent need to explain, she said, "My aunt got me interested in dancing when I was younger. I never pursued it, but I still keep up with the exercises to keep fit and limber. It also helps me to unwind. These tights are my aunt's. I have several pair just like these. You'll have to excuse my appearance. I must look frightful."

"Not at all," I said, meaning every word. I told her she could model the other pairs for me anytime. She smiled.

She looked phenomenal in this particular glassy outfit. The material gave a metallic polish to her figure. She resembled one of those curvaceous girls you see in Buck Rogers. Only this was no paper doll. Not by a long shot.

I gawked. I tried not to, but Britt had her back to me now so it was an epic struggle. Her form-fitting tights showed off capital-looking legs—the sinewy but shapely kind possessed by female dancers and trapeze artists. They seemed to go on forever. But where they finally did leave off, the solid roundness of a gymnast's rump took over. She seemed unaware of her sensuality, so frankly exhibited in the way she was standing—her full round hips tilting indifferently.

"While you wait, please make yourself a drink. There's wine, beer, and glasses in the kitchen. Or if you'd prefer," she pointed to a small dining nook off the living room, "you'll find something stronger in the credenza."

I brazenly ogled as she scurried off to her shower. If I were the delicate sort, I'd have fainted dead away from the experience. Luckily I was never so dainty.

Before shutting the bathroom door she called back, "Be a dear and roll out the rug for me, will you?"

I covered up Britt's makeshift dance floor and pulled a couple of pieces of furniture back where they seemed to belong. With her no longer distracting me, I was able to take in the tasteful surroundings. It was cozy. The facing of the credenza was decorated with ornate marquetry. It was doubtless an heirloom, as probably were the dining room table and chairs. But the furnishings in the living room were all recent acquisitions. She owned a television set. A 16-inch Philco. One of those consolette ensembles I'd seen advertised in the paper. All in all, I'd say the head honcho lady seemed to be doing all right for herself.

I could hear the shower was still going strong.

I found ice cubes for my tumbler in the refrigerator freezer. The mouth-slavering aroma of roasting chicken wafted up at me from the oven. As I poured myself some Scotch from the credenza I heard the shower go off.

I busied myself by finding plates and silverware. I set them on her small dining room table where she'd already spread a cloth. I couldn't find the butter plate, but I put out salt and pepper shakers. I also discovered some decorative napkins in the top drawer of the credenza.

Feeling pleased with myself, I took my drink back to the living room and planted my body in a club chair with big balloon cushions. It was the perfect spot for when she watched the television.

I parked my drink on the coffee table in front of me. What looked like a small family gallery took up one corner. I picked up two of the pictures that particularly caught my eye.

The first was of Blanche Arnot and a teenage version of Britt standing next to a woman maybe ten years Britt's senior. This had to be the Aunt Alexis she'd told me about. She too was a looker. The other photo was one I'd seen at Blanche Arnot's. It was a studio portrait of Aunt Alexis alone that had been oil-painted. She was fair-haired like her niece, but a strawberry blonde.

"She was beautiful, don't you think?" Britt asked from behind me.

"Definitely," I said.

I turned and saw my hostess just come from a showdown with her dressing table and wardrobe. She was the clear victor. Summer hadn't officially begun, but it had at Britt's place. She'd put a bow in her hair and wore a bolero dress with a texture that resembled a waffle-iron mold. She was wearing a smart pair of toeless sandals with wedge heels, but no nylons. The whole getup from head to foot was the color of ripe peaches and gave me a powerful yen for peach cobbler.

She headed for the kitchen.

I got up and followed her.

She poured herself a glass of wine and we talked while she prepared dinner. I finished my Scotch and replaced it with a bottle of Rainier Extra Pale.

I said that I liked her apartment.

"Do you? I'm glad. It was my aunt's place originally. It's been home since I came to Seattle. The rent has only been raised once. I've been lucky that way."

I told her in detail what had happened to Addison Darcy and me. I held back on my theories, but did tell her I was pretty confident that Len and his Packard weren't the culprits.

"That's a relief," she said, "although I was pretty sure that's what you'd determine. Which reminds me. So far none of the girls know a man who drives a newer Packard. But it's as you thought—they don't know automobiles very well. However, Peggy did explain her comment from earlier. She said she believed Christine might have been seeing someone other than Dirk, but that it didn't seem to be a serious relationship. One of the other girls had a similar feeling. I'll keep at it."

I thanked her for her efforts.

By the time we sat down to dinner I'd switched to wine. We ate roast game hen, stringed beans sautéed in butter, and leftover potato salad. It was excellent and I said so several times.

I told her a bit about myself. My upbringing by my grandparents in a little whistle stop upstate called Conway. I talked about my old partner Lou and our work at the Bristol Agency. At Britt's request, I made a few comments about the war. I stuck to humorous incidents. I usually revisited the horrific experiences only in my dreams. She told me a little about life growing up among the apple-growers of Wenatchee and her business schooling.

"I have four older brothers. After Mom died my dad thought I needed some female influences. So he shunted me off to Seattle. I hated it at first. But Aunt Alexis turned that around in a hurry."

She talked mainly about her Aunt Alexis, and how she'd idolized her. Alexis had worked as a legal secretary, but her real passion had been for performing.

"She could do it all. Act, sing, dance. Ask Blanche Arnot. She'll tell you the same thing."

Britt told me more details about what she called the dark times, when a man Alexis was madly in love with had abruptly ended their relationship. Britt's aunt had been devastated.

"She had a nervous breakdown. After that she never shook a malaise that led to a deterioration of her spirit. She sought refuge in drink."

Britt explained again how she'd curtailed her own plans in order to take care of her failing aunt. Alexis' alcoholic dementia worsened and led Britt to have her committed. After she'd died, Britt had taken the job as Len Pearson's aide-de-camp.

I helped her clear the table and put the dishes in the sink. She insisted on doing them the next morning. The wine bottle was a dead soldier, so I grabbed another beer. She didn't. We went into the living room and sank together on a daveno that matched her club chair for comfort.

We talked about poor Meredith. Britt said she'd called her when she got home from work, but there was no answer.

"If I were her I'd be making lots of Zs," I said.

She smiled, agreed, and then said, "This morning you mentioned you had a feeling Meredith had more to say than she did when you talked. You said it was as if she was holding something back. What did you mean by that?"

I told her of the telephone conversation Meredith had overheard—how she listened as Christine made plans to meet someone in Ballard, and had sounded hurt, like she'd been cheated. I added, "Meredith was pretty certain it wasn't Dirk she was talking to on the phone. She thinks Christine was having an affair with one of her customers."

I saw a brief flash of comprehension in her eyes. "Ah, *that's* the main reason why you wanted the list."

"Right."

"And so your suspicion springs from more than just a theory," she said.

"Right again. I also believe Meredith had more to say on the subject. I think she felt awkward talking about it at work. I'm going to call on her in the morning. I hope to get her to open up."

"Your line of work must be very exciting."

"It can be. It has been in the past twenty-four hours. More than I like."

We talked some more about the attempts on my life and Addison Darcy's. Then we shifted to nothing in particular. My beer was gone and our foreheads were maybe eight inches apart. We stared at each other for a while in silence—long enough for our breathing patterns to synchronize. We kissed. Her mouth was soft, her lips supple. We kissed several times.

Britt got up and took my hand. I followed her across the room like a dazed bovine led to shelter in a squall.

At work Britt was a little playful but she struck me as mainly officious, reserved, and genteel. I now met her alter ego. Bolero dress and undergarments hit the floor with a speed that would have horrified a veteran stripper like Mrs. Berger. I had no complaints. I was going to ask if she worked hot and did all the kicks, but I held my tongue. Sometimes you just don't ask questions.

At some point I drifted off to sleep. I dreamt Britt was talking on the phone. It was a dream made to seem real because I was awakened when she climbed back into bed.

She snuggled up close to me. Her clock said 11:45.

"I should probably be going," I said.

"So *soon*?" she purred, coaxing me with her kisses into a repeat performance. I was exhausted, but she *was* persuasive. And I was nothing if not persuadable.

I stayed in Britt's bed until almost 1:30 a.m. It was a welcome conclusion to the past couple of days of madness. I reluctantly pulled myself from the leg lock she had on me. As I dressed she got up and put on her bathrobe.

At the front door we kissed. Unbelievably, she wanted me to stay for an extra inning. But just as unbelievably, I graciously declined. I was done in. Plus, as much as the idea appealed to me, it went against my sense of propriety. I was concerned what the neighbors might think. I didn't want them to get the *right* impression.

So instead, I courteously thanked her for a great dinner and an even greater evening.

"I'll call you tomorrow," I said.

"You mean you'll call me *today*. And I'll expect you to," she replied. She then gave me a genuine goodbye kiss with cool lips and an elfin glance that disappeared coyly as she shut the door.

I hopped down her porch steps with Fred Astaire's light feet. Or so I liked to think.

Britt on the job was alluring. Britt at home was downright ambrosial. I could see that an intelligent and determined woman like her probably needed to compartmentalize her life at work and her personal life. But what a delectable contrast.

I was in love.

Well, I'd scratched a mighty lascivious itch, anyway.

I drove home slowly. The alcohol was long out of my bloodstream, but I had to fight nodding off. I wished that the Chevy could make its own way home like some faithful Cayuse with its frolic-sodden cowboy asleep in the saddle.

When I got to Mrs. Berger's, my light feet had grown heavy. I gave the street a reconnoitering scan before I went inside. No killer appeared to be lurking in the shadows. I didn't utter a peep as I made for the stairs. I didn't even glance at Mrs. Berger's cheesecake photos.

I went to brush my teeth and discovered vomit in the sink and on the floor. Poor Walter. He probably thought he'd hit his mark, but had been beguiled by the Black & White.

It saddened me and took away some of my zest from earlier.

The bathroom reeked of bile. I cleaned up the mess with fresh towels that I rinsed off in the tub before sending them down the laundry chute. I disinfected the area with Lysol and then showered.

Since Walter, my sentinel, had taken the night off, I set my .38 on the nightstand and wedged a chair in front of the door. I balanced a water glass on the doorknob as an added precaution.

It was 3:00 a.m. when I finally hit the sack.

I didn't go right to sleep. My clean-up duty had rekindled my feelings of guilt for abandoning Cissy and Walter in their time of need. I'd always intended to come up with a definite system of ethics for myself. I figured I'd use Benjamin Franklin's moral algebra when I finally got around to it. I'd weigh all actions with pros and cons. I figured that way I wouldn't be hounded by second guesses when these kinds of dilemmas occurred.

I managed to shake off my guilt. I reasoned that sometimes a guy's got to go his own way—look after himself. How else did he keep sane? I convinced myself that in a heartbeat Cissy and Walter would have done the same thing if they were wearing my ten-and-a-half Ds.

That last thought allowed me to drift off to sleep feeling a little less critical of Gunnar the Self-Seeker.

Chapter 11

—

"**H**AVE YOU EVER HEARD of Fletcherism, Kirsti?"
"Pardon me?"

She looked a little flushed in the face. I'd broken into her thoughts. Despite her modern views of sex and her claim that she was no prig, I think my escapade with Britt caused her prudish slip to show.

"Fletcherism. Ever heard of it?"

"No."

"Well, Mrs. Berger was a fanatical proponent of Fletcherism. The namesake of this practice was Horace Fletcher. He believed a person should eat only when he was hungry and that he should chew his food hundreds of times."

"Sounds radical."

"Very. Fanatically so. The practice was popularized but later rejected by John Harvey Kellogg, staff physician at that famous Battle Creek Sanitarium."

"The Cornflakes Kellogg?"

"The very same. I'm surprised you've heard of him."

"Oh, I get around. Why'd Kellogg later reject this Fletcherism stuff?"

"Something to do with too much chewing breaking down fibers."

"Sorry I asked."

"Uh-huh. Mrs. Berger had learned about Fletcherism years before from a dentist who'd wined and dined her when she was new to burlesque. He called her his 'greenhorn ecdysiast.' "

"His what?"

"Ecdysiast. It's a pompous way of saying stripper."

"Oh."

"According to Mrs. Berger, the dentist had encouraged her to become a star. She loved to tell the story of how he kept insisting that practice was the key. Of course, each time he took her out, he wanted her to do some practicing for him and give him a private performance when the evening was through."

"Yeah, right."

"In the words of Mrs. Berger: 'He was a damn good burlesque coach but had some funny ways when it came to the baser needs department.' She said she didn't love him. She knew she never could. As soon as he'd finished an overhaul on her teeth and helped her perfect her hitch kick, she broke it off."

"A real tragedy, I'm sure," Kirsti said, far from enthused.

"Mrs. Berger was a devoted Fletcherite ever after. I must have heard the dentist story a hundred times. She even had Walter weave it into the play they worked on. You see, her fictional heroine was a devoted Fletcherite."

"*Oookay* ...." Kirsti said in a slow hollow tone as she goggled at me.

"I mention Fletcherism and Mrs. Berger's play because as frequently happened, both came up in conversation at the breakfast that followed my return from Britt's."

I'd planned to call on Meredith Lane between 8:30 and 9:00 Saturday morning, but I didn't exit Dreamtown till 8:45.

I dreamt that Walter and I were in a pet store. We were buying a small cage. I insisted we needed one with a wheel. We argued. The next thing I knew we came home and walked in on Mrs. Berger teaching Britt Anderson and Len Pearson how to work her prized Sittenberg fans. Both were fully clothed—but Pearson was in drag. Mrs. Berger told Walter and me, "Strip down to your BVDs, boys, and join us."

I woke feeling disturbed by the dream and grateful it was over.

Mrs. Berger didn't serve a formal breakfast on the weekends. Still, we all hit the kitchen about the same time, which was a shocker, considering the shape we were in.

"Gunnar, were you ever in an opium den?" Mrs. Berger asked as I came in the kitchen.

I nodded.

"What was it like? Did they lurk? Was it like the ocean? You know, like moving waves of doped-up heads splashing into one another? Oh … I like that one, Walter. Try to remember it."

"I was running at the time," I said. "I didn't notice any waves or splashing heads."

Sten was busy at the stove. Sten was a hollow-legged leader in the art of downing schooners. He was scrambling eggs with the slow and calculating moves of a deluxe hangover. He had the pan on a back burner, safe from the ash-droppings from his cigarette.

I sidled up next to Sten and poured myself a cup of coffee and then stood leaning against the drain board.

Mrs. Berger sat at the table, chewing and re-chewing a mouthful of buttered toast as she read the *Post-Intelligencer*. Her struggle with nail-biting wasn't going well. Only the tips of her thumbs, pinkies, and one index finger wore tattered Band-Aid remains. She was wearing sun goggles, which meant she either had a migraine or a hangover. Whichever, it didn't stop her from jabbering.

"I was reading Sten's *Black Mask* magazine in the crapper yesterday. I got a wonderful idea for the opening of the second act. Walter, let's have Penny innocently flounce into an opium den."

"Innocently *flounce* is a bit oxymoronic, Nora," Walter said. "Huh?"

"What I mean is, it sounds a bit contradictory. Perhaps we should have Penny innocently *wander* instead of flounce."

"Whatever," she said waving the matter aside with her hand.

"Aunt Nora," Sten said, "I thought you had Penny the prisoner of a white slaver ring."

"I did. She escaped. Her cherry still intact."

Walter sat across from Mrs. Berger. He cleared his throat and said, "Nora, about Penny's escape from the white slavers …. When she expresses her gratitude to her deliverers for saving her from a fate worse than death … I think the word 'maidenhead,' or perhaps 'hymen,' would serve better than 'cherry.' I do wish we could discuss this some more before we go any further."

"No, no, Walter. It sounds just fine the way it is now. It's realer somehow," said Mrs. Berger.

"But consider your potential audience, Nora."

"Why, Walter Pangborn, no girl I ever knew would have said 'mainhead' to a police commissioner and a bunch of flatfeet. As for 'hymen,' I doubt one stripper in a thousand knows the word exists even."

Walter reluctantly conceded the point and resumed picking at a half slice of cantaloupe. He definitely had a hangover.

I hadn't gotten plastered, so except for a little grogginess, I felt pretty good. At least I thought so until a plate hit the floor with a jarring crash that united us all in a moment of keen misery.

My temples felt like they were imploding.

Walter winced.

Mrs. Berger moaned at the loss and scolded her nephew for breaking the plate.

Sten just held his head in his cigarette hand as he reached for the broom with the other.

"Help yourself to some cantaloupe, Gunnar. Shurfine had

'em two for thirty-nine cents," said Mrs. Berger.

I was working up to a bowl of Rice Krispies, but I did as she suggested and sat down at the table. Sten joined us after he swept up the debris.

"Walter, if a woman you loved were to innocently flounce into an opium den, how would you feel?"

"Nora, wouldn't it be better to stick with what *you* personally know?" Walter asked.

"Nonsense, Walter. What's the fun in that?"

"Well … we at least need to have a smoother transition. I really think we should go back and rework the last two scenes of act one."

"Oh, those scenes are perfect, Walter. They're just fine."

"But Nora, there are a few details that I fear will shatter your audience's suspension of disbelief. And—"

"Hell's bells and whistles, Walter. The people watching will know it's just a play. We're not fooling nobody. Besides, there's nothing we can't fix up later. Remember, it's supposed to be a love story and adventure both. We got to keep it moving. And you got to agree that if a shapely little bombshell like Penny flounces into a den full of drug-crazed Chinamen and assorted white riffraff, something exciting is bound to explode. The audience will love it. Trust me, Walter."

Sten winked at me and chimed in, "I don't know, Aunt Nora. I think a bunch of opium-eaters would be too hopped up to even take notice of a dollface like Penny. Why not keep her with the white slavers a little while longer?"

"Sten Larson, if we left our pretty Penny with those hard guys one moment longer, it'd be ground rations for her for sure." She went on for a few minutes rehashing Penny's past, her innocence, the mistakes she'd made, the doctor who treated her for the clap, the luck he brought her.

How the virgin Penny got gonorrhea was a mystery I never asked about. Some things you just accept as is. It's easier that way. At times it seemed like Penny was real—at least as real as Betty Grable or Rita Hayworth.

Mrs. Berger gingerly daubed the corners of her mouth with a napkin. Having finished her toast, she put a Chesterfield in her ivory holder and lit up.

"You know, you really need to slow down and chew your food more, Gunnar," Mrs. Berger said after I'd gobbled down half my cantaloupe. "You'll live a longer, more vital life. And it'll keep lead in your pencil," she added with a salacious grin.

I humored her as usual. I slowed my intake down to a bare nibble and began chewing rapidly. I noticed Walter ruminating with careful precision. He was a devoted Fletcherite, but only when our landlady was in the room.

Sten relished in his dissent, unblushingly bolting his scrambled eggs. After each forkful he'd quickly mash away with his tongue before each shameless gulp. He winked at me defiantly. His cigarette smoldered on the edge of his saucer.

"You're looking mighty relaxed this morning, Gunnar," Sten whispered between gulps. "Did you get your ashes hauled last night or *something*?"

"Or something," I said through a mouthful of orange pulp.

"Sten, that colon of yours is going to clog up and explode one of these days," his aunt said, getting up to pour herself a cup of coffee.

Sten puffed up his cheeks like a blowfish. Walter and I tried not to laugh. Mrs. Berger playfully whacked Sten on the head as she came back to the table, causing him to let out a blast of air.

"It's no joking matter," she went on. "Had your Uncle Otto listened to me and chewed his portions better, he'd still be alive today. I'm certain of it."

No one argued the point. Not even Sten. But he continued to shovel and gulp, unaffected by his aunt's withering look—that look a zealot reserves for the unabashed nonconformist. Even though Walter and I were mere *nominal* Fletcherites, it kept us safe for the time being. Walter had accurately summed up our situation on an earlier occasion:

"Thomas Jefferson wisely wrote, old top, that uniformity and coercion made half the populace fools and the other half hypocrites. When it comes to Fletcherism, I'm afraid you and I are, undeniably, hypocrites."

Most of the time I just felt like a fool.

As Walter and I got up from the table, Mrs. Berger beamed up at me, saying, "I made a batch of taffy yesterday afternoon, Gunnar. Be sure to grab a handful before you head out the door. Pass 'em out to people you know. Just tell 'em to eat around the little strip of paper. That idea about stuffing each piece with a fortune didn't work out like I hoped."

As we headed to the stairs, I heard my landlady ask, "Sten, are you sure you weren't ever in an opium den? Not even once?"

"There's a couple dens down on King Street in Chinatown," Sten said. "Hell, I'll take you down there some night if you want to do a little research for the play."

"I'd love that. Yes. Research for the play."

Walter and I went upstairs. I figured he'd spend the day in his room, reading, soldier-painting, or doctoring the perils of pretty Penny.

But the muse was not with Walter.

I slapped some cologne on my face, put on my hat and coat, and was making ready to leave when Walter's door opened. He was wearing his dark raincoat with the collar pulled up and his slouch hat in its usual position.

"Walter. You're dressed to go out."

He saw the surprise on my face. "I am indeed, Gunnar. You did me a kindness last night. I wish to repay it. I'd like to accompany you. Perhaps I can be of some small service." He patted his left side, where I guessed his Lebel revolver was holstered.

"Thanks, Walter, but you don't owe me a thing."

"Oh, but I do."

I knew how much he hated to venture out during daylight hours. But he had a sort of pleading look in his eyes. He wanted to come with me. Maybe he even *needed* to.

"Come on," I said.

MEREDITH LANE LIVED IN the Capitol Hill district.

The Ivy Lane Apartments might have had ivy growing around them at one time, but no longer. Not unless you counted a sickly looking vine on a rickety trellis curled over the front door. But the lawn was trim, and all in all the building was well-kept and nice enough to look at.

It had drizzled during the night and it was now foggy. The sun struggled to peek through the haze, but the feel in the air told me the rain would probably win out in the end.

I parked my Chevy out in front. The sidewalks were still wet. I got out of the car on what my grandpa Sven would have called an *uff-da* note. As my feet took their first steps on the concrete I stopped short and half-skipped to avoid stepping on a slug making his slimy escape. In the process I lost my fedora. I'd done this slug dance before. It was either dance the dance or go directly from *uff-da* to *ish-da*. The Greeks aren't the only ones with a word for it.

"Ever thought of dance lessons at Veloz and Yolanda?" Walter asked. "I see in the paper that their summer rates will be low."

"Very funny."

"Light of feet, light of heart, old socks."

"Yeah, and you should write Burma Shave ads," I said, picking up my hat. It had just missed the glossy trail left by the slug.

Meredith's apartment building was a four-story rectangular box on a side street off Cherry and smack-dab in a residential area. Built about 1900, it had probably seen some hodgepodge remodeling each decade thereafter. Its two large units per floor during its Victorian heyday had been converted to six smaller ones. It had a front and rear entrance and a staircase at each end.

Walter and I entered the front lobby and were immediately

hit with that stale fug no amount of paint, wallpaper, or Lysol can overcome and which residents become inured to.

"Oh, the landlord is missing out on an opportunity here," Walter said.

"How's that?" I asked as my nostrils relaxed their pucker.

"He really ought to bottle and sell this aroma. I'm confident he could find a market for it among innovative museum curators—or perhaps vacationing archaeologists lonesome for their digs."

We passed the bank of mailboxes along the wall and made our way up rubber-treaded stairs.

Walter's scars were mostly covered, but he kept close to the wall on his right. We only passed one tenant—a chesty woman in early middle age who shot Walter a curious glance after giving me a friendly nod.

Walter whispered, "It sounds like Miss Lane has been through quite a bit lately. Are you so sure this is a good idea?" By "this," he meant his face. He'd wanted to stay in the car as a lookout.

"Don't worry. It'll be fine," I said. "Once I've explained you to her, and she gets past the initial shock, I think your bedside manner might actually help get her to open up."

I figured the third floor was mainly occupied by single women; feminine door decorations and competing wisps of perfume in the hallway presented a definite womanly character.

I rapped on the door marked 304.

No answer.

I knocked again. No sound.

I eagle-clawed the prismatic glass doorknob. It turned easily and I let us in and shut the door behind us. There was no sign that the lock had been jimmied or the door forced open. The light was on in the small foyer that was directly neighbored by a tiny bathroom.

I called out for Meredith. Stillness.

I drew my gun.

I led Walter into the living room. We could readily see inside the kitchen and bedroom. They were average-sized rooms with high ceilings and walls that owed their shiny patina to countless layers of paint.

Britt had told me Meredith lived alone. Small as her apartment was, I was a little surprised she could afford it on a salesgirl's salary. I was more surprised by the expensive furnishings that didn't exactly suit her digs. But I was downright shocked at the aftermath of the small tornado that had struck the place.

Neither one of us moved from our spot. I made a quick visual sweep. In the living room, only her combination television-radio console was still standing—though it had been shifted from its location. A new armchair was overturned, and its jute under-fabric torn from the springs. The matching sofa had been similarly violated. Several books had their backs broken and their pages ripped. Pictures had been torn off the walls and the frames broken open. Vases and other knickknacks helped clutter the floor. The rug had been rolled up and flung to a corner. The kitchen was a jumble of dishtowels, silverware, plates, two pots and a pan, all tossed on the linoleum. From my glimpse of the bedroom it appeared to be a heap made up of clothes, a mattress, sheets, pillows, and down.

"What do you make of this?" Walter asked. He'd drawn his Lebel but was putting it away.

"I'd say the place was ransacked. Either that or Meredith's housekeeper quit on her with a vengeance."

"Have you been imbibing the humor vapors, old thing?"

Walter spotted her foot in the bedroom. Actually he saw a few toes peeking over the top of a big pillow. Our eyes followed the toes down a long, well-turned leg.

The leg led us to Meredith.

Chapter 12

—

MEREDITH WAS ON THE other side of the chaotic heap. Like her friend Christine, she was in that familiar puppet-with-its-strings-cut position. She'd no longer be worrying about losing her looks with age. The nylon stocking cinched tight around her neck had seen to that.

She was lying on the floor near the tasseled border of her bedroom carpet that had been rolled up against one wall. Her legs and arms were sprawled and bare. All she had on was a red satin chemise that had been torn wide open in front. Her red hair was tousled and tangled. Her full lips were parted and her eyes looked through and beyond us. Her face had the smoothed features that come with slackened muscles. There was no blood.

The sight sickened me.

"Meredith Lane, I presume," said Walter.

I nodded.

"Gunnar, it takes several hours for rigor mortis. From start to finish, I mean."

I knelt down and touched her neck. It was cold.

"She's stiff as a board. For all I know she was killed yesterday or in the early hours of this morning. We'll have to leave that detail for the medical boys."

It wasn't likely that someone came in through a three-story window, but I checked for signs of break-in anyway. I found none.

"The door has a peephole. She knew her killer, but freely let him in," I said.

"So she didn't expect to be killed."

"Looks that way."

We both stood in the living room again. We were being careful not to touch anything, but continued to look around.

"Any thoughts, Mr. Pangborn?"

"If we're dealing with the same fellow who killed Miss Johanson, then I'll wager Miss Lane wasn't raped. The murderer probably ripped open her chemise after she was dead to make it look like he'd had his way with her before he killed her."

"So then he tossed this place to make it also seem like robbery," I said.

"Yes, Gunnar, but tearing into the under-fabric of a chair indicates the murderer was looking for something, so it's very likely that Miss Lane had something in her possession that he wanted. He may also have been trying to make her talk and she died before she could do so."

"Makes sense. So then he rifles through her stuff in search and tries to pass it off as the action of a prowler turned rapist."

"Precisely. Our man *is* given to ruses and misdirection."

I scanned the disarray again. "Well, Walter, whatever the killer was looking for, it had to be flat enough to slide under a rug or into a picture frame, and small enough to shove in a book. Let's make our own search."

We were careful not to touch anything unless absolutely necessary, and then only while wearing one of Walter's leather gloves.

Your average house or apartment has numerous hiding places. We scouted the obvious ones first. Nothing in the toilet tank, and underneath the sinks yielded a big zilch.

Next we checked hiding places the killer might have missed that included possible false walls in closets, the tops of doors for keys, loose jambs, moldings or baseboards. Zip.

I was in Meredith's bedroom checking for loose floor covering when Walter called from the kitchen, "I think I've found something significant."

I'd started to get up off my knees when I also spotted something significant. It was a few feet to the right of Meredith's body. The killer probably flicked it there just before he strangled her. It was a toothpick. It was bent in half and V-shaped. I didn't touch it.

I found Walter pulling a manila envelope from under a loose strip of linoleum that was cover to a small cranny and had been anchored by one leg of the small kitchen table.

Walter handed me the envelope. I slit open its sealed edge with my penknife and took a quick peek inside.

"Your wish came true, Walter."

"How's that?"

"We didn't get it from Meredith's mouth, exactly, but she did give us the piece of the puzzle we needed." I stuffed the envelope inside my raincoat. "Let's scoot with the loot, my friend."

"If you don't mind, Gunnar, I'd much rather abscond to the nether region."

Chapter 13

—

SEATTLE USED TO GET a pretty bad rap for its rain, and it still does. But it actually rains less in Seattle than in New York, Baltimore, and Philadelphia. We just have more cloudy days.

Then, as now, no one ever mentioned the fog. The drizzles we got were nothing compared to the fog that rolled in off Elliott Bay. Sometimes our airports were socked in for days at a time. One time Sten Larson gave me a ride while carting a carload of friends to some shindig. For part of the way Sten had his buddy Kenny Flodine planted on the hood giving him signals with one hand while he pointed a flashlight with the other at the white shoulder line. Sten told me they did it all the time. It was so dense sometimes, it was sure to have made a Londoner homesick. Yet strangely, Seattle's rain got the spotlight.

The fog had lifted and the returning overnight drizzle had formed drops that merged into sheets when Walter and I left the Ivy Lane Apartments around noon that Saturday. We scampered out the back entrance that led to an alley. No one saw us leave as far as we could tell. In a meager attempt at obfuscation, we circled half the block in the rainstorm to get back to the Chevy. To any onlooker we were returning to our car from anywhere else but the Ivy Lane Apartments.

"I just hope that gal who saw us coming in doesn't make problems for us with the police," I said.

"What are the chances, old top? Let's analyze it. We've got a man-hungry woman living in an apartment house of mostly females, who happens to see two men callers dressed in raincoats, with one wearing a slouch hat to cover an obvious disfigurement and the other looking like the ravager of her dreams. I'd say we're home free."

"Shut up, Walter."

We headed for a phone booth. I called the police and gave them an anonymous tip and felt cheesy doing it. I always did.

To put some distance between us and the murder scene, I drove a few miles away before I pulled over so we could safely examine the items in the envelope. It contained a couple of news clippings and several eight-by-ten glossies.

I whistled softly as we fanned out the eye-popping photographs on the seat between us like so many playing cards. The pictures were the poorly lit and crude work of an amateur using a good camera. The antics and faces of the players were so clear, it moved us both to poetry.

"Lewd, rude, and nude," said Walter.

I added a rhyme from my army days. "Laid, relaid, and parlayed."

There were two sets of pictures: one of Christine Johanson and the other of Meredith Lane. All the shots were taken in the same bedroom, and showed them as enthusiastic party girls with different men at separate times. Judging from the clothes discarded by the girls and their varying hairdos, each had had two partners on completely different occasions. Some of the shots were of the girls and their respective admirers engaged in half-naked preambles to the sex act. Other shots were of the participants in nature's garb getting right down to business.

"Pretty raw stuff. Every one of these was snapped from the same angle," I said. "The cameraman was probably screened off and perched in a fixed hiding spot."

Walter was shuffling through the stack again, examining each shot with a clinical air. "These definitely make the women in those old French postcards seem like virtuous schoolgirls," he said. "If I didn't recognize two of these men, I'd think that these were stag pictures made to be sold covertly."

"Who do you make out, Walter?"

He pointed to one dallying with Meredith. "That's Ralph Colbourn. Local industrialist."

He pointed at another man frolicking with Christine. "Hugh ... Hugh *something*. Hugh *Rundquist*. That's the name. Rundquist. I've seen both these men in the newspaper over the years. Prosperous men. Society pillars, old socks. Members of Seattle's four hundred, don't you know. Were you aware, Gunnar, that it was a New York socialite named Ward McAllister, who is said to have come up with the original four hundred in the 1890s when—"

I stopped him and told him about the toothpick.

"Ah, then it's very likely that the black-hearted Mr. de Carter is also our shutterbug," he said.

I agreed.

We almost forgot about the two news clippings. The articles had been mostly cut away, but each showed a clear photo of Addison Darcy.

"Kind of odd, don't you think, Walter? The connection sort of jumps out at you, doesn't it?"

"Yes. I would say that Mr. Darcy was probably their next victim."

I held up a news clipping in each hand.

"And these were part of the briefings."

"Yes. So it would seem."

I headed us for home.

We discussed how it was that a couple of seemingly sweet young women could get caught up in such a sordid blackmail scheme.

"They were young but maybe not all that sweet," I said.

"Yes. Still, I imagine it was a progressive thing," Walter said. "They probably started off flirting with specific male customers. They accepted social invitations, and one thing just led to another."

"Yeah, but Walter, that's an awful slope to let yourself slide down."

"Admittedly. However, I'd guess that they were probably *pushed* sometime before that, Gunnar. Likely Mr. de Carter seduced these young women. Perhaps he raped them. Someone *did* tell you he abused women. It's also possible that Miss Johanson and Miss Lane were themselves initially blackmailed with compromising photos. Maybe they were even in love with Mr. de Carter. Who knows what tied them to him? There's several possibilities. Somehow he gained influence over them, and became a puppeteer procurer. In any event, these pictures don't lie. Those girls *were* most ... er, cooperative."

"Yeah, until something went very wrong."

"A labor strike perhaps?"

"Bingo. Meredith might have had seniority. Her new furniture indicates some sort of windfall. Maybe Christine insisted on a bigger cut."

"So, Miss Johanson accused Mr. de Carter of cheating her. They met and he ended the labor dispute."

"Looks that way."

A few things seemed clear. Guy de Carter had good reason to lie about Dirk. After murdering Christine, he'd probably scouted out Dirk's apartment, found the kid sleeping off his drunk, and planted the bloody shoes and gun. It also made sense that it was de Carter who tried to run me down. Failing that, he ventilated my office.

"At least now you know who to be on guard against, old thing."

"Yeah, but now that Meredith's dead and he didn't find what she'd stashed, maybe he feels a little safer. Maybe he thinks he's in the clear."

"You may be right. By themselves, these photos and clippings don't really point to Mr. de Carter."

"Uh-huh. But what I can't figure is why would de Carter try to kill Addison Darcy?"

"Maybe Mr. Darcy wouldn't pay the hush money. Maybe he threatened to go to the authorities."

"I don't think so, Walter. He was cozying up to Christine the very day she was killed. You'd think if he was being blackmailed he'd have steered clear of those girls and that store."

"You've got me there, Gunnar."

"I think your first thought was right. Darcy was probably their *next* target, and had yet to visit their studio love nest. I'm guessing that initially Meredith thought Christine might have been killed by one of the men she'd duped. Maybe Meredith worried that she was to be next, and that's why she suggested I check out some of the customers."

"Hmm. Yes, a preemptive action. And perhaps later Miss Lane began to suspect Mr. de Carter, and she threatened to expose him."

"Uh-huh. But whatever the case, Smilin' Jack stopped smiling and silenced the girl before she gave up the goods."

"So where are you off to now, old top?"

"I haven't quite figured that out yet."

We crossed the drawbridge leading into the Fremont district. The dilapidated houses and buildings made the area dreary under normal circumstances. Our findings and the wet weather made it more so.

We cruised toward Ballard, angling northwest on Leary Avenue. Raindrops the size of marbles battered the top of the Chevy. The pelting tattoo became a soothing distraction, however temporary. We drove in silence until we were a few blocks from Mrs. Berger's.

"I just wish that woman hadn't seen us on the stairs," I said. "Maybe she'll be gone when the police show up with their questions."

"I've learned not to bank on small favors, old socks. You'd better drop me off at Hardy Lindholm's. I'll lay low for a while. Besides, I could do with a couple of dozen games of checkers."

To Hardy's it was.

I DROPPED WALTER OFF at quarter to one. I drove to a drugstore on Market Street and used their payphone.

How to expose the guilty without hurting the innocent? Airing the story of the photos meant bad publicity for Fasciné Expressions—and that would mean trouble for both my client and Britt Anderson. I felt Britt deserved a heads up.

Fasciné Expressions was open for part of the day. I gave Britt's office a ring.

"You sound cheerful," I said when she answered.

She laughed. "Aside from some sore muscles and a slight hitch in my girlish gait, I feel wonderful. What took you so long to call me?"

"I had to regain my stamina."

"You weakling."

I didn't tell Britt about Meredith or about the envelope she'd been hiding, but I did want her opinion on what Walter and I had discovered. For now I just said I had something to show her that I believed was important, and asked if I could come right over.

Twenty minutes later I was knocking on her office door.

Britt looked smart in a teal blue office suit that matched her eyes as well as her high heels. A crisp blouse went with gray nylons, and her shoes had gold wrap-around ankle straps that tied in with her hair, watch, and earrings. She was a living, breathing, color-coordinated work of art. I was waved in and the door was shut.

"We'll need some privacy," I said.

She gave me a sly smile, pulled me close to her face by my lapels and gave me a tender kiss. "More privacy than this?" she asked.

"Nice. Very nice. But not what I meant, I'm afraid. With what I have to show you, it's best if we aren't interrupted and that you brace yourself."

She gave me a curious look and then motioned for me to follow her.

"We'll use Len's office. He's over on the peninsula for the weekend. He won't mind."

We entered Pearson's office and Britt locked the door. I walked over to his desk, flicked on the desk lamp and placed the envelope down on the blotter. I pulled Pearson's chair out for her and then slid a chair for me alongside her. I told her about Meredith.

Britt stared at me and put the back of her hand against her mouth. Her salmon-colored cheeks turned ashen. I thought she was going to cry, but she managed to keep it together. I reached for her hand and she clutched mine.

"I think Guy de Carter killed her," I said.

With my free hand I picked up the envelope.

"I apologize for what you're about to see, but I think it's best that you know. I also believe it explains why Christine and Meredith were murdered."

Letting go of her hand I took the photos out and quickly spread them on the desk in front of her. She made a small noise of surprise and gave me a questioning glance before she returned solemn eyes to the photos. I put my left palm on her shoulder and reached for her hand again.

She studied the pictures carefully, lips compressed, grimace lines between her golden brows.

"Wha ... why?" she said. She looked at me and asked, "What does it mean, Gunnar? Not *what* they're doing ... I can see that. I mean, what's the point of all this? Why photograph it?"

I kept my palm on her shoulder but freed my right hand from hers so I could collect the pictures. She helped me stuff them back in the envelope. I kept the news clippings out.

"The story that seems to go with these pictures is that Guy

de Carter, Christine, and Meredith were in cahoots. The girls seduced wealthy customers—men of some prominence, probably hand-picked by de Carter. The girls took them to some hideaway where de Carter captured their escapades on film in order to extort hush money."

"Blackmail." Her voice broke a bit and the shaking of her head became a small shudder. "How horrible. How dreadful." She didn't cry but her eyes were moist. She started to become angry. "How dare they use the rest of us? And how dare they involve the store."

I nodded. "Do me a favor," I said. "Don't tell anyone about these photos for a while. That includes the police. I wanted you to know before anyone else. Maybe there's a way we can contain the scandal. I hate to suggest it, but another one or two of your girls could be involved in this racket. Think hard. Try and recall anything that informed hindsight might now see as suspicious."

She shook her head slowly. "Gunnar, I didn't even know Christine and Meredith were doing this. I … I would hope they were the only ones involved."

"It *would* make things a lot simpler."

"I just don't know. This sort of thing makes me doubt my judgment. It makes me question what I believed was genuine. Does that make any sense?"

I told her it made perfect sense. What I didn't say was that it was the running commentary on my life. I decided to tell her how I'd met Christine at the movies.

"The night before she was killed she'd broke it off with Dirk Engstrom. Her feelings were running high. She might have had a squabble with Guy de Carter after that. Whatever the case, de Carter was tailing her in a Packard. Maybe he was intimidating her. I helped her shake him and drove her home. My theory is that Christine pressured Guy for more of the take. Maybe she threatened him. The next day de Carter witnessed Dirk's angry outburst in the store. That blowup was tailor-made for him. So, he met Christine and he killed her. Afterward he made it look like Dirk did it."

Britt took in a slow, deep breath and released it as deliberately. "And so that's *why* Guy de Carter tried to kill you … because you made him nervous. You're a big threat to him."

"That's how it looks all right. My guess is that after the dust settled, Meredith figured out that de Carter killed Christine. She may have tried to squeeze him for more money—or threatened to expose him just to protect herself. It would explain why he killed her and tossed her place looking for this envelope."

Britt was silent for a moment. Then she leaned her head on my chest and said, "But, why did he try and kill Addison Darcy?"

"I'm still trying to come up with the answer to that one. I hope to have it before the day is through."

I switched off the desk lamp and asked to use Pearson's telephone. I hadn't asked for privacy, but Britt left the office while I made a call to the home of Detective Sergeant Frank Milland. His wife said he'd been called in to work.

I gave his station number a ring.

"Gunnar," he said with a light-hearted lilt that sounded alien. "Just the man I wanted to talk to. Why don't you hop in that Chevy of yours and drive on down here to Fourth and Yesler?"

"Frank, I know who killed the Johanson girl. I'm pretty sure he also tried to kill me and Addison Darcy."

"Uh-huh. I'd love to have a nice long talk with you about it, Gunnar." Milland's voice was starting to sound like a brassy rumble. "I'd also like to know when your pal Lon Chaney started going around in broad daylight."

"*LON CHANEY*? WHO'S THAT?" Kirsti asked. It was an understandable interruption.

"Lon Chaney was a silent movie actor known for his portrayal of afflicted and grotesque characters. It was just

Milland's wisecrack way of referring to Walter."

I LET MILLAND'S CRACK slide. At least he hadn't called Walter
a freak. He obviously knew about Meredith's murder and I said
as much.

"Don't get cute with me, Gunnar. I hate cute." His voice was
gravelly and he teetered on furious.

"I called it in anonymously, Frank."

He moaned.

I didn't say anything. Milland cleared his throat and tried to
ratchet his tone back down to calm. "We've got a gal over at the
Ivy Lane Apartments who described that carnival sideshow
friend of yours to a tee. She said the guy he was with was a real
dreamboat. I figure that beauty and beast combination could
be no one else but you and Pangborn. So why not bring your
pal in, too? We three. We'll have us a fine chat."

"Frank, we didn't mess with the crime scene." I felt a little
twinge of guilt for lying to Milland, but it passed as quickly as
it came.

"That's good," he said. "Real good." He started to lose it again.

"The man you want is Guy de Carter."

I told him about the toothpick.

"De Carter planted the shoes and the gun. He lied about
Dirk threatening to kill Christine."

"Get your butt down here right now."

"I'll have something more concrete for you before the day is
through. I'll be in touch."

"Gunnar ...."

"Frank ...."

"Gunnar?"

"Frank?"

"Gunnar!"

I hung up.

The least I could do was cast some suspicion on de Carter
and maybe get him taken off the streets for a while. In the

meantime I had a couple of things I wanted to find out before I turned the photos over to the police. I had to discover why Addison Darcy was a liability—why he warranted killing. De Carter had borrowed that Packard. But *whose* Packard?

Britt returned and locked the door again. She smiled and came over to me. She took my hand and led me to a davenport on the far side of the room.

We sat. She tucked her face near the dip at the base of my throat and leaned on my shoulder. My arm encircled the pliant curve of her back, my fingers poised against the nape of her neck. All I could hear was our breathing. All I could smell was the tantalizing scent of her hair. That went on for one long minute before we started getting even more comfortable.

With her mouth three inches from mine and her eyelids starting to droop, I grinned and said, "Are you still sure Len won't mind our using his office?"

"Hush," she said, fastening tender lips to mine.

For several minutes she forgot about Fasciné Expressions and treacherous employees and I blocked from my mind the police, Guy de Carter, and blackmail. We would have been well on our way to making the Bard's beast with two backs, but I killed the mood by showing I was no longer in it when I said, "By now the police should have Guy de Carter in custody. Unless he's keeping clear of his apartment, that is."

I'd startled her. Our amour-divan became Len's daveno once more.

"You should have said something," she said. "Guy de Carter moved out of his apartment a week ago. I assumed you knew. He's staying on a houseboat on Lake Union for the summer. He gave us the phone number and address in case we needed to get hold of him. The police won't know to look for him there."

She stood up and said, "Wait here a moment." She left the office for two or three minutes. When she returned she handed me a slip of paper with a Lake Union address written on it.

"You'll call it in to the police, won't you? You aren't planning to go after him by yourself, are you?" she asked as she arranged her face into a pretty little grimace of concern.

It might have been her facial expression that did it. Or, maybe it was *libido-interruptus*. Whatever it was, I suddenly felt a need to act heroic. Plus, I didn't relish calling Milland again, and I wasn't about to pawn off that task on Britt. So I announced, "I'm going to go get him myself."

"Gunnar, is that wise?" she asked, furrowing her brow.

That made me even more determined. At that point, I wasn't about to waver or hesitate even if I'd wanted to.

Gunnar the Virile had committed himself.

Britt grabbed a coat and walked me down to my car.

Before I climbed in the Chevy, Britt gave me a lingering pat on the hand and a long parting kiss. "Call me later," she said, "and please be careful."

I said that I would. I made a mid-block U-turn and headed the Chevy in the direction of Lake Union.

I drove away feeling every bit like a Chinese puzzle: my feelings were inscrutable and contradictory. I was the strutting rooster leaving the henhouse. I was the lurking satyr, the despoiler of wood nymphs. I was confident, self-satisfied. I was sad and felt a tad criminal. I was male.

Wending my way by the lake I tooled along Fairview Avenue in search of the address Britt gave me.

Then, as now, Seattle had perfect spots to live if you were a free spirit or a beachcomber at heart. Hundreds of houseboats clustered along the shores of Seattle's bays and lakes—little communities with wooden walkways for streets. At the time some of these dwellings were actually homelike and cozy. Others were little better than floating ramshackle cabins. The east-shore houseboat that Guy de Carter was staying on was somewhere in between.

It shared a long wooden landing with several floating residences—some on one side, some on the other. De Carter's was the last one on the right, fronting the lake. I parked in back of a maroon Ford convertible that was snuggled alongside a late model Packard. Both cars were locked, but I made a visual search of their interiors. Nothing of interest.

I wandered down a winding footpath that steered me onto the landing. The rain had stopped. Across the lake stood the Aurora Bridge and a clustering of assorted craft cutting through water that looked murky because of the overcast. I spit a well-chewed clove in the water as I ambled along the landing.

None of de Carter's neighbors seemed to be at home. His place looked shut up and impenetrable—a castle waiting to be stormed. My storming experience was in the hedgerows of Normandy, with its feelings of an enemy menace only a few feet away, out of sight, waiting to pounce.

Bordering all four sides of his houseboat was a narrow catwalk that was skirted by a lattice fence about three feet high. The little gate fought me as I tried to open it, only to creak when I finally did.

I pulled my gun from its holster and kept it just inside my coat. I rapped on the door of what seemed like a buoyant tomb. Nobody answered.

I tried the door. It swung open with no resistance.

Sun from the windows showed me a nice place with a loutish ambiance. A coffee table made from cinderblocks and a smooth plank supported a stack of *Holiday* and *Esquire* magazines anchored in place with an overstuffed ashtray. Empty beer bottles and unwashed cups and plates rested in the corners and nooks generally reserved for photos and curios. The true masculine touch was the assortment of clothes not quite ripe enough for washing left hanging on the backs and arms of chairs, masquerading as slipcovers and covering up cigarette burns.

To my right was a bar that divided off the small kitchen from the living room. The kitchen clock said 2:20. Off the kitchen was a little hallway that led to a bedroom and bathroom. Those doors were closed. I figured if de Carter was at home he was either taking a quiet nap or a serene crap.

The stillness of the house bothered me. It was eerily quiet. The silence brought back inklings of the hedgerow terrors. I remained just inside the door with my gun leading the way.

Outside a nearby motorboat idled and made a rattletrap noise. I froze like a Bon Marché mannequin. The engine strained and chugged for a minute or so. The clamor grew louder as the boat came closer. The tumult short-circuited the usual bristly feeling I get when someone is behind me. It explained why I was such an oblivious target.

I felt the breeze of the first blow to my head. A nightstick smacking a melon. It stunned me and I began losing my balance. My vision was fuzzy and the room started to heave like waves churned up by an angry whale. Adrenaline induced a kind of supernatural alertness when the second blow hit. Then there was nothing but a black void, a sudden gust and a grand plunging ….

MRS. BERGER SHOVELED COOKIES in my mouth and told me to chew thoroughly. She wore a skimpy burlesque outfit and shivered. Guy de Carter held her fans in one hand and a camera in the other. He laughed and snapped shots of me being fed.

I chewed and chewed until the scene shifted and shells exploded around me. Mike hugged the ground and told me to do the same. The drumming of my heart serenaded the knot in my gut. The shelling stopped and Mike and I did an elbow and knee crawl over to what looked like a current of water. A machine gun crackled and small-arms fire erupted as we approached the stream. The air became filled with the shrill noise of flying lead as automatic fire moved through the ranks of soldiers around us like a tornado. A man was mowed down to my left. Ahead of me the storm reached a kid who couldn't have been more than eighteen. He gave me a questioning hurt look before he dropped to his knees in the water and slowly keeled over. Mike was transmogrified into Walter Pangborn.

Walter and I jumped into the stream for safety. We couldn't get deep enough. Artillery bombardment began again whipping up the water around us. I barely heard Walter scream, "They've got us zeroed in!"

I jerked awake. I was lying on my stomach. I raised my head and stared blurrily at a V for victory sign. It was a big one. I felt queasy.

My right hand was cradling something heavy. My fingers told my brain it was a gun. I managed to get up on my knees. It was *my* gun. I laid it on the floor.

A colossal ache began at the back of my head and flowed through my body down to my toes. A blackjack hangover. But it was a good sign. It meant I wasn't dead.

I almost lost my balance. I eased back, shifting haunches down on calves. I waited to see if the sick feeling would subside a bit. It didn't.

Eventually I lifted a resistant hand behind my head. Remarkably, my fedora was still in place. I felt for damage and touched a wet mushy spot. I brought my hand back and squinted at a mixture of hair strands and bloodied pomade.

I made feeble attempts to rub mutinous thoughts together to form conclusions. I wiped my hand with my handkerchief and repositioned my fedora. My watch said 2:50. I'd been out about half an hour. My hand leaped inside my raincoat. The envelope with the photos was gone.

Across the room the large V for victory sign started to take on freakish significance. It was the bottoms of a pair of shoes worn by the feet of someone lying on his back.

Drawing from a previously unknown energy reserve, I stood up. The shoes were Koolies, though not the pair from the day before. The same wearer though. It was Guy de Carter. He looked like he was saying something. His eyes had that unblinking apathy of a battle-savvy dogface. It went well with his chest and its ugly red blotch. I had a feeling my gun had made that blotch.

Scratch one drugstore cowboy.

My head tingled as if pricked by a thousand pins, but I was beginning to focus a little better. The bedroom door was wide open. I looked inside. I knew the room. It was the bedroom in the blackmail photos. As I entered I could tell that the pictures had been taken from the right side of the bed. In that direction was a closet. A little probing revealed a small space hidden by a false front where a stool sat in front of a peephole. The perfect perch for a candid cameraman. The marks had probably been brought here at night—too drunk or too rutted to later recall the location, or maybe just too afraid to try.

A siren wailed and whined in the distance.

It all began to make a sick sort of sense. Realization acted like a restorative, shoving aside the fog enfolding my mind, leading to alarm and a mild panic. Dead men tell no tales. De Carter knew a lot more of the tale than I did. Without the photos I didn't have much of a tale to tell. Not one I could prove anyway. I was to be the fall guy for Guy's murder.

The siren got closer.

I grabbed a dishtowel that sat on the kitchen bar. I wiped my gun thoroughly and placed it on the bar with the towel. Then I eased myself down to the floor and resumed the position I was in when I'd come to.

I closed my eyes and waited.

Chapter 14

—

"NO PRINTS ON THE gun," said Milland's partner from the houseboat landing.

Hanson's voice barely carried to where Milland and I leaned against the front of my Chevy. The medical examiner had given me a makeshift compress for the back of my head. I held it in place and did a fair imitation of dazed and miserable.

Milland gave Hanson a two-finger wave as he said to me, "I can't believe you didn't get the license plate of that Packard."

"Why would I? I thought I had him."

"What I can't figure," he said, giving me a sly smile, "is why the killer didn't put the gun in your hand. You know, make it a thoroughgoing frame-job."

I shrugged. "Oversight?"

He pulled on his cigarette. After he exhaled he said, "Uh-huh. Hell of an oversight. A real stupid one. Except I'm thinking this killer ain't that stupid."

I didn't say anything.

The uniformed cops who'd answered the call didn't know me. I'd struggled to regain consciousness for their benefit and mumbled "Call Detective Milland" before I passed out again. I miraculously revived when I heard a few insolent words from Milland's mouth.

"So you've got no idea who whacked Smilin' Jack over there?"

"Like I said, find the owner of that Packard and you've got your man."

"Yeah? Well, I'll tell you one of your bright boy guesses that didn't pan out. Nobody on that customer list owns a Packard."

I said it didn't surprise me.

I told him about the photos. I said I'd found them in the houseboat before my lights went out. It was an enhanced version of the truth. I figured de Carter would have taken the photos home if he'd found them. All I'd done was save him the trouble.

"I'll wager the men in those photos were patrons of Fasciné Expressions. I recognized a couple of Seattle's upper crust." I gave him the names Walter had mentioned. "Even money you'll find both of them on that repeat customer list. All the more reason to try and keep that end of things under wraps."

"Uh-huh," Milland said, not hiding his irritation. "Your client would just love that too, I bet."

"You'd win that bet."

"And maybe we'll get lucky and find a neat and tidy payment ledger or a list of shakedown victims inside that floating dump. Is that what you think?"

I didn't respond. My guess was that the killer would have tossed the place if he'd thought de Carter had that kind of evidence. De Carter's killer had likely been using him as liaison between himself and the blackmail victims. If he wanted more payments, he'd be forced now to start making direct contact for himself. It might be one way to catch him, if one of the victims could be made to cooperate. But I kept this to myself. I decided to let Milland figure that much out for himself. Besides, I was already poking away at his patience with a pretty sharp stick.

When he'd arrived, Milland had made opening salvos laced with several acerbic "You *shoulda* come in like I told you," and a series of "I *oughta* run your ass in, just on principle." I'd remained mute during the onslaught and only nodded at fit intervals. I learned that his informants had come up empty and that Meredith's estimated time of death was between 11:00 p.m. and 1:00 a.m.

"Frank, I'm convinced finding the owner of that Packard is the key. It wouldn't hurt to expand that registration search. Check on anyone connected with Fasciné Expressions and de Carter's ad agency."

He looked at me like I was a bug. But I knew I was a bug he'd listen to. I also knew he'd cut me loose after he finished questioning me. I knew Frank Milland from before the war, but I didn't meet his kid brother until he was sent to us as a replacement. Milland's brother and I had trudged through slush and muck together. We'd eaten the same inadequate chow together. We'd fought krauts side by side. I'd been there when Mike Milland bought it. I was the living link to Mike's final moments, and like it or not, Frank had a soft spot in his heart for me.

I tried not to take advantage of that soft spot.

Not too much, anyway.

Okay. Whenever I could.

"IT'S TIME FOR MY break. Care if I take a load off with you, hon?" Verna asked.

I told her I didn't mind at all.

The supper crowd hadn't yet hit Holger's Café when Verna brought me my chicken fried steak, french fries, and coffee. Her vacant stare told me she'd either had a grueling day of hash-slinging or something was weighing on her mind.

Verna headed over to where Holger was jawing with old Hjalmer Petersen at the counter. I watched in casual fascination as the fabric of her uniform stretched to bisect the fitness of her impressive bottom. She said something to her boss and pointed back my way, then poured herself a cup of coffee before returning to plant herself across from me in the booth.

"I'm thinkin' to call it quits," she announced solemnly.

"You're leaving Holger's?"

"Nah, not here. Quits with Hank."

"I take it your date didn't go well last night."

She laughed. "It didn't go at all. The big lug was a no show." She lifted her cup to puckered lips and blew. "I think he's taken up with that tramp I caught him with."

I told her I was sorry to hear it.

"Good riddance, I say," she said with a small shrug. Her eyes told me that the news about Hank was just her way of laying groundwork, as it hit me that when I'd ordered only the top button of her blouse had been unfastened and her red lips had looked faded. Now lipstick was refreshed and the second button undone, which invited a wee glimpse of brassiere tatting and cleavage. I pushed my back deeper into the red vinyl of the booth and nibbled on one of my fries. Verna's vacant stare had been replaced with a speculative one.

"I've always really liked you, Gunnar." She sipped her coffee and I saw the smooth vigor of her cream-colored neck work as she drank.

There was only a handful of people in Holger's, but Verna and I might as well have been alone given, the absolute noiselessness at our booth. As each second passed the quiet intensified. We gradually sensed our mutual understanding and I realized just how powerful my physical attraction was for this gorgeous virago—despite my Dutch headache.

Gunnar the Insatiable.

"I've always liked you too, Verna." It wasn't original, but for the moment it allowed my throbbing head and dulled mind to come to terms with what exactly she was after.

She put her cup down and leaned her head forward, which gave me a sightseer's view of her Grand Canyon. I quickly looked up to dreamy brown eyes and a pert smile that told me she approved of my sightseeing.

Glossy red lips moved unhurriedly as she said, "You talk real nice, but mainly you're a good listener. You make a girl feel ... well ... worth something." She took another sip of coffee before adding, "I was thinkin' how we really oughta get to know each other better. Better than we do now, I mean."

Her luscious mouth closed and she waited for me to take the next step.

I suspected what she had in mind. Either she wanted to strike back at Hank through me, or she just needed help to cut the umbilical cord once and for all. Believe you me, I was sorely tempted to help her do the cutting, but I could think of several good reasons not to. The trick was explaining things delicately. When you pass on a sumptuous three-course dinner, then you'd best word things just right if the cook knows you're suffering from hunger pangs.

I wasn't about to tell her I thought she was still in love with Hank. Too explosive a topic. And it wouldn't do to tell her my rule against getting involved with married women. She'd have dismissed it as a minor technicality. And there was no sense in telling her that I didn't want to risk ruining our friendship if things didn't work out between us. She'd have seen it as the lame dodge it would have been. So I decided to tell her a truth that would allow her to leave the field with dignity and make it so I'd still be welcome at Holger's.

Sounding as plaintive as I could, I said, "If this had only happened last week .... You see, Verna, I've met this girl, and well ... things are really going good between us." I gave her a grimace that turned into a weak smile and added, "You understand, don't you?"

There was always the chance she'd still be hurt and angry, despite my tact. Instead, the smile never left her pretty face. Her eyes became a little blank as she laughed and said, "Well, Gunnar, you're sure not givin' this girl much to write about in her diary tonight. I was hopin' for at least two paragraphs."

We made small talk awhile and then she stood up with

graceful ease and snatched tablet and pencil from her apron pocket. She scratched something on a corner of a page, tore it off and handed it to me.

"My new telephone number. You know, in case things go bust with your new girl."

She picked up her empty cup and went back on duty. Somehow she'd managed to refasten that second button when I wasn't looking.

As I got under the wheel of my Chevy, I applauded myself for my restraint. Another guy would have gone after Verna like a gin-fiend cut loose in a distillery. Still, my self-congratulations didn't stop a few erotic flights of fancy about what might have been. I even started to kick myself a little. But these thoughts were quickly swept away by something I remembered Verna had said. It gave me the idea I needed as to where to go next.

I got there at about 5:15. It proved to be a windfall.

Christine had been the navigator the night I drove her home. When you consider that my attention had been divided between the road and Christine's figure, eyes, and pouting lips, it was surprising I still remembered the street. Luckily Aunt Emelia's was the only two-story Victorian in sight.

The sky had cleared and it was a perfect day for combat. At least the local kids thought so. Boys wearing oversized sailor caps and army helmets had turned Aunt Emelia's street into a battleground while a cluster of noncombatant young girls hopscotched on a neutral sidewalk. I drove slowly to allow the pretend soldiers to fan out as they machine-gunned me and my make-believe Chevy-tank. Conveniently, Aunt Emelia lived a ways from the carnage.

The lines of the structure were familiar. Its daylight look was that of a smart gray house with a neatly manicured lawn. I turned into the driveway and parked. An elderly woman with carefully plaited gray hair sat on the verandah. She had the high cheekbones and almond eyes of her niece. But she was old and no longer beautiful. She knew it and she didn't like it.

She was knitting, her hands moving violently. As I stepped out of the car our eyes locked, and to my amusement, neither one of us broke off our gazes as I made my approach. Hers was a withering look that made me feel like *idiot du jour*.

As she and I continued our stare-down, Aunt Emelia feverishly worked her needles. She picked up her rhythm as I came in her direction and made me feel more and more like a scab crossing a picket line. I made out the closing refrains of "Don't Get Around Much Anymore," as I reached the bottom stair of her porch.

I wanted to search Christine's room. How to get past Aunt Emelia's formidable-looking defenses was the question.

"Good afternoon," I said, hat in hand. I was striving for a boyish grin to meet her stern expression, but a grimace was about all my sore face and aching head could muster.

She abruptly stopped her knitting and turned off her portable radio. She said, "Good afternoon," in a way that seemed anything but. Hers was the strong Scandinavian accent of my grandparents.

"*Ja, ja*, but I already talk to the police."

"I'm not the police," I said. I told her that I'd been hired by one of Christine's employers to look into her murder.

"*Ja*, I know nothing more to tell." A Scandinavian's "*ja*" can mean yes or no depending on the tone. Her "*ja*" was drawn out to two syllables. It was definitely a negative.

She looked down at the knitting she quickly resumed. I started climbing the porch steps. Nearby, three cats circled like buzzards the soured residue of a toppled milk bottle.

Aunt Emelia sat in a high-backed wicker chair, its white sheen worn away from use where her head and hands rested. "Do you mind if I sit with you as we talk?" I asked and pointed to the chair beside her—the twin of hers except its finish was still glossy. Visitors weren't exactly lining up for porch visits with Emelia—not *human* visitors anyway. I brushed a few hair balls off the chair's cushion and plopped down. She put her needles and yarn in a straw-colored basket at her feet.

I took it as a good sign.

Emelia Larson was a widow of ten years. She told me she had lived in Ballard for twenty-five years. Meanwhile the tabby cat crept closer to us.

"Christine should never have come to live with me."

"Why's that?"

She crinkled up her nose and eyes at me. "She was to go to school and work a little. Instead she work a lot and do no schooling." She shook her head. The basket at her feet was loaded with balls of yarn. The tabby made its way to it.

"What happened to school?" I asked.

"Fool business is what. *Ja*, that's what happened."

Aunt Emelia's right foot shot out as swiftly as a placekicker's. A blur of fur and a feline screech signaled the failure of the tabby's invasion of the yarn basket. It landed in a bush alongside the steps and scurried off as the old woman mumbled something in Swedish that I couldn't make out. The other cats were gone.

Aunt Emelia was definitely a rugged old bird. I saw no need to tread lightly. "I've seen photos of Christine. A pretty girl like her probably had a lot of suitors," I prompted.

"*Ja*," she said sighing. "Christine don't think I know what she be doing. I tell her more than once to stop acting like some *flyg skökan*."

It wasn't standard Swedish, but I knew enough Svensk jargon to recognize "flying whore" when I heard it.

"The night before she was killed, she come home late again. We have a fight. I tell her quit her fool business or she have to leave."

"What did she say?"

"She laugh and tell me she be leaving soon anyway. She expect *big money*," Aunt Emelia said as she slapped her left palm with the back of her right hand for emphasis. "She say she plan to move to New York City, and *so there*. *Ja*, that's what she say." Aunt Emelia's face showed the angry disgust that masks hurt.

"The police say robbery. But I think Christine come to no good. I think she be killed for something bad she done."

"What makes you say that?"

Worn shoulders heaved. "A feeling. Just a feeling."

"Did you tell the police about this feeling?"

"*Ja*, but why should I? They can't bring her back. Who knows what *skräp* the police dig up?"

I got the drift.

"Why break my brother's heart? He think his Christine was robbed. Let him think that. That's sorrow enough. *Ja*, let him be at peace with little sorrow."

I told her she was wise. I asked if the police had gone through Christine's things.

She shook her head. "What for? They were going to. But then one of them get a call that say they get the fella what killed her."

"Mrs. Larson, I believe the man they're holding is innocent. I think Christine was killed by someone else."

She considered that a moment. "*Ja*, and so what do *you* want?"

"I'd like to look through Christine's things. Maybe I'll find something that will help me find her murderer."

She gave me what my grandpa Sven used to call a *scrootinizing skvint*. "You won't make Christine look bad? You won't hurt her folks?" They were more commands than questions.

I told her I wouldn't. I said I just wanted to bring the murderer to justice.

"*Ja, dynga* justice," she said, spitting the words out through her once soft lips. She got up and indicated for me to follow her into the house. She was agile for her years but thumped when she walked. She led me upstairs and pointed to a closed door.

"That was *her* room. Do what you do," she said as she turned and thumped back downstairs.

Christine had adopted her aunt's sewing room. It had become the room of a girl in the intense wrench and stretch of life's sinews and muscles. A fluffy, stuffed kitten rested on her pillow. The pillowcase and bedspread were speckled with prints of Raggedy Ann. Had she brought these from home or had Aunt Emelia furnished them? Whatever the case, these were tokens of residual girlhood that had given way to another world and its symbols: the glut of lotions, rouge, jars, and perfumes piled in heaps on her dresser top, and the provocative finery in the closet. It was the burgeoning and prevailing domain of the demimonde.

It took me two minutes to find what I was looking for. It was in her dresser drawer, carefully wrapped in a pair of scented underwear in the middle of a stack of others.

I stuffed the item in my coat pocket. I rummaged around awhile longer for show. Then I bounced downstairs to where Aunt Emelia sat in her front room. She showed no signs of curiosity. She merely nodded as I bid her a solemn *farväl* and a sincere *tack sä mycket*.

After driving two blocks, I parked and started thumbing through Christine's diary.

It was more a daily log than a personal memoir. Any hints of self-analysis were absent. Lacking too were any Aesopian morals to her boring little stories. Most of it was tidbits of tedium: the stockings she'd purchased, the meals she'd eaten, the friends she'd met and what they wore.

But it wasn't all dull reading. She'd spelled my name as "Guner" and wrote only that I'd helped her out of a "tight spot." She described me as "a nice enough guy who was a little on the make."

But what really caught my eye were the periodic marginal entries. These were terse and written in a very small hand. She used no names—just nicknames and initials.

Armed with one of the names I'd learned from Walter, I studied a few of Christine's glosses until I thought I'd made sense of a couple from some months back.

G. called. H.R. in can. I interpreted this to mean that Guy had called to tell her his photos of Hugh Rundquist were good to go. Or maybe that he'd succeeded in shaking him down. Two weeks later I found an entry that read: *First payment from H.R.: $500.* De Carter was probably paymaster, but she had her own silly brand of bookkeeping.

I noted subsequent payments from H.R. in the months that followed. It was similar, with a few other initialed entries. For a little seductive flirting and a fervent one-nighter, Christine's cut was none too shabby. Not bad if you could still stand yourself afterward. I could only imagine what Guy de Carter's take was. I didn't find Christine's bankbook when I searched her room. My guess was de Carter stole it off her the night he'd killed her.

There were only a few such assignation entries over a stretch of several months, which told me that the girls had been selective and had apparently cultivated their prey slowly and carefully. In the entries for the last couple of weeks, Christine had written of a "special" project.

A few diary entries sandwiched in between shakedowns puzzled me. Then they started to trouble me. Finally they just made me ill.

> B. sensed trouble with Tubby. We backed off.
> B. wants M. to continue after Eyebrows and wants me on Slick.
> B. promises more $ for Slick. I think he's special somehow.

The note about Eyebrows was fairly recent and had to refer to Addison Darcy's bristly brows. Maybe both girls had been assigned to try and seduce Darcy, but for some reason Meredith had apparently seemed more suited to the task. Or perhaps Christine was a better choice for the man she called Slick. But why no initials for Eyebrows and Slick? And who was B?

I went back and studied the previous entries until something stood out. I looked for a peculiar quirk in her bookkeeping and found it. For some reason Christine didn't use the victims' initials until after a triumphal tryst and payment had been made. Prior to that she used pet names like Jowls, Bugeyes and Tubby—tags obviously drawn from the physical characteristics of the marks.

Her handlers were another matter. They were known simply as B and G throughout. I'd met only two people in Christine's circle these past few days whose first initial was B. Blanche Arnot and Britt Anderson.

I drove to the nearest payphone.

I didn't reach Milland, but got his partner Bernie Hanson.

"Do us both a favor, would you Bern?" I said.

"Oh yeah? And what favor might that be?" he asked in monotonic solemnity.

"It has to do with those registration records for late model Packards. Could you check on a name for me?"

"Well ...." he said, drawing out the word to two slow syllables. "I suppose I could do that."

Don't beat yourself up over it, Bern, I thought but didn't say. Self-control is the better part of favor-begging.

After five minutes that seemed like fifteen, Hanson returned to the phone and confirmed what I suspected.

I'd worked with Lou Boyd for almost a month, when in an outpouring of youthful idealism I'd told him that our job was to pursue the truth.

"Nah, Gunnar lad, it ain't as noble as all that," Lou had said with a wry smile. "We dismantle lies. If we're lucky, the truth—or a pretty close second—comes crawlin' out of the rubble."

In homage to Lou, I had my pile of rubble. And in a nod to Mrs. Berger's hootchie-cootchie days, my close second was slithering out from the debris on its belly like a reptile.

Chapter 15

—

HARDY LINDHOLM WAS CHAPFALLEN.

"Just in the nick of time, old thing," Walter said as we drove off. "It's my own fault. I know better. I should always let him win more than I do."

Walter was happy to take a ride. Relieved was more like it. He and Hardy had played a fatiguing thirty games of checkers. Walter had won most of them, but defeat didn't sit well with Hardy. The old Swede's identity and self-worth came from winning parlor games. Walter had agreed to a colossal rematch. A frazzle-haired Hardy had just put on a fresh pot of coffee when I showed up.

I updated Walter as we rode along.

"You said you wanted to meet her," I said, heading us to Laurelhurst.

"Yes," he said gravely, "but I had a different idea as to when and why. A very different idea."

I parked in her driveway. Her garage was a separate building outside her fence. The door had a series of small windows at the top. Before we passed through the wrought-iron gate, I peeked inside and saw the dark and unmistakable outline of a Packard.

I rang the buzzer.

Walter presented the left side of his face to the speakeasy peephole as its grated window rasped opened.

"Oh, it's *you*, Mr. Nilson," Blanche Arnot said in a cheerful voice.

"Yes. I've brought a friend. May we come in?"

"By all means."

She winced on seeing Walter's scars, but quickly reshaped her welcoming countenance. She didn't seem to need an explanation of my friend, and I didn't feel like offering one. She had a coat on and looked all dolled up and ready to leave.

"Are we keeping you from something?" I asked.

"No. Nothing that can't keep a little while longer."

She seated us in the living room.

"Now, to what do I owe this second visit—and so deliciously soon at that?" she asked.

"You drive a Packard."

"No … no, I don't."

"There's a Packard in your garage."

"Yes, that's correct."

"You're saying you don't drive. Is that the case, Mrs. Arnot?" said Walter.

She looked at Walter like an approving school marm. "That's correct. I regret I never bothered to learn. The car in the garage was my husband's. Henry bought it the fall before last, just before the heart attack took him."

"Has someone used your car recently, Mrs. Arnot?" Walter asked.

"Why yes. It was just returned today. It's been loaned out this past week."

"Who borrowed it?" I asked.

She noticed the edge in my voice and looked at me curiously. "I didn't meet the young man. He's one of Britt Anderson's friends. She told me his car is at the mechanic's. I loaned it out as a favor to her. I trust her completely."

I'd been pretty certain that my rough draft was ready to be inked in. When you've convinced yourself that all the evidence fits the way you want to look at something, you really hate anything that detracts.

"So, *Britt* dropped the car off?" I asked as my throat reached for my heart.

Mrs. Arnot shook her head. "I'd given her the keys. She passed them on. That way her friend could take the car and bring it back at his leisure. I saw it in the garage just a little while ago when I went to get my garden hose. It wasn't in there this morning, so I imagine the young man dropped it off this afternoon sometime. You see, I don't lock my garage. A thief is welcome to whatever he finds in there. Locks only dissuade the honest and the maladroit."

I was watching her closely. She was serene. Her equanimity was alarming. She might just as well have been talking about her grocery list. Her blithe comments came across with a convincing guilelessness. Another hypothesis began to bud that upset both my theories and my stomach.

My skin had those frosty quivers you get that start at the base of your spine and run to the back of your head. My neat little picture of things slipped right off its drawing board and went gliding to the floor, destined for the ash heap.

"But why all this interest in my Packard, Mr. Nilson?"

Walter Pangborn to the rescue.

"Because I might be interested in buying it," he said. "I'm afraid my DeSoto is on its last set of whitewalls."

She was deliciously amused.

Walter asked Mrs. Arnot a few more questions about her car, which gave me time to digest what I'd learned.

Sick. Disgusted. Those words work. Add a healthy dose of angry. That probably covers it.

It's the kind of thing that happens when you bring your glans in as a consultant. And I'd known better. A passionate bond and a protective male urge clouds the wits and any pretense to professional judgment.

I kept thinking how I'd screwed up and then some.

My mind was elsewhere, but I vaguely made out that Walter had shifted from automobiles to questions about Mrs. Arnot's days in the *Ziegfeld Follies*.

I forced myself to swap my prejudices for a stab at objectivity. My brain started sketching away at a new picture. It was impressionistic and it wasn't the least bit pretty. Revolting was more like it.

I struggled with the idea that Britt had used and manipulated me from the start. I rethought all my encounters with her. Innocent actions now seemed malevolent. That first day— those times she'd buttonholed Meredith. I had to figure that they had nothing to do with consoling or bucking up a friend. It now seemed clear that Britt had been cautioning Meredith— *warning* her. I envisioned Britt carefully choosing her girls— making sure they were the type who weren't likely to crack from the strains of the racket she was running, yet at the same time could be easily controlled by her and Guy de Carter.

I felt outclassed and outsmarted. Gunnar the Rube. It now appeared that Britt had set me up with Guy de Carter, and then gave him the lowdown on who I'd interviewed and when.

I remembered now her talking on the phone when I was in her bed, or so it had sounded. Talking with de Carter, no doubt. Probably warning him of my plans to squeeze Meredith for more information. Meredith had gone from asset to liability in a hurry. It made sense that she'd had de Carter go take care of Meredith while she'd waylaid me till morning.

I figured Britt had finagled me into going over to de Carter's houseboat and then called someone to bushwhack me. Either that or maybe she'd tailed me and sapped me herself. She'd killed de Carter and taken the photos from my coat. Then she'd tried to frame me. There was a disturbing kind of logic to it all.

And there was no point in asking why.

I had a sudden sense of knowing Britt less now than when we'd first met. It was like we'd become different people to each other—or at least she was different to me. A familiar stranger. A lethal one.

I don't remember if there was a lull in the conversation or whether I was rudely interrupting when I suddenly asked, "What was the name of Alexis' fiancé?"

"Pardon me?" said Mrs. Arnot.

"The man who broke up with Britt's aunt—what was his name?"

"Why, Mr. Nilson, she was engaged to Addison Darcy. Addison Darcy Junior, that is."

"Son of the same Addison Darcy in the store with you the other day?" I asked, knowing the answer.

"That's correct," she said, giving us a sad smile. "Alexis was devastated when her Addie—her Addison—broke off their engagement. But I think it was when she learned he'd been killed in the war that she was completely overcome with despair. Why do you ask, Mr. Nilson?"

"Why did he break off their engagement? Did Alexis ever say?" But again, I already knew.

Mrs. Arnot nodded.

Her mouth formed a sardonic smile. "His father pressured him into it. He didn't want his son to marry beneath him. He threatened to disinherit young Addison."

"Britt knew all this, of course?" I said.

"Why yes. Most definitely."

"It must have aggravated Britt to see the elder Darcy frequent the store."

"You mean did she blame him for Alexis' ruin?"

I nodded.

"Yes, I suppose she did. No, that's not correct. I *know* she did."

"Care to explain?"

Mrs. Arnot told us that as she watched Alexis begin to decline she also watched Britt nurture a hatred for both the Darcy men.

"I used to tell Britt that it was a foolish waste of emotion and energy. But you can imagine how that went over." Mrs. Arnot shook her head sadly, her lips puckering. "She became consumed by her feelings. At one point, I actually feared that she might do something rash."

I asked what she meant.

"Oh, I don't know. I've seen people try and take justice into their own hands before. I'm sure both of you have seen the same. Britt commented more than a few times how she'd like to see both the Darcy men dead. Her words disturbed me. Shook me up, really. I suppose I feared that she'd turn her words into action. It was foolish of me, though, the way matters have turned out. Why, had it been in operation a mere five years ago, Britt would never even have considered working at Fasciné Expressions—what with its affiliation with Darlund Apparels. Some young people can be so deliciously resilient. I'd say she's made a lot of progress. I suppose it was when word came of young Addison's death that things reached a turning point for Britt."

"A turning point?"

"Yes, I believe that correctly describes it. I'm sure that it was then when Britt finally let go of her anger. Seeing Alexis grow worse at the news of his death, she must have realized that her aunt had still been very much in love with Addison. As to Addison senior, I believe Britt saw his losing his son as punishment enough."

Not hardly, I thought, but kept it to myself.

"Oh, I don't like this at all," Kirsti said. She'd put her hand to her throat and was giving me a worried look. "This is taking an ugly turn, Gunnar."

"I know just what you mean, Blue Eyes. We might all see life through our own funhouse mirror, but what I thought I was seeing wasn't one bit amusing."

"I'm a happy ending kind of person, Gunnar."

"You're a romantic. A near-hopeless case, I'm afraid. It's part of your charm. Promise me you won't let life knock it out of you."

She looked at me like I was from the planet Mongo.

"I promise. Go ahead and go on with it."

I put my hands up with palms forward as if in surrender. "I'm afraid I'm all talked out for the day, young lady," I said matter-of-factly. "I'll have to finish this up another time."

Kirsti looked as deflated as a punctured and faded beach ball on the seashore in the pouring rain. She said something that sounded like "argh," and maybe it was "argh." "Oh, come on, Gunnar, you're leaving me hanging here," she protested shrilly. "At least give me a hint as to how things go from here."

I shook my head and said in a kind but determined tone, "You'll just have to wait. I know it's still light out, but it's almost eight thirty, which means we've been going at this for hours. In case you haven't noticed, I'm an old man, Blue Eyes. I've hit the wall. There's a night's sleep with my name on it waiting for me back in my room. We'll meet again when it's convenient for you, and I'll tell you the rest of it. I'll be fresh then and will be able to tell it far better than I would if I pushed on with it right now. Believe me."

"You're totally killing me here, Gunnar," she said in a high, twangy voice. "You've got to know that." But her frown soon became a lopsided grin of resignation.

I just smiled.

Chapter 16

—

Finecare Retirement Home, Everett, Washington, late afternoon Monday, June 23, 2003

KIRSTI AND I HAD agreed to meet up again the next afternoon when her shift ended at 2:30. She'd told me emphatically that she simply could not wait till the following Sunday to hear the rest of my story.

So by 2:40 I was in my wheelchair and Kirsti, still in her green scrubs, was once again giving me another bumpy ride over the gravel and flagstone walk leading to the outside courtyard.

"Tired out from talking or not, that was a dirty trick you played on me, ending your story where you did yesterday," Kirsti groused, but with her usual goodwill behind it. "I've been distracted all day wondering how it's all going to end."

Once Kirsti got me parked, she swung her tote bag from off her shoulder and retrieved her cassette recorder from it. As she took a seat on the wood bench across from me, she placed the recorder on her lap and put the bag right next to her. Then she pulled out a small, clear-plastic container that looked like it held gelatinous chunks, silvery-gray in color.

She waved the container at me and said, "This is pickled herring for later. You've said you miss it. Why exactly, I'll never know. It's really gross to look at. Also, the other day I had my mom pick up some of that Siljans hardtack you talk about so much."

"*Knäckebröd*," I said thoughtfully. "My grandmother used to simply call it *kaken.*"

"Uh-huh," she said evenly. "Anyway, I've got some pieces already buttered for you to eat with your herring."

"I'm speechless."

And I was. It had been some time since anyone had done something so kind and special for me. I mean the pastrami on rye sandwiches that she'd brought me the day before were great, but with hardtack and herring she'd taken her thoughtfulness to a new level.

"Kirsti, I really don't know how to thank you—"

"Finishing your story will be thanks enough."

I didn't say anything. I just looked at her a moment. Finally, I said impishly, "Oh yes, my story. Now *where was I?*"

Kirsti's bangs rose a bit as her eyebrows narrowed in a pretend scowl. "Uh-uh," she said in a smug tone. "I made sure I'd be ready in case you tried to pull something like this, Gunnar." She pulled out a slip of paper from a side pocket of her tote bag and glanced down at what from my angle looked to be shorthand scrawl, which she then proceeded to interpret:

"You met Christine Johanson on a Tuesday night. She was murdered Wednesday night. You were hired to look into it on Thursday and were almost killed that evening by a hit-and-run driver. Several interviews later on Friday, your office was riddled with bullets, but luckily you were in the office next door when it happened. That night things got more than a bit steamy between you and Britt Anderson. The next morning, Saturday, you and your friend Walter Pangborn found Meredith Lane murdered in her apartment along with evidence that she and Christine had been part of a blackmail racket with Guy de

Carter. A little later you shared this information with Britt and she steered you to de Carter's houseboat, where you found him murdered. A waitress named Verna happened to mention her diary, which gave you the idea to visit the house where Christine had lived with her aunt, where you located her diary. Christine's coded entries about the blackmail racket implicated de Carter but also pointed to someone else known simply by the initial B. Two people in Christine's life with names that started with B were Blanche Arnot and Britt Anderson."

"I'm impressed, Blue Eyes. Truly impressed," I said earnestly. "Don't tell me you listened to the tapes you made yesterday?"

She shook her head. "I made these brief notes from memory before I went to bed last night. Like I said, I wanted to be ready for you."

"Why, you were born to be a newspaper reporter."

"I've toyed some with becoming a journalist," she said in her usual sweet voice. "But anyway, you ended yesterday with telling me that when you and your friend Walter talked with Blanche Arnot, she went on about Britt Anderson's hatred for Addison Darcy and his son because of what had happened to her aunt."

"Uh-huh," I said, as I took a clove from my old Sucrets tin and put it in my mouth.

Kirsti suddenly clicked on her recorder like she was resetting a tripped circuit breaker. "Okay, Gunnar, I'm all set. Please continue."

Saturday, June 10, 1950

I WAS VIOLENTLY CHEWING on a clove when Walter and I pulled out of Blanche Arnot's part of Laurelhurst. We drove in silence for a while.

Walter started packing his pipe and said at last, "A very handsome woman. It's easy to get absorbed in her storytelling. She has a very engaging manner."

I agreed.

"So, where are we headed, old top?" he asked.

"Fasciné Expressions is closed by now, so we're off to Vista Court Apartments, to see one Miss Britt Anderson."

"Hmm."

I told Walter it seemed obvious to me that suspicions had now shifted from Blanche Arnot to Britt Anderson. I said nothing of my intimate relationship with Britt. When I'd finished, I glanced at my friend and said, "A penny for Walter Pangborn's thoughts."

Walter puffed away on his pipe, smoke escaping out the window he'd partly rolled down. I could see him going into one of his cogitating reveries, so I patiently waited. Well, maybe I wasn't exactly patient, but I held my tongue.

Finally Walter sighed and said, "On the face of it, it certainly seems that Aunt Alexis isn't the only actress in the family."

"Walter, Britt Anderson has got to be one of the best liars I've ever met. *The* absolute best."

"Either that, old socks, or her charms colored your view of the actual performance."

I didn't say anything.

"An attractive female *can* be a bane to the thinking male."

"I get the idea."

"A lovely lass can make one an ass."

"Shut up, Walter."

"It's your penny, old thing."

The Pangborn governess had not raised an idiot.

"What did you make of Mrs. Arnot?" I asked.

"A few things strike me as peculiar."

"I told you she was a bit otherworldly."

"Yes, that's part of it, I'm sure. She said her husband passed away almost two years ago. Did you notice that there wasn't one photo of him in the room? Not one I could see, anyway."

"People grieve differently, Walter. Maybe his photos are painful reminders to her."

"Possibly, but I doubt it, old top. I suspect that her husband was a very important figure to her. In fact, judging by Blanche Arnot's appearance and demeanor, I think males have played a prominent, if not a key role in her life."

"What are you driving at?"

"It's as if her husband no longer signifies to her in some way. It's as if she's … ignoring him. Purposely so."

"You base that simply on the absence of pictures? You're reaching, don't you think, Walter?"

"Perhaps, old socks, but consider how Mrs. Arnot carries herself. She's very much as you described her. She was clearly a beautiful woman when young, and is still quite attractive. She's extremely cognizant of herself as a female. Like most distinguished beauties, she grooms and carries herself in a formalistic way—but a way that is loaded with nuances and subtleties."

"Enlighten this aesthetic dullard, Walter."

"Why, old thing, Mrs. Arnot gives her looks a ceremonial attention that practically smacks of religious fervor. Notice the precise part in her hair. The artistic application of lip rouge. Her lustrous manicure. Even her shoes are carefully shined. She's more than just mindful of her appearance, old top. All of this care really speaks to the self-regard she has in being a female, and in her need to make a calculated impact as a woman."

"So?"

"So, old socks, she wasn't wearing her wedding ring. I take that as significant. It has to have been a deliberate decision *not* to wear it—given how calculating she is about her appearance. Her husband is dead and gone, and she's closed the chapter on him for some reason. *Why*, I have no idea. But it's as though he had been a commodity that's fulfilled its use. Or, perhaps seeing his face and the wedding ring would be a troubling reminder of something she chooses to ignore."

"Walter, this is too much."

But it reminded me that Britt had said Blanche seemed cut from her moorings when her husband died. I told this to Walter.

"Hmm. That *is* interesting. Perhaps she doesn't want to be reminded of those moorings. Maybe she prefers being adrift. I wonder why."

For a few moments the only noise we heard was the Chevy's motor. Finally Walter continued, "Even the way she spoke with us is telling, Gunnar. Like I said, she's very engaging. However, I must say that while a little flicker in her eyes bespoke a subtle mind geared for intrigue, I sensed instability. And I had the distinct feeling several times that I was being carefully handled. As if she was talking to an inferior. I don't think she has a very high opinion of men."

"I don't know. I think she liked me well enough. I think she liked both of us, Walter."

"You can *like* a chimpanzee, Gunnar. You might even train one to mix drinks. It's been done, you know. However, you wouldn't seek its advice if you were making an investment. Mrs. Arnot may *like* men, but I don't think she respects them too much. Why, she actually seemed quite surprised when a couple of times I grasped her unspoken meaning."

"Give me an example."

"She told me the same woeful tale she'd told you the other night. The story of poor Sally Miller and her tragic death in prison."

"What of it, Walter?"

"When Mrs. Arnot finished telling me the story, I made one of my comments that you dislike so much. I said, 'Diamonds and pearls have been the bane of many working girls.' "

"Say it ain't so, Walter."

"But I did, old thing. Unthinkingly, I'm afraid. I followed it up with another one that is equally inane. You know how they just come to me. I said, 'A man's power and lechery lead often to treachery.' "

I groaned.

"But it was amazing, old top. Instead of a polite smile and eyebrow roll as you might expect, it's as if I'd validated her by the remark. I noticed in Mrs. Arnot's interior eyes a small, crazed flash of respect and reappraisal. As if to say that before she'd considered me a mere cypher. It was very strange, old socks. And I must say a little unnerving."

I felt that my first talk with Mrs. Arnot had been fairly straightforward. So I was a little annoyed that Walter could have picked up on something I might have missed. I glanced over at him to make sure he was earnest in what he said.

He went on, "I also find it a bit odd that Mrs. Arnot would retell that Sally Miller story again so soon. Generally people only do that when a matter is particularly close to their heart."

"Well, Walter, maybe it is. She told me she and the girl were very close."

"No doubt. But, what happened to her friend Sally took place some thirty years ago. By the furnishings of her home and her modern attire, she doesn't strike me as someone who cares to live in the past. And Mrs. Arnot is far from her dotage and the reminiscences that accompany it."

"So what are you trying to say, Walter?"

"I guess I don't know, old thing. But I've just got a hunch that Mrs. Arnot may be every bit the actress that your Miss Anderson seems to be."

"You think she's lying to us about something?"

"Something's definitely amiss. You told me that Mrs. Arnot had made Christine Johanson out to be a girl of poor judgment. But from your own encounter with the girl, she seemed to be quite shrewd. Wasn't that your conclusion?"

I agreed.

"It suggests that Mrs. Arnot was trying to color your perception of the murder victim. Recall, she described Mr. de Carter as a harmless drugstore cowboy. Later, another source made him out to be a ruffian. And a ruffian he was, indeed."

Walter added, "And, you must admit, Mrs. Arnot did appear more than willing to put Miss Anderson in a bad light."

"But I'm the one who brought up Britt and her aunt."

"True. You gave her opportunity. All the same, casting aspersions is not something a person readily does regarding a genuine friend. Not without some hesitation, anyway. Especially when she's talking to someone investigating a murder, and her words might indict that friend."

I weighed his words.

"Another thing, Gunnar. We'd clearly interrupted her departure when we arrived. Yet there was no taxi waiting outside. So, unless she'd planned to take a walk—"

"She was planning to drive the Packard."

"That would be my surmise, old top."

Walter's words had a strange and soothing effect on my psyche. All of a sudden, my discarded first draft started to look salvageable—at least parts of it. Enough so as to pick it up off the floor and dust it off.

Maybe, I thought, Blanche Arnot *was* involved with this whole mess after all. Ordinarily money would have been motive enough, but I sensed there had to be another factor with Blanche Arnot. While Britt hadn't exactly come out from under suspicion's shadow, I now had some reason to hope that she might. At least that's the attitude I had when we parked near the Vista Court Apartments.

"Any suggestions, for when we talk to Britt?" I asked.

"There's still reason to harbor misgivings about Miss Anderson, of course. For all we know, Mrs. Arnot telephoned her immediately after we left. And, if she has been warned, I doubt we'll find her at home. If she is home, and she *is* somehow in league with Mrs. Arnot, then clearly Miss Anderson has been hung out to dry, as they say. But if she's completely ignorant and innocent, I believe we can quickly determine it by asking her a few simple questions."

Chapter 17

⸺

IT WASN'T THE NEED for a drink of water or a pee break or a question from Kirsti that got me to stop talking this time. It was the anguished look on her youthful face. My pause prompted her to say:

"Man, Gunnar, I'd think at this point … I mean, with what had gone on between you and Britt and all … you'd want to talk to her in private."

I shook my head. "Believe me, I was tempted to suggest as much to Walter, but I didn't dare."

"Why not?"

"By then I didn't trust myself, is why not. Besides, Blue Eyes, Walter seemed to have figured out how to cut this Gordian knot."

"Gordian knot?"

"It refers to a complicated problem, which like a knot is hard to unravel but that someone clever might know how to quickly cut through, so to speak. And right then I felt I needed Walter along with me, because he seemed to have just the right questions in mind to ask Britt to get things unraveling."

"You make him sound like some kind of psychologist."

I laughed. "No. Walter Pangborn really liked people. He was a keen student of them. And it also didn't hurt that he was well read."

"For sure."

"Now where was I? Oh yes …."

WE STOOD ON THE small enclosed porch. Walter admired the hanging fuchsias and carefully fingered a few of the blossoms.

Britt opened the door and wore that far off, besieged look she'd had while sitting at her desk the day we met. She flinched infinitesimally on seeing Walter's face but recovered beautifully. When she saw me her troubled face transformed into a smile beaming nothing but warm welcome.

I introduced Walter as one of my good friends. "I sometimes consult with Walter in some of my investigations."

She invited us in, no questions asked.

"I stopped at the market after work," Britt explained. "I just finished putting a few things away and was changing clothes when I heard your knock. Would you like some coffee? Or perhaps something stronger?"

Thanks but no thanks, we said.

Britt was wearing red denim pedal pushers and a white halter-top with yellow polka dots. She looked marvelous in spite of my suspicions about her. Walter and I sank deeply into the balloon cushions of her daveno. She plunged into the club chair.

"I hoped you'd get back to me, Gunnar," she said. "I was really worried when you went after Guy de Carter alone. I trust the police have him in custody."

"You could say that," I said.

Britt studied my face and one blond eyebrow lifted, telling me she sensed something was wrong.

"What's the matter, Gunnar? You look like you've come from a funeral."

"In a way. Someone shot and killed Guy de Carter."

She looked genuinely alarmed. "How dreadful. Is … is *that* how you found him?"

"Not exactly," I said. "Before I explain more, Walter and I would first like to ask you a few questions, if you don't mind."

She looked puzzled but readily agreed.

"Miss Anderson," Walter said, "in your dealings with Christine Johanson, would you have characterized her as a shrewd young woman?"

"Yes, I suppose so," Britt said. "Yes, I'd say Christine was fairly bright."

"Have you ever been driven anywhere by Blanche Arnot?" Walter asked.

"What … what's this all about?" she said, looking from Walter to me.

"We're not sure yet, Britt," I said. "Humor us. Please."

"About Mrs. Arnot's driving ability, Miss Anderson, would you say she's a *good* driver?"

"Yes … I suppose so. Perhaps a little on the slow side for my taste. Maybe a little too quick on the brakes. But yes, overall I'd say she's a good driver." Walter signaled me with a look.

"Britt, could you tell us how Blanche Arnot viewed the Darcy men after young Addison ended his relationship with your aunt?"

"I … I don't understand. Where are you going with all this?"

"Please, Britt. It's important. What was Blanche's reaction?"

She hesitated, her face grew pale. "I … I suppose she was upset with them."

"You *suppose*? Only suppose?" I said.

"No. They upset her."

"That was it? They upset her? She had no other emotion?" I asked.

"Gunnar … why—?"

"Indulge me. Please."

She sighed. "All right. Blanche hated them. She despised them." I looked in vain for any sign of lying.

"And when Alexis died?"

"Even more so. But I suppose I did too, for a time. Why wouldn't we?"

"Did Mrs. Arnot ever speak of wanting to exact some sort of vengeance?" Walter asked.

Britt didn't say anything for a moment but then nodded. "But it was all just talk. You know how people go on sometimes. She loved my aunt as much as I did. We were both extremely agitated. You know how people say things. We all say things we don't really mean."

"But she talked about it often, didn't she?" Walter said.

"Yes. Yes, she did. But she would never do anything rash—if that's where you're going with this. It was all just talk."

"What was Blanche's husband like?" I asked.

"Henry? Henry was a kind and mild-mannered man." Britt laughed. "He used to say he was a mare yoked to a stallion. But he was good for Blanche. Blanche respects few men. She really respected Henry."

"A stabling influence on her, would you say?" Walter asked.

"Yes. Yes, that would describe it, I think. Definitely."

"Stabling in what way?" I asked.

Britt thought for a few seconds. "Blanche used to laugh and say that Henry kept her reined in and on track. She still says he kept her an honest woman. Why, she said as much less than a week ago. As I told you the other day, Gunnar, I sensed the difference in her since her loss. It's one of the reasons I offered her a job."

As the saying goes, it takes some time to see the patently obvious. What's right in front of your face takes even longer. An eerie notion jolted me. Blanche Arnot's quaint, otherworldly air took on another meaning. Apparently the same notion had also struck Walter.

"Did Blanche Arnot ever tell you the sad story of her friend, Sally Miller?" he asked.

Britt was jarred by the question.

"Yes. Often."

"Did she ever tell you the name of Sally's lover? The man who treated her so shamelessly?" I asked.

A gleam of troubled realization showed in Britt's eyes. "Oh, yes. Right after my aunt took up with Addie. Oh, yes. She mentioned him many times."

Chapter 18

—

"THIS WAS THAT BOLT out the blue you talked about earlier, wasn't it?" Kirsti said. "We're talking critical mass time, aren't we?"

"Uh-huh. None of us is that remarkable, Kirsti. It doesn't matter how exceptional a person feels they are. Most everything we all do is totally foreseeable, if the interested onlookers are armed with a few particulars. The trick is coming up with those particulars. And we three had come up with those particulars."

"And then it must have seemed so obvious, huh?"

"Without question."

"I'm just glad Britt turned out to be on your team."

"Uh-huh."

"MRS. ARNOT HAD TO know that we'd probably confute her story rather quickly," Walter said. "So the only reason for her to lie so brazenly and cast suspicion on Miss Anderson here—"

"Is if she were planning some immediate and drastic action," I said, standing up. Walter rose with me. "She was getting ready to leave when we showed up."

"Precisely," he said heading for the door. "She knew that

whatever she told us wasn't going to matter one whit."

I followed after Walter with Britt trailing behind me, demanding an explanation. We told her there was no time. She insisted on coming along.

The three of us crammed into my Chevy, with Britt in the middle. I headed the coupe in the direction of The Highlands. En route we gave Britt the thin version of our suspicions regarding Blanche Arnot and the blackmail racket. She sat between Walter and me, and I caught snatches of her face in the rearview mirror. She listened calmly. She interrupted only with an occasional clarifying question. Her mouth looked pale and she searched my face when learning a horrid detail. I soon recognized her working-woman compartment—the pragmatic, reserved, and well-behaved box that probably helped keep her sane at such moments.

After our tale was told, we all rode in a silence imposed by Britt's need to digest what she'd heard. I kept up my furtive glances at her in the mirror. She sat composed but with a sour mouth for most of the trip north. A time or two I saw her quickly pin down her bottom lip with her teeth as it started to tremble. The unfolding events had shaken her world. I empathized.

I finally broke the quiet when I saw the gatehouse in the distance. "How would Mrs. Arnot have gotten past the guard?"

"She has friends in this community," Britt said blankly, in almost a whisper. "She'll have gained entrance easily. I'm sure of it."

"The question is, old top, just how are *we* going to get in?" asked Walter.

I was hoping that the ex-bouncer Charlie would be on duty and remember me from before. But Charlie had been replaced by a guard named Bill. He approached the passenger side of my Chevy as Walter rolled down the window.

Bill looked at Walter without any kind of reaction. "Costume party at the Nudell's?" he asked. "Go right on in, sir."

And so we did. When we rounded the first turn I picked up the speed.

Swinging into the driveway, we saw Blanche's Packard parked closer to the house than the garage.

The front door was open, the foyer empty.

We made our way to the parlor where I'd had my talk with Addison Darcy. Hildy, the lean and scary housekeeper, was lying on the floor. I felt for a pulse. She was alive but now quite immune to more than just charming smiles.

Walter picked Hildy up and placed her on a couch as I took my .38 from its holster. A telephone sat on a small table near the doorway. I picked up the receiver. The line was dead.

A carpeted corridor shot off to our left and another corridor with a bare hardwood floor ran in the opposite direction. Britt and I took the latter. Walter whispered after us that he'd catch up after tending to Hildy.

The corridor led to a sliding door with polished mahogany panels. The door was open partway.

We headed for it.

We didn't think to kick our shoes off. We clattered and clacked on the hardwood despite our best efforts. A trumpet blast wouldn't have announced our arrival any better.

"Whoever you are, if you have a weapon, I advise you to drop it before you enter," said a feminine voice that still sounded half its age.

I slipped my gun in its holster and took Britt's purse from her and let it fall to the floor. It made a fair *cluh-thump* noise. We waited a few seconds before she spoke again, "Well, don't just stand there. Come in. Come in."

Britt and I obeyed.

Addison Darcy's study was huge and impressive, with soft rugs, dark-paneled walls, carved furniture and floor-to-ceiling bookshelves. Blanche Arnot sat on a leather-upholstered settee built into the nook of a large bay window. She was pointing a small automatic at us. On the rug in the middle of the room sat Addison Darcy. His hands were tied behind his back. His hair was tousled. He'd aged since our chat. He looked very old and very frightened.

Mrs. Arnot gave us a courtly little nod as we entered. "Ah, Mr. Nilson, and you too, Britt dear. How delicious. I suppose I'm not really surprised that you've joined us," she said. Her casual tone gave me a chill. "Mr. Darcy and I were just discussing old times. Reminiscing, you might say. I think it wise if you both put your hands in the air." Her request was cordial, even motherly, but to disobey would have been deadly.

The ultimate way of classifying people is by the acts they're willing to commit. A pending act was evident. But was Blanche Arnot evil or just maniacal? Or maybe both?

"It doesn't need to happen like this, Mrs. Arnot," I said.

"Please, call me Blanche, Gunnar. You don't mind if I call you Gunnar, do you? The way things are shaping up, we really should be on a first name basis, don't you think?" She smiled. It was an expansive though intimate smile, but the madness in her eyes was just enough to make her look ugly.

"Mrs. Arnot—*Blanche*. There's no need for this. There are other ways to get justice," I said.

She sniffed derisively. "*His* kind buys justice," she said, nodding her head at Darcy. "They always have. They always will. It's been a long time coming, but this one's luck has finally run out."

Britt and I traded glances. Startled eyes looked at me under the narrow crooks of her brows. When Britt spoke, her voice was unsteady.

"Blanche … please. Why don't you just put that gun away?"

Blanche's pale mouth seemed to detect an unwelcome taste. "You of all people should be grateful to me for this, my dear. It was this lustful animal who killed Alexis."

Addison Darcy was shaking slightly. He looked pleadingly at Britt. His cheeks glistened from the tear trails. Where the hell was Walter? I wondered.

Blanche looked at the floor. I toyed with the idea of reaching for my .38, but gave it up as a bad job just as she raised her eyes.

"It was you that knocked me out. And then you killed Guy de Carter," I said.

"That's correct," she said.

Britt's body braced as if absorbing a blow.

I continued, "And after you killed him, you left me to be the patsy."

Blanche's mouth spread out into an apologetic smile. "That's correct, Gunnar. No hard feelings I hope. My, but you are deliciously astute. What else have you deduced?"

"Enough, I think. You, Guy de Carter, Christine, and Meredith were in cahoots. Blackmail. The girls seduced 'em. de Carter took their pictures. And you collected the hush money. Discreetly, of course. Things were going just swell until Christine got greedy. Maybe she even figured she could strike out on her own and eliminate management. Whatever the case, de Carter killed her and tried to make it look like Dirk Engstrom did it. Dirk's angry outburst in the store was an opportunity to pin the blame on him that de Carter couldn't pass up."

Blanche gave me the approving look a teacher reserves for her star pupil. "I misjudged Guy de Carter. He merely possessed a kind of raw cunning. The cunning of an alley rat." She shrugged. "Both Guy and I were in the store that day by sheer coincidence. I was hoping to negotiate with Christine. She got greedy, just as you say. And Meredith … well, she had way too much pluck for her own good. But greed can be dealt with and pluck is a virtue, after all. The girls weren't supposed to die. I didn't want that. Guy just got too nervous, that's all. That's the trouble with womanizers. They don't know women in the ways that really matter." She looked menacingly at Darcy.

Britt remained quiet. Her eyes were as big as prize cherries.

I continued, "You tried to make me think de Carter was a harmless ladies' man. Did *you* sic him on me, Blanche? Did you want him to kill me?"

"Gracious no, Gunnar. Like I said, Guy got nervous about the girls, and he grew absolutely frantic when you began poking and probing. I must say, his attempts on your life were clumsy and amateurish at best. But I never intended for you to die. Not at first, anyway. I was mainly after *this* pathetic excuse for a man," she said, pointing the automatic at Addison Darcy.

Darcy's eyes shifted from the floor to the gun and back again.

"How did you know I'd come calling at the houseboat to see de Carter?" I asked.

"I didn't. It was another delicious coincidence. Guy was getting antsy and out of control. His precious car was being serviced so he'd borrowed my Packard. But he was derelict in returning it. Finally, I told him I wanted to meet to get my car back, and to talk things over. So I took a taxi to his place. I didn't want a witness to my true destination, so I had the cabbie drop me a few blocks away. As I walked up, seeing you on the landing was a total surprise, I assure you."

"You'd planned to kill de Carter?"

"Oh, yes. By then it was quite necessary. He'd become a loose cannon, I'm afraid."

"And you figured the cops would nail me as his killer."

Blanche nodded. "I hoped they would. I didn't think you had any way to connect me to any of it. The houseboat belongs to Guy's grandmother, who now spends her dotage in a Portland old folk's home. I relieved you of those photos you'd stolen. Without them, I didn't think you had much in the way of real evidence to go along with whatever tall tale you planned for the police. Besides, Gunnar, I rather liked you."

"I'd have preferred flowers or maybe a necktie," I said.

"But *why*, Blanche?" asked Britt, anguish in her voice. "You ... you certainly don't need the money. I thought Henry left you well off."

Blanche dismissed her remark with the wave of her free hand. "Don't be naïve, my dear. It's never been about the money." Blanche looked from Britt to me. "*You* understand that, don't you, Gunnar?"

"I think I do. The blackmail racket was a means to an end. You probably had some plan to eventually have the whole thing come out in the open to besmirch Darcy's enterprises and shame his family. But first, you hoped Darcy himself would become one of your victims. You planned to string him along. You wanted to torment him."

"That's correct," Blanche said, giving me another smile of approval. "Both of the girls started out cultivating this randy old goat. But he seemed particularly taken with Meredith. He always did like full-bosomed women. So I switched Christine to another mark. That Christine was a clever one. She sensed Darcy and her new target were particularly important to me. I think that's what sparked her greed. She demanded more money. The little tart even insisted that her raise be retroactive. It was fine with me, but not Guy de Carter. He lacked my sense of fair play, I'm afraid."

I said, "You deliberately tried to confuse me with your talk of foolish young women and vindictive rich men. And you made Christine out to be anything but shrewd."

Blanche was silent and thoughtful for long moments. Finally I pointed to Addison Darcy. "You're not doing this to him just for Alexis, are you Blanche?"

She fixed her gaze on me.

"You're avenging Sally Miller. You're avenging your friend Sal, aren't you?"

She pointed the gun at Darcy again. "I detest him," said Blanch with a twisted smile. "I loathe him for what he did to Sal. I had a long and drawn-out revenge planned ... but, the precipitous actions of Guy de Carter have necessitated ... innovation. Guy stupidly tried to make amends by taking a potshot at this worm. Foolish man. He thought I'd be pleased. But he botched that too. He really should have stuck with his strong suits."

Blanche fixed her eyes on the shrinking old man on the floor as she resumed speaking. "Sal didn't deserve what he did to her. Not at all. She was one of my dearest friends. We shared dreams. We helped each other. She was like a sister to me. Closer than that, really. She had the talent and the looks. She'd had an offer to make motion pictures. She could have been another Gloria Swanson." Blanche again motioned to Darcy with the gun. She shook her head and made an incredulous face. "*He* didn't even remember Sal at first … not until I reminded him of a few things. Can you believe it?"

I heard a whimper come from Darcy.

"Sal believed his lies," Blanche continued, her mouth pulling tight to her teeth and her brow getting taut. "She passed up that movie contract. She said she just knew this rich scum would marry her. She said she knew it just as sure as night follows day. Instead, he beguiled her and treated her despicably, like she was dirt under his feet. Sal withered away. The betrayal, the prison sentence … it killed her."

I didn't know what to do. I figured to just keep her talking.

"How long did it take you to trace Darcy to Seattle?" My question penetrated the dreamlike state she'd entered. Her face muscles slackened and her countenance smoothed out.

"But I *wasn't* looking for him, Gunnar. Not at all. I happened to see his picture in the newspaper the first year after I married Henry and moved here to Seattle. Henry … he told me to forget about it. Henry didn't fully understand. Not at all."

"But *you* couldn't forget about it," I said.

"*Never*. And then, irony of ironies, Alexis took up with his son. So this bastard ruined Alexis' life, as well. When he did that, everything that happened to Sal got raked up all over again. But still, I did nothing. Henry told me it wasn't worth it. Sal used to say, just as sure as night follows day. No, Henry just didn't understand. Not one bit."

I had a weird epiphany. "But when Henry passed away and Alexis died in Steilacoom, you couldn't stand it any longer. You had to act. You came up with a plan."

"That's correct," said Blanche, her voice full of bitter scorn.

"It was a rather delicious plan. I had to finally rid the earth of this vermin. And after him, it will be his old buddy's turn." She glared at Darcy. Then her eyes shifted to Britt and me. Blanche got up off the settee, and as she took a step toward her intended victim, she pointed her gun at us in warning.

Darcy was sobbing and barely managed to mutter, "Please ..." as Blanche grabbed him by the scruff of the neck as if to put down a dog.

I had few options. I stood ten feet from them. I watched and waited for her eyes to leave me a second so I could leap at her to plow her over. As a plan it didn't even qualify as a long shot.

"Put the gun down, Mrs. Arnot."

The command came from Walter Pangborn. He stood in the doorway in his stocking feet holding his 8mm Lebel revolver. It was leveled at Blanche.

"*No!*" Blanche screamed in rage. Her automatic had been pointed at Darcy's head, but Walter's intrusion caused her to aim it in his direction and fire.

The crack of Blanche's automatic was followed almost immediately by the report from Walter's Lebel so that the two noises made a protracted sound like crackling thunder. For a fraction of a second it looked as though they'd each missed, as both posed in a kind of frozen showdown.

Nothing made sense. Then everything made complete sense. The doorjamb next to Walter's shoulder was shredded and splintered by the slug from Blanche's gun. I noticed it just as Blanche crumpled to the floor.

Britt screamed.

Walter stood motionless, still holding his revolver. It's a peculiar thing about the Lebel. Its cartridges were grievously underpowered. So much so that a Frenchman had to hit a Boche in a critical part of his body to knock him down.

I walked over to Blanche Arnot and felt for vital signs. A futile gesture. The slug from the Lebel had taken her in the chest.

I looked over at Walter. His twisted face told me that he already knew what I went ahead and said anyway, "She's gone."

I helped Darcy to his feet. "Help me with him, will you, Britt?"

She was in a daze, her eyes fixed on Blanche. I padded over to the settee and grabbed a folded afghan. I used it to cover the body. Some people need a gesture like that as much as they do a period at the end of a sentence. Britt's daze ended.

Britt attended to Darcy while Walter went to check on Hildy. I went to a neighbor's house to use the phone. I reached Frank Milland at home.

Chapter 19

—

A T THAT POINT KIRSTI'S face was ice-pale. She certainly didn't want me to suddenly break off when I did, but I told her that at that moment my old bladder trumped all the youthful curiosity she could muster. And then, after I'd taken care of business and she'd wheeled me back from the men's room, I told her I was in desperate need of some of that hardtack and pickled herring she'd brought me.

"That Blanche Arnot was a real sicko," Kirsti said. Her face was its normal color again. "So what happened next?"

I held a hand up palm forward to let her know I needed to finish chewing and swallow. After doing so, I took a sip from the water bottle she handed me and said, "The cops took our statements separately. After the housekeeper Hildy was checked over by the medical examiner and told what little she knew, she went off to bed. We learned from her that Mrs. Darcy was away visiting family in New Hampshire. She'd been forced to tie up her employer and then Blanche knocked her out."

"How did Addison Darcy handle it all?"

"The last I saw of him, he was taking a bottle from a liquor niche. Doctor's orders be damned, he had a more immediate ailment to reckon with and so he went and buried himself in some remote corner to empty his mind."

"What about Britt and Walter?"

"After the cops quizzed them they went to the kitchen to drink coffee while they waited for me."

I WAS QUESTIONED IN Addison Darcy's parlor. Frank Milland sat where Darcy had the day I'd visited and I was planted in the armchair across from him. Bernie Hanson joined us seated on a muslin-covered ottoman he'd found in some far-off corner.

"Walter and the Anderson dame both heard the Arnot woman confess to killing de Carter," Milland said, lighting a cigarette and cupping his hands to shelter the match from a nonexistent breeze. "Darcy's a mess. He won't say a peep without his lawyer present. He don't seem to know shit from Shinola right now, anyway."

"But you've got enough to let Dirk Engstrom walk," I said.

Milland sniffed the air and nodded. "And between your client and Darcy, none of this is going to get in the papers. No juicy details, anyway. You can bet on it."

"The rich have their own ideas about the free press," I said, but no one saw the humor.

"So was this Arnot broad whacky-brained or what?" Milland asked.

"My guess is she's always been a little … *pixilated*."

"Yeah … ain't we all," said Milland, laughing.

"You might look into her medical records, but chances are there aren't any. Her husband was a medical doctor. From what I've learned he was a stabling influence on her. My guess is he was probably more than that. Maybe he kept her medicated. Who knows? Something sure went haywire with her when he died."

I told them the stories of Sally Miller and Britt's Aunt Alexis and the tie-in to Addison Darcy.

"So what you're saying is that the Arnot broad nursed a grudge that turned into a Frankenstein monster," said Hanson.

"It looks that way. Alexis' death opened an old wound that had never really healed."

"And how. I'd say it opened and festered," Milland said. "So when her old man croaked, the Arnot broad snapped. Is that the idea?"

"Sure looks that way. I don't know how she ever got teamed up with Guy de Carter. She'd been a chorus girl and had worked in Hollywood in her youth. So she'd been around. She might have sized him up and saw his potential. It's hard to know. But together they hatched a pretty sordid shakedown racket. De Carter was in it strictly for money and probably for the kicks. But Blanche Arnot was hoping to parlay it into a diabolical act of revenge."

"And it probably would have worked, too," Milland said before giving out with a triple *tsk*. "Some people's children."

"How's Walter going to fare on the shooting?" I asked.

"He fares okay. By all accounts it was self-defense," said Milland. I could hear respect in his voice when he added, "A dead shot, that Pangborn. And a cool customer to boot."

Hanson looked at his notebook. "The Anderson gal told us that when the Arnot broad was about to shoot Darcy, she muttered something about it being his old buddy's turn next. Did you catch that too?"

I nodded.

"With Darcy all clammed up, we were hoping it might make sense to you. The 'old buddy' part, I mean," said Hanson.

They'd found the pack of blackmail photos in Blanche's coat pocket. I'd also given them Christine's diary. Both items sat on the ottoman next to Hanson. I pointed over to them.

"You might find the answer in those," I said.

But I knew otherwise.

WALTER ASKED MILLAND FOR a ride home. He'd rightly sensed

that I wanted some time alone with the dazed Britt Anderson.

She wore a small, formal smile as she got in the car. I popped a couple of cloves in my mouth to occupy my tongue. Neither one of us spoke for at least five minutes. Finally she did.

"I never thought … I mean, *my* anger had passed. I no longer felt vengeful …. I just naturally assumed …." She stopped. She was struggling to retain composure.

We all do it. Even when we know better, we still do it. We impose our ego on others. It's as though our individuality is like a shoe that's supposed to fit all feet, even though we know damn well it's as unique as a tailor-made boot that's been broken in and well-worn. So I sympathized with Britt, but didn't voice it.

After a few more minutes of silence I said, "I want to apologize for suspecting you for even a moment. I—"

She cut me off with a wave of her hand. "There's no need to explain, Gunnar. If I were in your position, I probably would have concluded similarly, given how things developed. You were only doing your job."

She said it with a clinical detachment. She looked very calm. The silence resumed until we were parked outside her place on Queen Anne Avenue. I didn't expect her to invite me in, and she didn't. But she didn't leave right away either. She wanted me close a little longer, but not too close.

"I suppose I've been more than a little naïve. It … it's unsettling. Embarrassing even. It kind of makes me doubt all my relationships. I guess I never really knew Blanche Arnot."

"You knew what you knew. People are polychrome. You were just ignorant of Blanche's darker shades, that's all."

"It's so confusing …."

"She was a very sick woman."

Britt thought about that, took a deep breath and let it out slowly.

"Do you run into this kind of thing often?" she asked, looking at me with gloomy speculation.

"At times. But it's not the usual or always this extreme."

"How can you stand it?"

I thought a moment before I answered. It wouldn't do to tell her I'd become inured. Too cavalier.

"Maybe I fool myself into thinking that I *can* stand it. Walter says I'm gifted with a little spark of dogged idealism. He says it keeps me from going crazy."

She shuddered. "I couldn't do what you do."

Suddenly the atmosphere was tinged with a mixture of apprehension and sexual tension. For a time she even became coy and mildly flirtatious. At one point I had the distinct feeling that the least little glance or touch from me would squeeze her out of halter-top and pedal pushers like toothpaste leaving a new tube.

But there was to be no clinging together. No putting red-blooded distance between ourselves and the earlier nightmare. For just as suddenly, she changed the mood with a barrage of friendly questions about trivial things. She talked about a few old school chums. I told a humorous story from my army days.

Finally Britt stifled a yawn with her fingertips, giving me the signal as universal as a thumbs-down or an index finger pulled across the neck. After a quick but gentle kiss, we exchanged courteous goodnights and she got out of the car.

It wasn't déjà vu. I *had* experienced something like this before.

I watched as she began her ascending walk up the slope leading to her apartment. Britt's unhurried strides reminded me of the night I dropped Christine off and watched her climb her aunt's footpath. As I had then, I now stared in forlorn fascination as Britt's denim pedal pushers defined the back of each shapely thigh as one leg darted out in front of the other.

I watched until she disappeared inside her place. Like Christine, she didn't turn to wave. I didn't expect her to.

This time I didn't feel like Fred Astaire as I drove away from her. I felt a keen detachment from everyone and everything.

And I was pretty sure I'd later be turning disappointment into virtue by means of a bone-chilling shower.

But before I took that shower I checked in with Walter Pangborn. He was busy painting toy soldiers at his workbench and listening to *Music Till Midnight* on KRSC. The bottle of Black & White and a half-empty shot glass were nearby as well.

He offered me a drink. I declined, and kept standing by the door.

"French Imperial Guard," he said, holding up the soldier he was working on. "The grand saga continues."

He meant life in general or his project for Perry. Probably both. I just smiled what had to be an exhausted-looking smile. Walter put the toy man down and took a sip from his shot glass.

"My only hope, old socks, is that she died immediately … that there was not even a split-second comprehension that I'd killed her."

"I understand," I said. I really did.

I bid Walter goodnight and headed for that long, cold shower.

Chapter 20

—

I DREAMT I WAS at a burlesque show with my old partner Lou Boyd. Several people in the audience were smoking opium. Mrs. Berger was on stage keeping rhythm with the music being played as she artfully hid her nakedness with ostrich feathers. Just as she was about to show all, the scene shifted and I was hugging trees in the Hurtgen with Guy de Carter. He was outfitted for combat and between explosions was shouting, "We gotta go, sport. We gotta go." He took off running and I woke up. It was one of those sleeps that leaves you more exhausted than before you went to bed.

Sunday morning I strolled into the kitchen long after everyone else had breakfasted. Mrs. Berger and Walter were at the table.

Mrs. Berger was saying, "Then we'll have the big fella say to Penny, 'That's a colossal lookin' run you got in your hose, girlie-girl.' "

Like a dutiful stenographer, Walter scrawled the banal drivel in his tablet stuffed with notes.

"Then Penny gives him a bugged look that as good as tells him, 'What's it to you, bub?' But then the guy says next, 'I know

just the place to have that run fixed for free, darlin." So now
Penny's sort of curious. Her face has gone from being bugged
to a look that says maybe this man knows something about
stockings that I don't. Do you know what I mean, Walter?"

Walter nodded and continued to write furiously.

It sounded to me like they were revising the act about the
white slavers. I went over to the stove and poured myself a cup
of coffee just as Mrs. Berger said, "Well, look what the cat in
her pity drug in."

When I realized she was talking to me I smiled and asked,
"Was it a billiards or church Sunday for the young and
perplexed?"

"Sten decided on church, judging by his costume," said Mrs.
Berger.

At least twice a month Sten attended a Lutheran church over
on Twentieth. He was the only churchgoer in the house. But I
don't think it was because he was particularly devout. He told
me once it just gave him a good feeling when he went. The
only religion I ever heard Mrs. Berger spout was Fletcherism.
Walter was a deist in the manner of Thomas Jefferson. As
for me, I'd been a non-practicing Lutheran since my teens.
Before the war, while holed up alone at a friend's beach house
in Nelscott, Oregon, I came across a stack of old newspapers
dating back to the 1910s. To kill time I read some sermons
by a popular syndicated preacher. He had a rational and lucid
style that I liked and that forever spoiled me when it came to
religious discourse.

I sipped my coffee and tuned out the conversation between
Walter and Mrs. Berger. It had something to do with Penny
having trouble reading a street guide of San Francisco. Walter
busily jotted down whatever was deemed pertinent for later use
at his typewriter keys. I was just glad to see him happily back at
it. I knew he'd spend part of the day in his room, going over his
notes, writing, editing and rewriting—thoroughly engrossed
in his labor of love. We all have our ways of offsetting hysteria
and dulling pain.

I washed and rinsed my cup and put it back in its spot on the drain board. Turning toward the pantry, I swear I caught a glimpse of Mrs. Berger kneading Walter's instep with the toes of her right foot. But when I did a double take both of Mrs. Berger's feet were sheathed in their pink fuzzy slippers and reposed under her chair.

Footsie. On a Sunday no less. *Mrs. Berger and Walter*. I went upstairs wondering if I really knew these people. After a shave and a fresh change of clothes, I telephoned Rikard Lundeen.

I apologized for not calling sooner, but he told me he'd already learned quite a few of the details. It was no surprise, what with his city hall connections and his tie to the Engstroms and their attorney.

We talked for a few minutes, and I agreed to visit him the next day in the afternoon to submit my full report and my bill. I wasn't looking forward to it.

After we hung up I went back to bed and slept till 3:00 p.m.

WHEN I ENTERED THE Hanstad Building Monday morning, I went straight to Olga Peterson's shop.

Miss Peterson gave me the curious and approving look all saleswomen give a man when he buys flowers. I think she was also tickled to finally know the exact nature of one of my purchases without having to ask. Still, there was a quiz.

"Has a particular young woman caught your fancy, Mr. Vance?" she asked. Her eyes sparkled but she sounded like she was auditioning for a spot on a parole board.

"My office needs a little cheering."

My answer disappointed, but it didn't stop her from giving me an accompanying card or from wishing me good luck as I edged away from her.

"I'm glad to see your jungle fever isn't bothering you, Mr. Vance. Did you remember about the molasses?" she called after me.

"Every night. Two tablespoons. *Heaping*," I said over my shoulder.

"And, by the way, did you happen to pass my greeting on to Mr. Pangborn?"

"Western Union couldn't have done better."

My Longines told me it was a little after 9:00, but the door to Dag's suite was locked. I was more than happy to postpone my encounter with Cissy Paget. I opened the card Miss Peterson had given me, and wrote, "With apologies to Sweet Knees." I tucked the card in the flowers and set them in front of the doorsill.

The maintenance man must have made an emergency weekend stop because the frosted glass in my door had been replaced. Cissy's thoughtfulness further indicted me.

A solitary letter was nestled in my mail slot. The name of the sender gave it the dreadful attraction of a telegram in wartime. It was missing both stamp and postmark, which meant Britt probably delivered it herself when the building opened.

The door to the inner pigeonhole was also repaired and I noticed fresh plaster on the back wall. I left the inner door open and sat down to open my letter.

Britt's handwriting was beautiful. The message was short but definitely not sweet.

> Dear Gunnar,
>
> Recent events have made me realize that I'm in need of a big change in my life. I've decided to move to New York City and see about finding that "throne" of my own that we talked about.
>
> If I don't get a chance to see you before I leave, please know that I enjoyed our brief time together and hope to keep in touch.

It was signed "Yours Always, Britt."

Yours, *what*? Always, *how*?

"Ah, that's sad, Gunnar," Kirsti said in a feeble voice. Her eyes actually had tears in them, and she was gingerly dabbing at them with a Kleenex.

"Yeah. A dimwitted lout just might fail to pick up on her unwritten 'I'll call you; don't call me.' "

After a few seconds of calf eyes and parted lips, Kirsti said, "I'm sure it was hard for her to do. It's not easy for a girl to break things off, you know. It can be a ... challenge."

"At the moment, Blue Eyes, I wasn't exactly thinking of the challenge I posed. However, I did try and figure Britt out. On our drive over to Addison Darcy's, I'd picked up a few pieces of the puzzle from her."

"What do you mean?"

"Well, that first day we'd met, when she'd buttonholed Meredith, it had been out of genuine concern."

"I thought so. Sure," Kirsti said.

"And Britt had honestly been interested in my investigation all along."

"She liked you, silly. Women get men to talk about what they do if they like them. You men fall for it every time."

"Uh-huh. Well, come to find out, Britt had been on the phone that night I was in her bed. Blanche Arnot had called her on some pretext, probably trying to find out my whereabouts from Britt, while de Carter paid his deadly visit to Meredith. According to Britt, she and Blanche talked on the phone all the time. Britt had unwittingly passed on my every move to de Carter through Blanche."

She nodded. "So, why did she go to New York?"

"Times were different. Britt was a gifted businesswoman with a truckload of promise and the ambition for far more. Not to mention she was stellar in the looks department. But a talented and attractive woman still had it tough in those days. The achievements of the feminist movement were yet to come. She probably saw New York as a city where she stood a better chance of advancing herself."

"Is that the only reason she took off, do you think?"

"Britt was only human. For a long time, Blanche Arnot had been part of her life—probably more a part than I realized. Blanche had nurtured both Britt and Alexis. And while their roles had reversed in many respects, I'm sure Blanche had been a kind of respected role model to Britt. But none of that mattered now. Not anymore. Not ever again."

Kirsti remained quiet.

"You understand, Kirsti, I was mainly left with my guesses as to Britt's feelings. Finding out she'd misjudged Blanche and misplaced her confidence in members of her sales staff had to have been a painful shock."

"It probably blew her away!"

"Yeah. I could see when I took her home that night she was having a rough time of it. Some people are unable to love and trust in the same way after an experience like that. I hoped better for Britt. But I didn't think I'd ever know. She didn't want to talk about it. At least not with me."

I REREAD BRITT'S NOTE three times. I read between lines, stayed alert for loaded words, hunted for ambiguity, and tried to sniff out any hidden implications. It was pointless. Its plain message bit and twisted my heart in a way I couldn't define.

No matter how much I might have wanted to be Britt's shoulder to cry on, or fix the hurt she felt, I wouldn't be able to make it better overnight—if ever. Maybe that's what she believed. That's one of my guesses anyway.

Everyone uses somebody. Sometimes several somebodies. The trouble is getting somebody to use you when you want to be used.

I carefully put the note back in the envelope and sailed it into the spilth receptacle just as someone rapped on the outer door.

The rap was too forceful to be Cissy Paget's, no matter how mad at me she might be, and the cloudy figure through the frosted glass was definitely too large. I told my caller to enter.

It was Dirk Engstrom.

He shook my hand and I told him to take a seat. He wore a sheepish grin as he studied me and then my office.

"I … I wanted to thank you for clearing me, Mr. Nilson," he said. His crisp dark suit told me he was dressed to sell jewelry.

"Glad I could help, Dirk."

"I … I want to pay you for your time."

"That's not necessary. Rikard Lundeen's footing the bill."

"Still—"

"It's not necessary."

I would have liked for him to insist one more time. If he had, I'd have let him pay me something. But he didn't. He was of that budding post-war generation with its ever-diminishing list of ought-to-dos.

He cleared his throat and shifted uncomfortably in his chair. His unruly lock was slicked in place, and all traces of belligerence seemed to have evaporated. I wondered if he'd been told about Christine's part in the blackmail racket. He didn't leave me hanging.

"I feel … like such a … jackass," he said looking at the floor.

I didn't disagree. I didn't say anything.

"I … I loved her. At least I thought I did. Now I … I don't know what to think."

I still didn't say anything. It's easy to do when a person isn't looking at you.

Dirk raised his eyes from the linoleum to me. I saw tears. Now I had to say something.

"It was what it was. It just wasn't what you thought it was. There's a lot of that in life, kid. The earlier you learn it the better."

"I … I suppose so. It's just so hard to accept that she used me."

"We're all users, kid. You both used each other. It's a primordial instinct. That's the way it is."

He gave me a grim smile and slowly nodded. Then he looked at the floor again so I gladly returned to being mute. But I couldn't maintain it.

"If it means anything to you, at least Christine tried in her way to warn you off."

"Wha ... what do you mean?" he asked looking at me again.

"You said she bawled her head off when you talked marriage. She *did* tell you she wasn't good enough for you. A guy might take that to mean that at heart she really cared for him."

Dirk was dumbstruck. I actually believed what I'd just told him. But I didn't believe what I said next.

"It looked like she was being coerced somehow to do what she did."

"You mean like a white slavery racket?"

"Something like that. Who knows? If she hadn't gotten killed she might have worked up the courage to ask for your help."

He liked the sound of that. He thought in silence for a while, recharting his mental and emotional map. Suddenly he stood up and reached over to shake my hand once more. This time he did so more heartily.

"If there's anything I can do for you, please don't hesitate to call."

He needed to say it. I knew it just as sure as I knew I'd never call him.

The back of my head still hurt when I put my hat on in the hallway. I noticed the bouquet of roses was gone as I walked away from my office. I slipped a clove in my mouth and opened Dag Erickson's door to take a friendly reconnoitering peek.

The flowers sat on Cissy's desk. A good sign.

She was at her typewriter. I studied her pondering profile, noted the brow knotted into a scowl, the lower lip pinned down by front teeth. She turned to me as I entered.

It was probably my imagination, but I thought I saw a fleeting tenderness in her eyes before they turned stormy. She fixed me with a venomous stare and said in almost a whisper, "May I help you?"

"Peace offering okay?" I asked, nodding to the roses.

"Let me make something perfectly clear. It's not like I own you or anything. You're over twenty-one. It's just that I expect a wee bit of consideration if you're not going to show up when you say you are. I mean, what was I to think? Especially after what had happened the last time I saw you? For all I knew you'd been killed and were lying in some gutter. How do you think I felt?"

She bit her lip petulantly. I said I was sorry.

Knowing Cissy, she probably hadn't seen the newspapers—generally too much lunacy and heartache for her taste. But, even if she had, thanks to Rikard Lundeen and Addison Darcy, certain details never saw ink. I apologized again and told her those details.

She listened respectfully and I watched her thin-lipped pout give way to shock and sorrow.

"Does it help at all to say again that I'm sorry?" I said.

The first sign of absolution was a small and rather formal smile.

I checked my watch and started for the door.

"Listen, Sweet Knees, I really want to make amends. Let me buy you dinner tomorrow night."

"I don't know—"

"I'd take you out tonight, but I've got a feeling I'll be grim company later. But how about a prime rib feast in the Georgian Room over at the Olympic? Cocktails and all the trimmings. What do you say?"

That won her over.

"Great. We'll talk more then. Right now, I've got to go meet a man with a checkered past."

EVEN THOUGH MY STORY was winding down to a close, I insisted on taking a short break. After chewing and swallowing the last of the hardtack with herring, I said to Kirsti, "It still dumbfounds me, Blue Eyes, how many irrational people make up the world. I'm convinced that most humans are lunatics to some degree."

Kirsti's look was more sympathy than understanding. Like my grandmother used to say, you can't put an old head on a young body.

Still, I felt a need to explain.

"I don't mean it like it sounds, Kirsti. Most people aren't crazy enough so as to spot it, or to where they'd get themselves locked away in a mental hospital. They're just crazy when it comes to some important or critical issues."

She gave me a charitable smile.

"I'm serious. How else do you account for the way people live their lives? How else can you explain the huge gap between the beliefs and opinions people mouth and their personal choices and behavior?"

She stayed silent.

"I rest my case."

THE DRIVE TO RIKARD Lundeen's was disquieting. It meant a return to The Highlands and to thoughts of Blanche Arnot and Britt Anderson. Britt would be haunting me for quite a while. That I knew.

Charlie was at the gatehouse again. He dutifully found me on his clipboard and sent me on through.

I parked my Chevy in front of Rikard Lundeen's stately New England-style manor house. It was way too big for a widower to rattle around in.

Lundeen's old manservant gave me a suit-off-the-rack look before he let me in. His quick appraisal told me that if I were a dinner guest I'd be seated way down table and out of reach of the salt. He left me waiting in a living room with floor-to-ceiling draperies and furniture with sapphire-colored upholstery and blond woodwork. The décor was but one of many bothersome details Lundeen had turned over to hired help.

I spent ten minutes studying the original works of art that

adorned the white walls around me. Abstract expressionism. All I saw was a jumble of colored blotches, slashes, and twirls that some visionary had splashed on canvas, put into frames, and then taken money for his perversity. Had these somehow spoken to Rikard Lundeen? Or were they just high-priced window-dressing?

I sat on a hybrid daveno that lengthwise could easily have slept two. Rikard Lundeen entered the room, followed by his manservant carrying a metal tray that held cups and a porcelain decanter.

I stood to meet him. He clasped my hand in both of his and wagged it in the air a full ten seconds.

"Masterfully done, son. Masterfully done," he said.

When he let go of me I handed him my bill with itemized expenses and made the obligatory by-all-means-check-it-over comment.

"That won't be necessary, son. Not at all." He glanced at the total, shoved the paper into his pocket and took his checkbook from his coat and made me out a check.

I thanked him and put the check in my wallet. I resumed my spot on the daveno and he sat in a chair across from me. The manservant left after pouring us coffee.

We talked about some of the events of the past several days and how they'd unfolded. I was tempted to let it go at that. After all, I reasoned, what difference did it make? But then Lundeen went and gave me an opening I couldn't ignore.

"Addison Darcy, that randy old son of a bitch. It looks like his wicked ways almost caught up with him."

"Funny thing that," I said, positioning a fresh clove with teeth and tongue to the left side of my mouth. "Just as Blanche Arnot was about to shoot your friend Addison, she said something about ridding the earth of him, and afterward it would be his old buddy's turn. Any idea whom she meant by that?"

Lundeen didn't say anything.

"It got the police curious. They asked me if I knew who this old buddy Blanche referred to might be," I said.

"And what did you tell them?"

"That they might find the answer in the blackmail photos or in Christine Johanson's diary."

"And will they?" His voice had dropped an octave.

"No. Guy de Carter had yet to take photos of you and Christine, and she didn't name you in her diary."

"How long have you known?"

"About your budding affair with Christine?"

He gave a nod.

"I had a few inklings along the way. Her diary refers to you as Slick, as in slicked-back hair," I said, pointing to his head. "You're not listed as a repeat customer at Fasciné Expressions, but then I remembered you telling me that you stopped by the place from time to time to take its pulse. But it really wasn't until Blanche Arnot made her 'old buddy' comment that I made a solid connection. You live just down the road from Darcy. You were going to be her next stop."

"I see."

"It made me rethink a few conversations. You told me that you and Darcy made trips together and raised hell when you were younger. Darcy told me that he practically lived in New York City due to business, and that he liked to take in the shows. As you must know by now, Blanche Arnot had been a Ziegfeld Girl."

That news didn't surprise him.

"At the Moonglow Eats the other day, you told me that the golddigger I'd helped you with previously had gotten off easy because you'd mellowed with age. I understand better now what you meant by that comment. You *have* mellowed.

"Blanche Arnot told me a pitiful tale about her good friend Sally Miller, a fellow chorine who'd been betrayed, framed, and sent to prison by her lover and his friend. Both were businessmen. Out-of-towners with local pull. The Miller girl died in prison. Addison Darcy had been her lover. And *you*,

Mr. Lundeen, were his old buddy. You helped him to get rid of the girl once she'd become a liability."

He closed his eyes for a second, opened them and looked at me speculatively.

I continued, "Blanche Arnot never forgot you two. When she married and came to Seattle, she recognized both of you. She was an unstable woman, kept reasonably stable by a man who loved her—her physician husband. But then he died. If that didn't push her over the edge, I think it at least allowed her to jump. She hatched an elaborate revenge for you and your old pal. She chose a trap that fit your crime and that she was sure would snare you both. And whaddaya know? She almost pulled it off."

Lundeen's breathing was shallow and his rugged cheeks had reddened. He regained possession of himself with no little effort, deliberately taking slow deep breaths. I stood up to leave. He stayed seated, watching me.

"Blackmail was to be only stage one. But the murder of Christine Johanson set everything and everyone connected to her reeling. Including you. I believed your spiel about concern for family. But you weren't really too interested in clearing Dirk. Mind you, I don't think you have anything against the boy, but it probably would have suited your purposes just as well had Dirk quickly been found guilty. You hired me for insurance. What you really wanted was a plausible explanation to spoon-feed the police and any of the press you don't already have in your pocket. How was it you put it again? You wanted me to 'contain anything disturbing.' Wasn't that it?"

He stood and gave me a level stare with his slate blue eyes. I kept thinking about all his sanctimonious talk of family, when but a day or two before he'd been making moves on his godson's girlfriend, getting set to jump her bones.

"So, what do you propose to do now?" he asked flatly.

"Not a thing," I said. "That chorus girl's been dead for over thirty years. Anything resembling a case against you died with a madwoman. And the last time I checked there's no law on the books against being a jerk or a conniving old roué. Not on *man's* books anyway."

Then I gave him a glassy-eyed smile and got the hell out of there. I found my hat in the anteroom before the smarmy manservant made his showing.

Outside, heavy drizzle doused the grounds and shrubbery. Everything had a dismal, disenchanting look, like a fairy kingdom gone sour. I got in my Chevy and edged down the driveway until the windshield wipers started to make a difference. I stopped at the border of Lundeen's property and let the engine noise compete with the sound of rain battering the car body.

"Like a tiger getting beat out of the brush." Lundeen had said that right after de Carter had tried to kill Darcy and me. But Lundeen knew better. It wasn't just scandal he worried about. His instincts for self-preservation were strong. He sensed a personal danger from the very start. I was the baby goat. The bleating kid. I was hired to be the tiger bait.

Lundeen hadn't mellowed with age at all. I was wrong about that. He'd merely slowed.

I rolled down the window. As my sleeve and shoulder got wet I took from my wallet the card with Rikard Lundeen's private number scrawled on it. I tore it into little pieces and tossed them in a nearby Thuja hedge. Or was it Viburnum? They all look the same in the rain.

"Good for you, Gunnar," Kirsti said sweetly, her eyes shiny. She suddenly looked extraordinarily lovely and alive to a guy who'd already reached for more than his share of brass rings. "That was awesome. I'm proud of you for tearing up his phone number like that. That Lundeen was pond scum. Lower than the low."

Kirsti was beaming at me. I liked being beamed at. So, I fudged a little. She probably would have too, if she were in my shoes. I much preferred Gunnar the Noble to Gunnar the Abject. Besides, she was recording things for posterity.

"Tell me again, Blue Eyes, what kind of paper did you say you might parlay these memories of mine into?" I asked.

Kirsti switched her recorder off and pulled in her lower lip with her teeth and then slowly let it go. "Well, actually, Gunnar, I wanted to talk to you about that," she said in a sweet melodic purr.

It was a classic female purr with which I was long familiar. It was harbinger to a request.

Kirsti went on, "At first, I thought of simply writing a human interest paper. That sort of thing."

"But *now*?" I said warily.

She was beaming again. "Well, you have to admit, that was quite a week you've told me about. So now I'm thinking that I might like to type up what I've recorded *as is*. You know, a transcript. With your permission, of course. In fact, I'd love to record and transcribe any other cases of yours that you'd care to tell me about. For instance, last week you mentioned some guy who had been killed 'out of character.' Maybe you could tell me all about that one, and what exactly you meant. I think making written records of your private eye days would be cool, and that others would like to read them. What do you think, Gunnar?"

"Hmm.... You want to play Watson to my Holmes?"

Her smooth forehead creased as she thought about that. "No... more like I'd be Boswell to your Dr. Johnson," she said in a satisfied tone. "But you don't need to decide right now. Just promise me you'll think about it, okay?"

I promised I'd think about it.

"So, getting back to what happened," she said forming a cheery smile as she switched on the recorder. "You'd just finished talking with Rikard Lundeen, and when you got back to your car you tore up his card with his private phone number on it. So let me guess what happened next. You hooked up with

Cissy Paget like you told her you would, and probably sooner than you planned to, I bet. You made up for being rude and missing your date. Right?"

"Yeah … something like that. Sure."

"I knew it. I just knew that's what you'd do."

The recorder was clicked off and put away, and Kirsti started to roll me back to my room.

Mind you, I was tempted, but when it came right down to it, I didn't have the heart to tell Kirsti the whole story, including how after I tore up Lundeen's card, I waited a minute before I got out of my Chevy and picked up all the pieces; and how later I taped them together with Mrs. Berger's help. That woman just loved jigsaw puzzles.

However, I did follow through on my promised amends-making to Cissy Paget, but as I'd told Cissy, not till the next evening. So, Kirsti's guess was correct, even though she was a little bit far afield of what really happened that day I gave Lundeen my bill.

I'm pretty sure Dr. Johnson didn't tell Boswell every little thing. Besides, sometimes you want to keep people from getting the right impression.

THE SNORING WOKE ME. But it was the rhythm of her hoarse sputter that kept me awake. I knew after five minutes there was no point in trying to get back to sleep. I just stared across the room at the wallpaper and fought an urge to count faded daisies.

The bed was small and I was about to be pushed off my side of it. Verna Vordahl's shapely rump was pressed in the small of my back like warm lead in a plaster mold. She was every bit the hot and spry Amazon of her customers' fantasies. Her Tuesday shift didn't start till 10:00 a.m. At the moment she needed her sleep. So I carefully pried free of her clinging silkiness and our short-lived closeness.

I got up, quietly pulled my pants on, and tucked in my shirt.

Verna rolled over and nuzzled the corner of the mattress where I'd been. Her snoring halted. A disheveled cluster of reddish brown hair hid her face. Only her mouth showed, her lipstick worn colorless from a necking session the night before that left both of us eager and gasping. My head ached from our little charade at dinner and the stiff drinks we used to make it credible.

From the roadhouse, we came to her place for another drink and more alchemy that temporarily transformed our grief-affirming bedpost rattling into something honest. For a few hours we lost ourselves in sensation, lessened our loneliness, and became oblivious to the events of the past week. In our grip of mutual affection we each forgot about Hank Vordahl for our own reasons. Verna briefly forgot how much she still loved him, and I was able to put from my mind the enemy I'd make when the two of them got back together.

But I also managed to forget all about Britt Anderson.

Well, almost, anyway.

Gunnar the Self-Deluded.

BORN INTO A BLUE collar family in Seattle, Washington, and raised in the suburbs of the greater Seattle area, **T.W. Emory** has been an avid reader since his early teens. In addition to fiction, he likes biographies, autobiographies, and the writings of certain essayists. He also enjoys reading secular and religious history, and is a dabbler in philosophy and sociology. Moreover, he likes reading reprinted collections of old comic strips such as *Thimble Theatre* (aka *Popeye*), *Moon Mullins*, *Captain Easy*, and *Li'l Abner*.

After taking on various odd jobs that included brief stints assisting a grounds-keeper, working in a laundry, washing dishes, waiting on tables, and doing inside and outside painting, he got into drywall finishing and eventually became a small-time drywall contractor.

In addition to writing, T.W. enjoys cartooning as a hobby. He is second-generation Swede on his mother's side and third-generation Norwegian on his father's, which helps explain the Scandinavian flavoring in his first novel, *Trouble in Rooster Paradise*.

He currently lives north of Seattle with his wife, two sons, one cat that is companionable and another that is aloof and rather ditsy.

For more information, go to www.twemoryauthor.com.

43227931R00155

Made in the USA
Charleston, SC
18 June 2015